CW01066742

Keep The Home Fires Burning

MARILYS EDWARDS

Bloomington, IN Milton Keynes, UK

authorHOUSE

AuthorHouse™
1663 Liberty Drive, Suite 200
Bloomington, IN 47403
www.authorhouse.com
Phone: 1-800-839-8640

AuthorHouse™ UK Ltd.
500 Avebury Boulevard
Central Milton Keynes, MK9 2BE
www.authorhouse.co.uk
Phone: 08001974150

This book is a work of fiction. People, places, events, and situations
are the product of the author's imagination. Any resemblance to actual
persons, living or dead, or historical events, is purely coincidental.

© 2007 Marilys Edwards. All rights reserved.

Cover Photograph: Annette Bishop
Author Photograph: Annette Bishop
Cover Design: Mary Parker

No part of this book may be reproduced, stored in a retrieval system, or
transmitted by any means without the written permission of the author.

First published by AuthorHouse 2/20/2007

ISBN: 978-1-4259-3085-1 (sc)

Printed in the United States of America
Bloomington, Indiana

This book is printed on acid-free paper.

ACKNOWLEDGEMENTS

Judith Lappin: M.G.C. Association

Jim Parker: M.G.C. Old Comrades Association

Mark Offord BA (Hons). Researcher

Landlords of The Griffin Hotel: Llandrindod Wells

The Waterloo Hotel: Bury

The Hotel de Lac: Camiers

Tony Sprason: Wellington Barracks Museum, Bury

Bury Registrar

Bury County Records Office

Vin-Mag Archive: Hackney

Llandrindod Wells Information Bureau

Llandrindod Wells Archives

Llandrindod Wells Library

Members of Ithon Road Presbyterion Chapel Llandrindod Wells

The lady next door to the Griffin Hotel who was a friend of Tom's from years back:

Mrs. Maisie Powell

Nan/Rodge/Mac. who told me it was my duty to write this tale down.

REFERENCES

"With A Machine Gun to Combrai." George Coppard

"To The Last Man, Spring 1918." Lyn MacDonald

"The First World War." John Keegan

"Back To The Front." Stephen O'Shea

"The 1916 Battle of the Somme: A Reappraisal." Peter H. Liddle

"Dreadnought. Britain, Germany, and the coming of the Great War." Robert K. Massie

"The 1910 Scrapbook. The Decade of The Great War." Compiled by Robert Opie

For Annette, Jackqui and Little Brian whose hero was his Grandfather: Tom.

In 1899 Conrad's Friend
Cunningham Graham
Wrote to Edward Garnett: "My life
Is almost the same as yours. It is a
Joke, a black joke of course, but we
Must laugh at our own efforts."

(Watts p.26)

(Joseph Conrad. Victory. Everyman. P.338)

Keep The Home Fires Burning

O N E

The ladder leans against the middle bay of the Little Barn. It is dusty up there with that exiting smell that comes off the hay. Motes dance in the shafts of sunlight filtering through cracks in the huge, black-tarred, wooden doors.

Tom sits at the foot of the ladder dapping at the dust with his infant hands but looking up to where the roof-beams are almost lost in the shadows. Old redbrick and roughened-wood colours tumble into his eyes as he strains to see if Eloise and Ivor have reappeared. They are up there playing tunnelling-games. They will dig deep one side of the bay and try and get out the other. Tom knows the order of things. It can be quite a frightening game especially if you feel the roof might collapse in on you or that you're going to get stuck halfway.

It is not allowed really. Father will be very cross if they are caught but Tom is supposed to be listening out for Ida in case she comes across the yard searching for Eloise and warn them to get down in time when they can pretend they have been looking after him.

They have been looking after him anyway. They told him to sit still and not go wandering off and he has done what they said hasn't he? He loves Eloise desperately. She is on his side always and so funny.

"That gel would make a CAT laugh!" His father will sometimes chuckle, wiping his hand across his big moustache and putting on the Radnorshire accent to make the others laugh even more; but Eloise is high-spirited and has to be kept in order – hence Ida Owen, who when she is not being Bernard's nursemaid, is supposed to keep her eye on Eloise's activities.

Tom hates Ida and he is not too fond of Bernard either. Bernard has taken his place in his mother's affections. Not that she has had much affection for him up to now: it has been apparent; but BernARD, as she pronounces him, BernARD – is her little darling with his huge dark-brown eyes and his gurgling and cooing and pulling at her chestnut, curly hair with his chubby little hands while he, Tom, has never been allowed to even touch and is always viewed with a suspicion he is unable to understand, whatever he does: always somehow OUTSIDE. There is no explanation.

He and Eloise both have deep-set green: green and hazel, hedge-row eyes. They are wild and wiry creatures, both of them, swift moving, agile….. always in trouble: a nuisance to Mary Ellen who prizes order and saintliness above much else. Tom adores Mary Ellen and Arthur, his father, but Bernard suits them best. He is docile, accommodating. A charmer.

Their mother has made an exception with Bernard. Hating the process of 'carrying' before the birth: the distortion of her hourglass figure, the inevitable bloating of her fine features, she has not turned a cold profile towards him since he was safely delivered, not completely dumped him on one of the maids as a nurse the same as Tom himself had been on Nellie Davies.

The effect this has had on Tom is a certain alienation. For instance, he would prefer the servants' quarters at Mainstone, to the stifling depression of the family rooms – the only bright spark in his existence there being Eloise and her shameless laughing fits, her taking-off of the 'elders' her sometimes quite pathological letting-off-steam performances.

Once she took him to Rhayader in the gig with Ida Owen alongside riding "shot-gun", as Eloise laughed, and Tom had been thrilled almost out of life at the pace she had managed to get Arthur's prize, Hackney-cob up to as they careered along. "You're not allowed to gallop the cob, gel!" Ida kept shouting. "You'll ruin his pace! Break his stride!" but Eloise wouldn't listen.

They had swept into Rhayader like a tornado, Eloise yelling to ladies crossing the street to "Lift yer skirts, Missus! – out the way!" in the most frightful parody of one of the Radnor yokels while Ida Owen cursed and swore as she held on to her hat with one hand, on to the seat with the other, Eloise cracking the whip over Flash's hindquarters until she pulled him up sharp outside their cousins' hotel, The Golden Lion, on the corner where Tom was lifted down to safety by Auntie Corys who loved him dearly – and was never afraid to show it.

"Eloise dear – you've come", Auntie Corys exclaimed without turning a hair. She hated a show of feelings…. "and little Tom: my Tom! Come on in my dears."

They followed her into the parlour that had that peculiar 'ancient' smell of old country places: ferns, damp stone walls, a hint of outside lavatories. She had a plate in there with a beautiful blue pattern on it. She would bring it down off the wall always for Tom to touch and exclaim over. He had always loved it. The blue was pale with the light shining through it: the blue of angels. She went through this routine now before feeding them by the enormous fireplace in the Snug and then Eloise had conveyed them back to Llandrindod Wells. Eleven miles as the crow flies.

Tom picks up his stick off the stone flags and starts trying to draw a pattern in the dust. He will make a picture of the sun setting over Dolfan if he can, though he knows he will have a job to get it right. It is a sight to see from beneath the eaves at Mainstone: the sky on fire, so exiting – if only he could DO something with it; but what? ….. the hills outlined with boulders black against – CRASH! - the barn doors are flung open with a terrible clatter. Ida must have tiptoed over the cobblestones. She is here. Now!

"Eloise!" he calls. "Ivor!" but Ida is on him, wrenching the stick out of his left hand viciously. "You're NOT to use your left hand – you great booby!" she yells in the 'Radnor'. She is still half-savage. Mary-Ellen had her brought over straight from Nantmel, near Rhayader, when she was twelve. She is fourteen now, but the streak in her is like a snake. Yellow. It will dart out from her low-slung, Celtic frame without the least provocation. She is set back on wide hips for such a skinny frame and Tom hates the sight of her. He scrambles to his feet and rushes forwards nearly knocking her off hers. He kicks and kicks at her so that she has to turn away to defend her shins but Tom won't let up now. Just because he is not allowed to do things left-handed, why should SHE take it on herself to correct him? Who DOES she think she is? Always hanging around his mother too - and trying to curry favour. Always sneaking on him.

Eloise is behind him, pulling him off. Ida turns.

"Where've you been gel?" she yells at Eloise but Eloise is hugging Tom to her and wiping the tears of rage from his face.

"What's the matter Tom?" she asks

"What did she do to you?"

She tries to pick him up but he has grown too heavy. Tom doesn't answer. He is no sneak.

"Come on Ivor!" she calls over her shoulder as Ivor comes sliding down the ladder.

"Let's take him home".

But Ida has become an open-mouthed effigy of suspicion and lets out a fresh stream of invective at this proof of some sort of mis-behaviour.

"What the hell have you been doing up there – the pair of you?" she screams. "You ought to be ashamed of yourself Eloise Edwards! .... You and this great long streak of NOTHING: this ...... this pansy-wansy, little mother's darling – this CREATURE who can't do anything else but fiddle around on the bloody piano! - what have you been up to eh? EH?

"What on earth do you mean, Miss Owen?" Ivor enquires super-ciliously enough to make Eloise splutter with laughter.

"What are you implying?" he goes on while Ida struggles for breath, but before she can reply, Eloise looks her straight in the eye and says

"Get this Owen. One word out of you to the Old Man that Ivor and I have been tunnelling through the hay – and I'm going to ask his mother: MADAME – if you don't mind – Novello-Davies – to put in a word against you with mine. We'll see how long you last then."

The suspicion drops from the wide cheekbones facing her and the hooded eyes slide sideways almost in embarrassment as Ida mutters semi-apologetically "Oh, I see – hay-tunnelling is it my lad? Right. Right-oh then. Yes ..... well there we are. It's time you were coming back home anyway.

"Tom – run and say 'goodbye' to your grandparents ...... to your Aunties – and you Eloise! Go on. Go on! Ivor ...... good boy – that's it! We'll all go back up town for a nice lunch now in a minute – shall we? Come on then."

Like a cloud passing from the face of the sun, her mood has lightened (childish-games still – that's all. Ah well…..).

The fields are sunlit. The farm lies in its dip, open to the summer day.

TWO

Grandmother Anne is in the back-kitchen cooking a ham over the high, black-leaded grate. "Supper for the harvesters later on", she says. She has on her lace bonnet over thick dark hair, parted in the middle and scraped back into a bun. She is very tidy in a voluminous, grey, cotton skirt with the print apron over it tied round the waist, her cross-over bodice with its shawl-like fringe disguising part of her enormous bosom. She is very much like Tom's father to look at with the same piercing green eyes and oval-shaped face. A strong woman.

She was a widow from Llandegly when Tom's grandfather married her. They must have met when he was living in the stationmaster's house at Pen-y-Bont, though Tom has never really found out what he was doing there. All he knows is that Grandad is a very important man. You mustn't swear in front of him. Everything belongs to him. He built the Presbyterian Chapel where they go 3 times on a Sunday. Tom wonders sometimes how he lifted all the stones and pillars. Still – it ought not to have been too much of a job for him after he tore all those gorse-bushes out of the common-land (he had rented off the Gibson-Watts) with his bare hands, planted and hedged his fields, put in the wind-break of firs they call the Plantation before founding the first milk-round with a donkey and cart in 1872.

Now he rents the 3 farms, strategically placed around the county: Bryn-Gros, out near Newbridge, Three Wells, on the way to Builth where Uncle Tom, his favourite uncle, lives – and this one: TyCanol, Father's pride and joy. Father will inherit it all one day but meanwhile Grandfather had Mainstone built for him as a wedding present so that he and Mother could run it, supplied with produce from the farms, as a superior boarding-house with the help of the 7 maids: Big Annie, Thin Annie, Hannah, Nellie, Margaret, Club Foot Joanna and – Ida Owen.

This is how Ivor comes into it. His parents bring him to stay every summer now. They think it's nice for him to play with Eloise who puts on her good-girl act beautifully when they are about though at the same time muttering awful things about them out of the side of her mouth. How she has the nerve to do it, Tom has no idea.

"Oh yes – Mrs. Novello-Davies …. Oops – sorry! MADAME Novello-Davies", she will smile, blinking her eyes. "Ivor is SUCH delightful company" (then to Tom, raising her thin black eyebrows farcically) - as long as he hides his boney-shanks under the table AHEM! – Pardon, Madame Novello-Davies ….. you were saying? - Oh, he has SO been looking forward to coming up from Cardiff! ….. Yes – I'm sure. Well" (and to Tom again, by now rolling in an agony of laughter on the floor) – "I can tell you we are going to give the bugger the time of his life YERE (Radnor) – ain't we Tom? – No Madame Novello-Davies – I said – I hope it will TRIGGER (as if to the deaf) – the TIME OF HIS LIFE. Yers ….. only 12 ….. like me – yet writing music. Songs! Mrs. – sorry MADAME Novello-Davies – and singing so wonderfully. I know M.E. (her mother's nickname to intimates) is delighted to have him here and so am I!

He's good-looking like his father isn't he!" (glaring coyly up beneath Novello-Davies's moustache). "Oh, I could kiss him" (to Tom) "and often do ….. and he can kiss my arse – can't he Tom?" (Back to the Novello-Davies's) "PASS ANY EXAM going – I'll wager Madam Nov–", but Tom is now thumping the floor with his feet, almost sick with laughing – so thank Heavens for Nellie Davies who is still on hand though he is now nearly six. She will haul him to his feet and take him by the hand into the kitchen, change his knickerbockers, get him clean underpants if he has peed himself.

"That Eloise! – Full of it". She will grin and them compliment him on his size. He looks down, chuckles and is restored.

"Mother says I'm a freak," he said once and Nellie, remembering, feels sad for a moment: worried for him. He is so beautiful in a house of prudes – though sometimes she wonders about Arthur. He always had such an eye for the girls. Secretly she wishes Mary Ellen would take a bit more time with the little boy. He has a sweet nature – but it could so easily be ruined if he gets the wrong messages about YOU KNOW WHAT. Ah well!

"Where's Grandfather?" he now asks his grandmother. "Where's Willie? I've got to say goodbye to everyone".

"Well you saw the girls in the milk-shed as you came by Tom, didn't you? So you can call to them from the back door as you go. Willie's in the parlour and your Father and Grandfather are down in the water-meadows breaking in Davies Cer-y-Croes's colt".

"O-o-oh! Can I run down and see ….. Grandma?"

"No dear – not today. It's time you went home now. Go on – say hello and goodbye to Uncle Willie, there's a pet. Don't keep Ida wait-ing. She'll have plenty to do at Mainstone".

He knows better than to argue, even though he loves watching Arthur and his father schooling one of the colts on its long rein.

Round and round they go, stepping gingerly, ears pricked forwards, that lovely smell coming off their coats, their eyes blue and sideways in their heads like Greek legends.

Farmers bring their horses from miles around for the Edwards's to break-in. They have a way with the animals. Tom's heart nearly bursts with pride when he realises his place in the scheme of things: Arthur's oldest son – even though he doesn't seem able to please the elders too often.

Willie is in the parlour carving a stick.

"Oh, that's a good one, Uncle Willie," Tom says cheerfully and Willie holds out the whittled end towards him, smiling. Tom takes it willingly enough. He likes to please his uncle. He is a kind boy. There is something wrong with Willie. He is SIMPLE, his grandparents say – and not to be taken advantage of, never to be made fun of or to become the butt of any jokes or pranks. He is very pale and short. Very sweet-natured.

"You can have that one", he says so Tom thanks him profusely.

"Oh thankyou Uncle Willie", he says. "I've got to go early I'm afraid …. Sorry I can't stay. Goodbye now."

"Bye boy", Willie grins and Tom slams out of the room before running into the kitchen again.

"Bye Grandma", he calls, rushing out the back door, then seeing his aunts in the milk-shed opposite, shouts "Hello Auntie Lucy. Hello Aunt Agnes. Where's Auntie Alice?"

"She's up in bed today boy", Auntie Lucy says softly. "Got a bad cough again."

She and Agnes are washing milk-tins and sterilising the bottles brought back from the first round. They put them down and come to give him a hug. He loves them, Lucy especially. They are very kind and tidy. They smell nice – of warm, clean cotton, of milk and roses;

even if they are not all that beautiful to look at. Auntie Lucy's face is long like a horse though she has the softest skin and warm brown eyes; almost ginger-striped eyes, like bees buzzing in her face. She will laugh and laugh if you say anything funny and is forever trying to urge Eloise into more and more outrageous remarks.

Agnes is pale as a little ghost and her face is flat like a frying pan. Tom doesn't quite know what to make of Agnes. She has an inner sadness that he can't fathom. He would like to cheer her up but she seems to live in the back of her eyes. You can't always get at her.

Eloise comes hurtling around the corner of the house, Ivor at her heels.

"Hello gels …." She greets her aunts cheekily and they both laugh. Their soft, freckled hands go out to catch her as she flies past them into the back kitchen.

"How's Annie today?" she dares to utter once inside the house and even Tom is apprehensive as she comes giggling back out again with the broom, flying through the air behind her – but it's all right. His grandmother is on the scrubbed step, hands on hips, one little buttoned boot up on the foot-scraper, heel down but laughing.

"That gel!" she exclaims. "what we going to do with her – eh Tom?"

He touches his cap and nods to the women before they go. Ivor shoves his hands into his pockets and saunters behind the other two after saying "Goodbye to you ladies, one and all", touching his cap respectfully also and giving them his sophisticated Cardiff smile.

"Nice lad", Lucy says when the children have turned the corner.

"Very." Anne agrees primly. "Like his mother. Very talented too".

"Remember her playing the organ at Mary Ellen and Arthur's wedding?" Lucy smiles sweetly and the three of them agree what a lovely day that had been before returning to their tasks: the old chapel at the end of a long sling between wild-rose bushes at Cefnllys, beneath the hill, Mary-Ellen so beautiful that people had journeyed from miles away just to see her the night before the ceremony, done up in her wedding-regalia and sitting in her mother's front parlour at Llanfawr. A tradition of the times. The bride on display. Raymond Cox, the new Botany Master at the County School had gone along. Years later he told his daughter he had never, ever again, seen such a beautiful sight. Her hair had been a mass of chestnut curls, he said.

Anne re-enters the house; the two girls turn back to the soapsuds and the wooden racks. Agnes's eyes to their unseen horizons.

THREE

Tom wakes. There is uproar coming from the chicken run. He sits up in his room beneath the eaves and yanks the lined cretonne-curtain across to get an idea of the time. It is light and going to be a hot day. The mist isn't rolling up the hills; it is hanging in the valley.

He gets out of bed in his nightshirt and quietly opens the bedroom door before tiptoeing barefoot along the landing to the window overlooking the side of the house but can't see a thing out of place. The clamour goes on, hens squawking and he can hear Mary Ellen remonstrating with someone.

If his mother is in danger – to hell with it … he will risk all and rush to the rescue straight away even if it means a hiding from the old man for parading around on his bare feet; for daring to get out of bed before he is called. There are so many rules and regulations: no shoes on and you could end up with kidney trouble – they say – "just like old Pugh the Barber: got all swollen up round the ankles first, then spreading all over. And WHEN THEY BURIED HIM – the coffin leaked a brown fluid!" The very thought terrifies Tom and Eloise. Also you are not allowed to run around with anything sharp in your hand pointing upwards. You could get your eye out – "like Amy

Morrison's boy" – and as for getting up before time – well you're just a damned nuisance then under the grown-ups' feet. Children should be seen when necessary but not heard. Don't answer back! Sit up straight – you'll get curvature of the spine otherwise! Don't sprawl! Don't eat with your mouth open! Elbows in at the table. Drink the soup out of the side of the spoon. Stand up when a woman enters the room and always in front of the elders. Don't cough unless into a handkerchief. Blow your nose, don't sniff, spit, hawk phlegm and make damn sure you leave the cans in the outside lavatories in a fit state for the next person. You have to learn how to behave. Don't play with yourself boy. Take your hands out of your pockets! My stars! Thank Heavens for Chinny, his best friend, and Co.

He flies, thumping now around the corner. Further along the second landing and down the back-stairs, both hands on the banisters; propelling himself two or three steps at a time past the kitchen door at the bottom but he doesn't go in.

The door is open and Nellie is helping Rosa with the breakfasts in there so he darts past and to the left, out through the back-door and left again down the gravel-path through the rhododendron bushes into the kitchen-garden.

"Tom! – Where the hell are you going?" Nellie shouts behind him but he doesn't answer. He's nine isn't he? Why should these women always be after him? He runs on through the bean-sticks with the leaves curling up on their tendrils out of the dew, their little red flowers sparkled with moisture.

It is a beautiful morning with that early-morning smell. The spiderwebs on the hedges and wires strung between posts separating them from the huge Victorian, red-brick and ochre-coloured cliff of a house next door are outlined with a thousand drops and the wild-roses are unfurling into wet, pale, pale pink and white petals like stars shining through the mist: serrated leaf-edges, thorns, long, trailing brambles and stalks stiff and pulsing with sap almost grinding into music like one of Ivor's symphonies. No time to think. Tom shoves his head above the bushes to see where all the noise is coming from and catches a glimpse of Mary-Ellen bending over inside the hen-run and tugging at something on the ground. She has a print-pinafore over her black dress and the egg-basket is at her feet. What on earth is going on? Is it a fox? He'll get Arthur's shotgun and shoot the bugger if so. It had better not bite Mother.

He dives around the last of the currant-bushes and crashes into Ida Owen. "What the devil are you doing here?" She shouts but he can't be bothered with her nonsense this morning. He heaves her aside and she goes sprawling into the raspberry canes as he rushes on.

And then he sees the cause of all the trouble and commotion: Jim Corp has come home. He must have been asleep in the hen house when Mary-Ellen came down to get the eggs. She is furious. She is tugging at Jim's booted feet and trying to drag him out and now he edges himself into sight and sits up grinning, passing an enormous hand over his face in a wiping-motion, Tom remembers from long ago, as he does so.

" 'Morning M. E-E-E", he chuckles quietly while Mary-Ellen berates him for daring to turn up like this, unannounced and having the effrontery to ensconce himself in the hen-house.

"Well, the big house was locked, gel – I wasn't going to knock you up. It was late," Jim explains gently in his slow accent but Mary-Ellen is not grateful for his thoughtfulness. She is at her sarcastic-worst.

"Hem! Hem" – she goes. "Imbibing in the back-bar of the Llanerch? Oh yes! – After hours of course. That Leslie! – Drinks all round….. on the house, I'll warrant. Carousing into the small hours. Oh dear. Poor you."

"Now Mary-Ellen – that's no way to welcome back the wanderer from over the ocean." Still smiling, Jim rises to his full height, brushing off feathers and hen-shit as he unfolds. He is a giant. Tom steps forward. "Jim!" he cries delightedly.

"Tom boy! – Tom ….". Jim rushes towards him and big as he has become, picks the child up one-handed and holds him splayed and balanced flat on an enormous palm as he would when Tom was a baby. They turn in the golden glow growing rapidly through the mist over the lawns; almost a ballet-movement of perfect symmetry before Jim gives a tremendous shout of joy and returns Tom to his feet at which Mary-Ellen scolds: "Where are your SHOES?"

She is in a real fret, Tom can tell. She has gone red from below the black, velvet band she always wears around her slender neck – right up into her hair.

"Go in AT ONCE and get dressed. Put your shoes on! Don't want to catch kidney-trouble do you? - Ida! Ida! – come and get Tom ….. and you – stop SHOUTING. You'll wake the guests. Into that downstairs washhouse with you and clean yourself up before anyone sees! Have you no shame? Brush those hen-feathers off you – and out of your hair. Oh, what have I done to deserve this?"

They move towards the house, Tom looking back admiringly over his shoulder at Jim as Ida tugs him, viciously as usual, towards the back door.

"Jim? Jim? Where've you been this time Jim?" he calls as softly as he can so that he won't annoy Mary-Ellen more than he can help – but he has to know. He stops. Ida tugs in a licensed manner now his mother has ordered her to take him in but he resists her pull until Jim mouths "Ca –a-n-a-d-a!" making Tom's eyes widen with anticipation for all the adventures Jim is now sure to relate before allowing himself to be rough-handled back upstairs and into the family-bathroom. Jim Corp is Mary Ellen's half-brother. She is ashamed of him because of his ways: he is wild. Tom adores him. Jim is his hero. He is the strongest man in Radnorshire and champion prize-fighter at all the 1d-booths in fairgrounds up and down the county. Tom has seen him send men resembling gorillas to the floorboards, bare-knuckled at Builth Wells, without any trouble at all. The boy is not supposed to have witnessed these sights because Mary Ellen and Arthur are against any such competitions; even though Father himself was a champion wrestler renowned throughout the hay-fields of his youth – and no-one: no-one at all could 'throw' him, according to Jim. But that was different evidently … for fun rather than for money.

Arthur, in fact, loves going to the circus when it is in town. He is a great circus-lover and even went to see Bill Cody with his Wild-West Show plus Indians at Liverpool when he came over from the States with his outfit – though now, he appears to have become more and more respectable since marrying Mary-Ellen: the both of them full of new responsibilities especially since the 'awful year' when Tom was either five or six (he can't quite remember now… was he still five or was it the year after?) he will have to search out the Death-Cards to make certain though they're all locked up in Mother's rosewood writing-desk … but do things matter anyway … the exactitudes?

That year Auntie Alice's cough became much worse before she started spitting blood and died, then Little Willie got pneumonia – and he died. Agnes was next. Got a cough. Died. Tom feels frightened even thinking about it. The two girls had caught T.B. whatever that might be. He hoped they wouldn't get it at Mainstone. It was rumoured they were infected as a result of drinking river-water – still Grandmother Anne has had a tap put in the back-kitchen lately, (too late for the others) but at least they are safely switched on to the mains down there now. He can drink water if he wants to.

The Family always seemed to be trotting in procession that year: the horses done up with black-plumes on their headbands out to the family burial-plot at Pen-y-Bont. It was as if one of them would get ill and the next thing you knew, these black-bordered cards would appear on the black-oak dresser after breakfast:

'Alice. Beloved Daughter of Thomas and Anne Edwards.'
'Willie. Beloved Son of Thomas and Anne Edwards.'
'Agnes. Beloved Daughter of Thomas and Anne Edwards.'

No, it didn't do to think about it. You needed people like Jim Corp around the place to cheer you up a bit: to take you out of yourself and your horrible worries; though Jim was away then even so.

When he left on that occasion, two police officers had attempted to accompany him, handcuffed, to the Lock-Up, that was also in Pen-y-Bont in those days. They were walking, Jim head and shoulders above the members of the <u>Force</u> (, as he would refer to the constables, grinning, when indulging Tom by relating his activities afterwards). He was on a charge for fighting when drunk – but his natural good humour was very much in evidence as usual now he had sobered-up.

They had strolled about half way and Jim was remarking on the quality of the morning – when he saw a goods train coming along the line making for Shrewsbury.

"Well lads …." He said agreeably, raising his two hands above his head and hauling them half off their feet in the process,

" – I reckon we've gone far enough together now ….." and with a laugh and a tremendous jerk, he had snapped the handcuffs in two and running off towards the line, clambered into an open truck and started on his journey – to <u>Canada</u>, he said. But at the farm, there was more to come. That same winter, the almost unbelievable happened. Grandfather became ill. He had been delirious in that end room at TyCanol, overlooking the three hills. Tom could imagine the chattering of voices in his head as the winds raged and buffeted around the old chimneys and the intense cold froze the rooms into cubes of ice. You could only ever get one side of yourself warm at the farm: the side nearest the grate and the grand, old man had ended-up with pneumonia, like Willie. He had begged the doctors to "Bleed him, bleed him!" as he would have one of his horses but they refused and he too had succumbed before the year was out.

The town was stunned. Thomas Edwards had been well liked by most. Before he had built the Presbyterian Chapel in Ithon Road, he would go out preaching himself, as a lay-preacher, on horseback to outlying farms and villages in the area. Later, some wondered if maybe he had listened to disciples of the Wesleyans or some other forceful evangelists preaching somewhere in the days before he landed in Radnorshire and that the occasion had ignited his own passion for the Word. Or could it be that anyone preaching at others with that intensity was really aiming arrows at his own shortcomings? It was whispered in kitchens (especially those he owned in houses he had been wise enough to buy and rent out to tenants who commiserated one with the other concerning the exorbitant rents, - in their nodding opinions – they were meant to pay for the privilege) and some even would go as far as to mouth behind palms, held backwards, fingers spread half-way across the lower visage allowing only the spitting envy and malevolence in their eyes to impress any listeners gullible enough to be half-hearted in the acceptance of these revelations;

that the family was CURSED because of the way they treated their workmen. Sometimes these questions are unanswerable.

He worked hard, anyway. He had founded the milk-round after putting his fields in order but had soon progressed from delivery by donkey and cart to ponies and traps, horses and milk-floats, then when the three farms were operational, there were teams of cart-horses (Clydesdales and Percherons) to plough and harrow, to harvest the crops, to rake the stubble and drag logs out of his woods and hedgerows.

When the teams of workhorses were moved from one farm to the other they were never brought through town in the rough. They were brushed and groomed, their manes and tails plaited and braided, polished horse-brasses jingling down their Roman-noses, down over the whitened hair of their great barrel-chests, their hoofs blackened while their silver-shod feet would strike sparks up off the flints in the roads; more feathery strands of hair falling over their huge fetlocks.

The whole neighbourhood would turn out to see them passing through the streets with grooms and farmhands in attendance. There must have been an element of unresolved pride in the old man: of showmanship almost. It was carnival. Tom, his grandson, didn't care a damn about the sinning side, was only too glad to be part of it. On the whole he was quietly mischievous but he appreciated the banging of the big drum, same as Bernard with his perpetual, smiling-charm. Eloise, of course, was a real case and little Billy (christened John Richmond) the toddler, Tom's fervent admirer and shaping up well to become a hell of a case himself in spite of the adoring Ida Owen's efforts to subdue any discernible Tom-influences in this laughing little boy, would spin his rattle round and round before ending up throwing it at Ida herself, more often than not.

The elders of the chapel had Thomas Edwards' name engraved on a brass-plaque and put down left near the Big Pew as one entered through the doors with brass-handles at the back – after the Funeral. It is still there. Honoured in death. Also when alive, for the bank had wanted to lend him the money to actually BUY the three farms and the land off the Gibson-Watts, all the way from TyCanol right up to the edge of town; but unfortunately it was against the Righteous-One's principles: 'Neither a lender or a borrower be', his philosophy – so the family continued to rent from the local land-owners (who were probably as fed-up about the old boy's carefulness as Tom would inevitably become). A pity, as it turned out.

Auntie Lucy was left at the farm with the widow Anne but Arthur's working-days became progressively longer now as he undertook the overseeing of the three farms plus the upkeep of Mainstone and the family and staff there.

He was fortunate in Mary-Ellen who had a talent for bookkeeping and kept tight reins on the business-side of things. She would need to for Arthur, having a generous nature was inclined to listen to tales of woe, especially if another farmer was failing and would arrange loans, let off payments, advise what was best to do backed up with cash (money where mouth is) and was altogether too much of a soft touch in some ways. Mary Ellen loved him dearly (except for physicalities ahem!) but had to keep this trait in him under constant surveillance – and as for Tom, well – it seemed that he had inherited Arthur's gregariousness albeit in a quiet way to quite an alarming degree.

That Chinny-Lloyd, next door, Lance Milward, Stan Harris! Turks! It must be stopped. Arthur would have to discipline the boy. He had always been 'difficult' while BernARD was such a sweet little angel. Why oh why was the whole thing so disgusting, then so difficult rearing the results? Mary Ellen hated the 'submissions' of the marriage-bed, the ruination of her figure, having so much to do when she would rather sit down and read if the truth were known, visit friends: the Prices , the other lady-friends who would call her M.E. or best of all – drive out to the Forest Inn in her gig by herself, the lively little Welsh-cob trotting high, alone with the pony, the curlews calling, the turf springing under the flaming gorse. It smelled of tinned-peaches. Her favourite place was up the path by the side of the inn – then over to the pond in the dip between ragged pines and fir-trees. Going over the crown before the descent, the whole of Cefnllys was outlined below against the south-west: the hills booming all the way down to Abergavenny, black against restless skies or dove-grey merging into blue. Whatever. She loved it: the tomb of seven ancient kings or warriors to the right in the foreground, the weathered remains of seven tree-trunks bent by the wind sticking out of the tump. Yes, she loved THIS: the wind, the hills, and the warrior-kings. It must be ancestral or ancestral-in-law for Arthur's mother Anne had lived in shadow of that hill leaning down towards the main road back to Pen-y-Bont before she married the old one: the Righteous, may God rest him. Mary Ellen was pious. Would send arrow-like prayers to the Almighty as she rode along. She was only able to snatch moments to herself now.

Sometimes she suspected she had not been made for marriage. It was her beauty that had marred her, Pride. Her profile held up in silhouette attending the concert-hall. Her little hands on the keyboard of the rosewood grand piano. It had been essential to gain a position – could not allow all that beauty to go to waste. Apart from that, she had the soul of a nun. Yes. She confessed as much to herself sometimes, sighing with frustrations she had no idea how to assuage.

That his wife was skilled in book-keeping was undoubtedly a re-lief to Arthur who had a love of pleasant company and liked to attend council-meetings and to be in the know of what was going on around the county: any urgent matters that might need attention. He soon became a J.P. having his seat on The Bench. As a magistrate, local criminals were brought before him as one of the worthies officiating at the courthouse. It was said that matters of incest were listened to with the <u>utmost interest</u> so that often offenders were asked to repeat statements made but a few seconds before. Hardly any prisoners at all were sent 'up the line' (to Shrewsbury) for further interrogations. The assembly being exclusively Christian, whatever the domination, worked mainly on the principle that justice is inferior to mercy, and most penitents, to their intense pleasure and amazement, were let off. 'There but for the Grace of God, go I' ...... being paramount in the hearts of Arthur and Co. He was elected Chairman of the Council on more than one occasion and also was approached by the local Masonic-Lodge, eventually becoming Worshipful Master (photographed in an apron with medals – but that of course was many years later.)

Meanwhile, when Lloyd George came to stay at the Gwalia Hotel, he would send down to ask Arthur to come up after dinner and sing to him. Arthur had the most beautiful singing voice. It was untrained but the sound was deep and melodious, never to be forgot-ten once listened to. He had charm. When he sang he would smile and his eyes would sparkle green, the brown flecks in them catching the light to turn gold under the lamps.

He loved it when Clara Novello-Davies came to stay with them in the summers and they would have musical evenings around the piano with either Nellie accompanying the singers or Mary-Ellen in turn when Ivor and his parents were performing.

Brushed and combed to perfection, their thick, black hair smoothed down over their crowns, framing the healthy planes of their faces above the Eton collars, the Norfolk-jackets, the knickerbockers, socks and polished shoes, Tom and Bernard, now up to his shoulder, would stand together pretending to snatch the sheet-music one from the other before settling down, looking as much like Arthur as they could possibly manage (for they adored him) to sing a duet: their favourites were 'Because' and 'Watchman What Of The Night?'. They were able to make themselves look very soulful especially mouthing out "Have the Orient skies a border of light, like the f-r-i-n-g-e of a fun-er-al PALL?" and like their father, were natural performers. Also Eloise was by now quite beautiful with long, black ringlets almost to her waist and when dressed in a dark-green, velvet dress with lace collar and cuffs, white stockings and black buttoned boots, could sometimes be persuaded to sing solo.

Last year, she had picked up the new baby, Billy, out of his cot and brought him downstairs (an unheard of liberty) and ordered Ivor to plonk out 'Two Little Boys' before treating them all to a really theatrical turn involving Eloise swaying tenderly above the swaddled bundle with Tom and Bernard swiftly picking up the notes and supporting her by harmonising in all the right places. Afterwards Eloise had ascended the stairs without glancing back as the applause mounted: A diva! But Madame Novello-Davies had begged Arthur to sing 'Because' himself, once the baby was in bed. It was his song, she insisted – and if he would sing, she would accompany. Last year. 1908. A wonderful evening. A wonderful era ...... but running out Fast. Running out.

FOUR

Jim and Tom are lying on their stomachs, half-hidden beneath great rhododendron bushes bordering the lawns. Jim is telling Tom about his time in Canada: how easy it had been to find work. He had worked on the Prairies, drilling wheat. "You don't merely have a horse between the shafts, Tom – you have 6 or 8 of 'em. 6 or 8 lines in each hand. It's like ploughing the sea."

Tom is captivated. He will probably try something like that when he grows up. He is sure he will travel and have adventures as they do in 'The Gem' every Wednesday or 'The Magnet' on a Monday (Both 1d). Once he read a complete story about Redskins in the 'Boys' Own Paper' ….. but at 6d a copy, he is fortunate to be allowed that one every month. Mary-Ellen and Arthur consider those 3 publications suitable for boys to read though they have no idea that Tom shares his with Eloise for it would be frowned on, so they keep that between themselves. Bernard is still reading 'The Dreadnought' – (1d) every Thursday while little Billy happily squashes up 'Chuckles' (1d) between his podgy hands on Saturdays so no swapping can take place there even if the others wanted to. At first the older boys were supposed to share the comics but it was asking too much. The ensuing fights between Tom and the unspeakable Bernard became so vicious when one or the other had snatched a copy out of an unwilling hand, having finished with their own, that even Mary Ellen had agreed to the extra 1d in the cause of peace. Before order was restored and the armed-truce shakily in place, BernARD on not being allowed immediate access to 'The Gem' would taunt Tom with having a certain facial resemblance to Gussy in Tom Merry and Co's tales: Arthur Augustus D'Arcy in other words. The unfairness of this assertion was so great, even if there was some vague similarity between smooth, boyish cheeks and hair waved across the forehead (because the likeness was more to Bernard anyway than to Tom) – that Tom would react with flying fists directed accurately towards Bernard's smug smile, before reaping Mary Ellen's full wrath leading to the usual hiding from Arthur when he returned home from TyCanol.

The long wait in his room under the eaves, knowing he was in for it was far more than the actual punishment. The feeling of injustice could be physically painful. Inside, it was almost as if his organs were being scraped with a rake: red-raw down through the trachea, lungs, gut, and bowels. He kept trying to please Mary -Ellen and his father – but things just would not seem to go in the right direction. (Deflected by that bloody, bloody Bernard). Why should she favour him so when she had often told him, the older brother too! – that he had been nothing but trouble ever since he had been born? Once even that she WISHED he had never been born! – and that was only because he had been unable to stop laughing when the 'faithful' were having a 'united' prayer-meeting down at the Quakers.

Yes, it was a good idea. Once a month all the different Non-Conformist denominations in the town, that is Wesleyans, Congregationalists, Baptists, Friends (as the Quakers were known) and Presbyterians (them) would meet in the host chapel to show solidarity before the Lord. Tom loved going to the Friends. He found it acceptable, even exiting. "You have to sit there quiet-like and wait for the Spirit to move", he told Chinny and Co. later – "then someone will rise and give off a communication". He had not meant to laugh. It was the furthest thing from his imagination or intention…"But old Elwyn came in the back, full of beer, as usual. I couldn't help noticing. He'd had a few before…you know that big, fat chap who works down the gas-works? – him. Anyway – it was just as the silence was at its deepest and although I should have had my eyes shut, I <u>observed</u> Mr. Watkins: Hardware – preparing to rise – when Elwyn couldn't hold it in a moment longer – and this TREMENDOUS fart went reverberating round and round the room. I thought it would never end.

Poor old Elwyn. I felt sorry for him but I couldn't stop laughing either, especially with Eloise just by me and you know what she's like if anything tickles her. It was awful. Eloise tried, same as me, to stop it but she started YELPING like a puppy and ended up on the floor between the seats while I …..?" He sniffed. " 'nuff said".

But now Jim asks "- and how have things been here Tom ….. with <u>you</u> boy? Got anything to tell old Jim? Been playing any football?"

"Sh! Sh!" – Tom signs and after Jim lowers his great, curly head nearer, tells him how he is not really allowed to play but will stuff his togs and football-boots up inside his jersey and get going by sneaking down the back stairs and out that way.

"I duck through the fence and get into Chinny Lloyd's place to put the stuff on – but for Heaven's sake don't tell will you? I'll get another thrashing."

"Why?"

"Well they don't like me playing. It's wrong for some reason – and I'm not allowed to chum up with Chinny and the boys either – but I do".

"They all right?"

"Right as rain, Jim; but Mother and Pa think they're too rough".

"You like 'em? You get on with them?"

"Of course. Don't know what I'd do without them really."

"Bernard play with them too?"

"What d'you think?"

"No."

"Right."

"You've been in Cardiff, I hear – for a spell".

Tom grins ironically while Jim chews the inside of his mouth suggestively, half-laughing as if in the know.

"I was sent".

"Sent?"

"Yes."

"Why? What you do, boy?"

"I upset things."

"How?"

"Well, that sap from Cardiff was up here staying –"

"Ivor?"

"No. Our cousin, Jack."

"Oh – Betty and Zachariah's son, is it?"

"That's him"

"You don't like him?"

"Can't stand the sight of him – or his stupid sister. They're spoiled to death. Damned sissies".

"What happened?"

"We were supposed to be playing with them the whole time – but I wanted to go and be with my friends."

"Chinny and his lot?"

"Yes. We've got a club-house in the attic – above Old Humphries – The-Pony-King's place."

"What – 2 doors up? That mean old pisser who conveys invalids up and down to the Pump-Rooms when they're taking the waters?"

"Yes, him. He's got all sorts of nags and that in his stables. Donkeys! Old hacks. My stars, you should see some of the Jim! Bones sticking out – but on the whole ….. not too bad a state. Piebalds, two of Daggerfield's Skewbalds – 14 hands, those, ….. nice lines – and some dumpy, little Welsh cobs for pulling the bath-chairs."

"Not a bad business then."

"Cor' – not much! He's raking it in. Well, just look how busy we get in the summer – and he's got all the big hotels to cater for as well. Can't go wrong."

"Like Arthur and the milk-rounds."

"Well yes. Old Gramps knew what he was doing in 1872, Jim."

"No doubt about it boy – what did you do to get on the wrong side of young cousin Jack's lot?"

"Huh! Well that was the last straw, I suppose. He wouldn't join in our game for a start."

"What game be that, Tom?"

"Oh, Chinny and some of 'em come over when nobody's looking and we get up in the branches of those crab-apple trees overlapping the 'arrangements' – other side of the first lawn."

"What – the outside latrines?"

"Yes – for the visitors. As you know, they're open-topped – so if you're up in the trees, you're looking straight down the holes in the planks over the buckets - ."

"Unless some poor bugger's squatting on the seat ..... is that it?"

Tom shakes with laughter. His head goes down on to his hands. His toes drum into the grass."

"Y-e .. Y-e ... Yes! – that's about it. What we do, Jim, we wait for the invalids to be conveyed back from the Rock Park where they've been imbibing the waters, we know they'll be in a hell of a hurry – so when the crab-apples are ripe – we get up in those branches, hide in the leaves and wait for Humphries-The-Pony-King's team to deposit them out the front, full of 'sulphur' and chalibeate water as they are .... Oh, you know – all the fluid they're topped-up with until they can hardly wait to get out of the bath chairs and pony-carts.

Well, they come rushing down the side of the house, practically lifting their skirts or unbuttoning the flies before they can unlatch the doors and -------."

"Poor buggers. Poor buggers."

"I ... I – know, oh dear ..... sorry Jim but it has its funny side .... Gor – you should see them scratting to get on with it – heads down, up with the skirts then down with drawers ..... bare bums sticking up before AA-A-H ..... just about to sit down and let it all out when BAM, BAM, BAM – we let loose with the crab-apples. Oh, I can't tell you how funny it is. Chinny laughed so much he fell out of the tree and went slithering down almost into the can with some old trout -------".

"Oh don't! DON'T!" Jim has turned over on to his back, knees up, rolling from side to side in a paroxysm of unseemly mirth.

"Oh, I shouldn't encourage you boy. Mary-Ellen would kill me if she could only see me now."

"I know, but.....". Tom sits up wiping the tears of laughter and the snot from his face with his bare hands. Jim hands him his clean handkerchief.

"Here boy. Use this for goodness sake."

"Thanks Jim."

"So was that it? Was that why they sent you to school in Cardiff?"

"No. That was leading to it – but it had been a bad summer for me. Apart from the crab-apple stunts, there had been other things. Father was always having to give me the strap and half the time I hadn't meant any harm at all."

"What had you done, Tom?"

"Well, do you remember Mrs. Heighway – friend of Mother and Father ….. her husband died?"

"Not that pretty little woman who used to – "

"Yes her."

"He's never dead?"

"Yes he is. He died suddenly. Everbody dies Jim."

"Only when their time's up boy."

"That so Jim?"

"That's it Tom. Don't do to worry about it now. Just make sure you're right with the Lord boy – and keep beggaring on."

"COR' Jim – that's practically what old Gramps used to tell us …. " 'er without the buggering bit, I might add."

"Yes, - well you know what I mean, young 'un."

"Thanks Jim. It's a help that."

"What about her then?"

"Who?"

"The Heighway woman."

"Oh yes. She and John Heighway, her son, came to stay here for a time after Mr. Heighway died. The next Summer, they both came again for a few days before Mother and Pa took her over to Aberystwyth for a week – to get some sea air into her while John stayed with us."

"Is he to your liking?"

"Oh aye. John's fine."

"Yes? Well go on."

" – She had brought some old buckskin pony with her and asked Father if he would stable him for a time and of course he said yes –"

"Um-m-m?"

"Well just listen to this Jim and see if you can get it from my point of view."

"Uh huh."

" – a funny thing occurred. They were all done up out on the 1st back lawn before they set off for Aber. ... but just before leaving, little Mrs. Heighway turned to look over her shoulder towards the stables where the buckskin was quartered and suddenly she started crying; or nearly."

"Oh Arthur!" – she said to Pa.

"Arthur – what are we going to do with Hector?" (The pony). "We are going to have to get rid of him – but I just don't know HOW I'm going to do it."

"Yes ….. go on. What did Arthur and Mary-Ellen say?"

"They tried to comfort her. They put their arms round her and Father said – 'Don't you worry, my dear, we will think of something.' Then they went off for the week in Aberystwyth"

"What in hell are you supposed to have done wrong Tom?"

"I meant to help Jim, that's all. I could tell the old man was worried – same as Mother and I felt so sorry for Mrs. Heighway that – to cut a long story short – a meeting was convened."

"What kind of a meeting you talking about boy?"

"John Heighway and I, Chinny and the gang – above Humphries's shop. I told you we have our den up there."

"So you called the meeting?"

"I did – yes."

"Why?"

"To see what could be done. Mrs. Heighway had been nearly crying, as I told you, that she would have to get rid of Hector – but she didn't know how to do it – so I convened the meeting to see if the boys and I could come up with some ideas – and anyhow, poor, thin, little John Heighway, one of the nicest blokes you could ever wish to meet, was really concerned – ".

"So what did you decide?"

"Shoot him – to save Mrs. Heighway having to do it."

"What?"

"Yes – shoot him and bury him in the garden. We thought it would take a load off Father's mind too."

"You didn't SHOOT him!"

"We did."

"Who actually shot him?"

"I did. I was chosen by the others because I know how to fire Father's shot-gun so we took it down off the rack – I got the cartridges, we dug this huge hole in the back-lawn, out of sight of the house .... in case Ida and Co. .... Then John Heighway brought Hector out, stood him alongside the pit, I shot him through the head then we pushed him in and tried to bury him before they came back.

We thought they would be no-end pleased except we were worried that we hadn't made a very smooth job of putting back the lawn."

"What the hell happened?"

"Huh! – They came home and after tea, Mrs. Heighway went off to the stables. I was quite exited thinking how relieved they would all be. She came running in. "Where's HECTOR?" she cried and Father stood up suddenly putting his china moustache-cup down on the oak with the tea in it, untouched. "Tom?" – he said quite fiercely – so of course I had to tell them there and then instead of keeping it as a nice surprise for later on."

"And what did Arthur say, Tom?"

"He was MAD – I can tell you. Furious with me. He wouldn't listen. I had the biggest hiding I've ever had. I couldn't understand why they were so cross with me."

"Did you manage to explain?"

"Oh – the next day. But it was too late then …. Huh! For my backside Jim.

Mary-Ellen was in a real huff and although Pa had cooled off, I could tell he was as impatient as hell to get me out of the way. Evidently Mrs. Heighway had only been worried about how to SELL Hector – not destroy him."

"Well they haven't broken thy spirit yet lad, have they? Don't you let 'em."

"Nuff said again Jim. Another lesson learned the damned hard way."

"So that was why you were sent to Cardiff?"

"No. Not that either. It was Mother's decision I suppose, – after the Three Wells episode. I suspect, if the truth were only known, that she was worried about my unwelcome influence on BernARD."

"So?"

"We were invited out to Uncle Tom's place for the weekend: Bernard, Jack and I."

"And?"

" – I knew I wouldn't be able to stick it without seeing some of my own friends – I mean …. not even Eloise was coming out there – just Bernard, that prat Jack and me, so I arranged for Chinny and Co. to show up mid-morning – as if they were passing and just dropped in, kind of."

"What? Right out towards Builth wells?"

"Well, you never know Jim."

"Pushing it a bit boy."

"Ah. I s'pose. Anyway – we were all dressed up in our knicker-bockers and best shirts, hair pomaded down like lounge-lizards, I thought, before being taken over to Three Wells by Shaky Davies: Bran-Mash, in the trap, Arthur's prize Hackney-Cob between the yellow shafts: an honour ….. or maybe that bit of Edwards' pride surfacing, Jim."

Jim chuckles. "You've got 'em, boy." His hand swipes over his face, forehead to chin. "Bran-Mash …. him who sees to Mary Ellen's fowls?"

"Him."

"What transpired?"

"We were returned without thanks, same evening."

"Why?"

"Afraid we mistakenly drowned a lot of Uncle Tom's hens, to start with."

"How the hell - ?"

"Tried to get 'em to swim on that great duck-pond they've got – but the buggers all sank before we could get them out."

"Then what?"

"We got over that – and had been called in for hot milk and cakes about 11 o'clock when here come Chinny and Co. Boy was I glad to see them."

"Did they come in?"

"Oh yes. Uncle Tom and Aunty – invited them in all right, got the maid to boil up some more milk and bring the cakes back out."

"Did Bernard know you'd asked 'em to call?"

"I think he guessed. He looked – watchful. He's a bit frightened of Chinny, I think. Probably Mother keeping on about him being 'unpleasant' or something."

"HA. Ha. So – did you get up to some pranks then, to get sent home – or what? I thought you said you were there for the week-end."

"We were SUPPOSED to have been. No – it was just ….. well 'er – Chinny and Co. can't stand the sight of Jack either. I think I told you before. He's such a ninny. Should be in a frock, I think – so do they."

"Bit of bullying was there?"

"I suppose."

"What you do?"

"'nother meeting. Concerning Jack."

"And what was the outcome?"

"'ANG 'IM, Chinny ordained."

"What? ….. WHAT ----?"

"We were in the barn. There was a rope in the corner – one of the joho-lines. Chinny's decision was final …. So we slung the rope round his neck and the other end over a beam and were just about to haul him off his feet when the door came flying open and Uncle Tom came thundering in."

"Was he shocked?"

"Foaming! Anyway, Chinny and Co. went tumbling in all directions and adding it all up – hens drowned etcetera, Bernard and I were sent back to Mainstone, post-haste."

"Well boy – you could have killed him, you know."

"I know now."

"You didn't then?"

"Well 'course not. Thought we'd just dangle him for a bit and let him down after we'd given him a fright."

"And that's why you were sent to Cardiff?"

"Yes. It was all arranged. I was to go and learn book-keeping at Bloggs of Cardiff – my Alma Mater: BLOGGS …. S'trewth! And the worst part was a total come-uppance: that I would be staying at Aunty Betty's and Uncle Zac's with that precious pair, Jack and his sister – for company."

"How long did you stick it?"

"2 months."

"Learn anything?"

"No."

"Did you get a report?"

"Brief one."

"What did it say?"

"One word."

"What was it?"

"HOSTILE."

"What you want to do when you grow up, Tom?"

"Help Father – that's all."

"On the farm?"

"Yes – of course."

"Could you manage that d'you think?"

"Oh aye. Easy. As long as Mother sticks to the books."

"Ah yes. It's nice here Tom, isn't it?"

"I love it. Especially when Eloise's on form – though she doesn't seem quite so interested in our games now ….. fooling around, you know. She's always in company with Maggie Price: Boot and Shoe - or the Davies girls from the Limes these days. Don't see much of her then do we?"

Growing up, I suppose. How old is Eloise now, Tom?"

"Umm. – let's see. I'll be 10 in October – then she must be getting on for 15, I suppose – and she's kept more or less under constant <u>surveillance</u> Jim."

"I like the way you emphasise certain words, Tom. Makes me chuckle."

"Yes, but sometimes if you say a certain word in a certain way – it seems to exactly describe an attitude – don't you think, Jim?"

"I <u>do</u> lad: indubitably."

"Ah – good 'un. Yes I can almost <u>see</u> Ida Owen peering over the top of some windowsill as I say that one. Poor Eloise – to have that stuck to you all the time. I don't know why she puts up with it."

"Has to I suppose, lad."

"I wouldn't."

"No, I know you wouldn't Tom – but it's different for girls."

"Don't see why it should be."

"You'll learn."

"Just reminds me Jim. I've been invited down to a party at Maggie Price's – Eloise's best friend – next week. Mother says I've got to go and Bernard is to come with me. What in hell will I do there, Jim?"

"Enjoy thyself, I trust."

"Hast <u>thou</u> ever enjoyed <u>thy</u>self at a bloody birthday-party, Jim?"

"Frequently my friend – and don't swear. You'll get <u>me</u> into trouble for influencing you – I'll wager. But as for enjoying thyself lad …. Depends on the company don't it? - What the hell's THIS?"

Suddenly a great sorrel mare comes galloping round the corner of the house. She is flecked with foam and slobbering at the mouth for she has been ridden hard and is blowing.

Archy Lewis, the Llanerch is on her back. He has his crop out and is urging her up the wide, concrete steps to Mainstone's back entrance. The door is wide-open leading into the polished hall-way. Archie is cheering and whooping like a maniac.

"We've won! We've won!" he bellows and shoves the mare forward with his knees and heels so that she plunges up the steps, her quarters quivering with fright as her shoes loose grip on the polished tiles of the back porch.

Jim rises in one fluid movement, huge hand swiping over his grinning face and makes a dive towards the house.

"Conservatives have got in then!" – he says quietly to Tom. "He's come to crow over Arthur. Local elections."

"Yes." Tom mutters. Father's all for Lloyd George's lot."

"Stay there Tom boy," Jim orders over his shoulder, keep well back."

He follows the rider across the threshold as Tom hovers at the edge of the shrubbery, intent on what Jim means to do: what <u>can</u> he do now?

He has not long to wonder. There is a commotion and then here come horse, rider, crop, hat and boots backwards, thrown unceremoniously from the mighty arms of Jim Corp – down once again on to the gravel path skirting the flower-beds around the 1ˢᵗ lawn. A scarlet flower flares and spins in the corner of Tom's eye.

"Get from here!" Jim advises Archie in his soft voice as the mare regains her back feet and springs up off her white fetlocks towards the dark, ivied corner of the house with a mightily subdued Archie, ... older, second-cousin to Tom, brother of the one they call <u>Aunty</u> Corys in Rhayader: (more polite, it is thought), readjusting his small, green hat having the brown feather stuck in its band, with the handle of his riding-crop, as he is bounced off and away sideways then out of sight and only the clatter of the mare's hoofs left as they hit the road and fade into the distance down Station Crescent.

1909. In the borders, the dark velvet flowers nod in a gentle breeze and tall blue delphiniums spike towards the burning sky, a furry, yellow-striped bee goes burrowing into the spires and a sudden gust stirs the deep-green firs guarding the back lawns from Chinny's place, next door. A singead-black crow flops over the tall chimneys, over the gardens and down towards the Crossing. Tom gives a sudden shiver.

"Someone walking over my grave, Jim," he laughs when Jim tells him he surely can't be cold on a day like this. They re-enter the house and walk through into the front parlour to wait for Arthur to come home for tea.

To Jim, who has been away, the rooms are full of what he always thinks of as the 'Edwards' Smell': a mixture of flowers and fruit, polish, blue and white willow-patterned china and the lingering odour of good, cooked food. A welcoming smell. He only wishes that he were welcome here. He knows he is not and Tom knows though he has not yet learned – that neither is he.

Mary-Ellen is across the hallway in the other room teaching Bernard percentages. He is smiling out of his brown-moth eyes right into her love-lit face, while Ida Owen rocks Billy (christened John Richmond), the baby, upstairs out of the heat and Eloise ducks her head and giggles over a letter she is writing to Ivor Novello-Davies in Cardiff. He is a nice pal though not as exiting to be with as some she hopes to see at Maggie Price's birthday-party next week.

She raises her dark head, after a time and looks out of the open window. All the windows are right down to the sash this afternoon, it is so close. There will be a storm later. She can sense it: feel it coming above the scent of the roses covering the stone walls between them and the street.

When Ivor was staying, if they had a storm brewing, the three of them, Tom, Ivor and herself would snatch an eiderdown off one of the beds not in use and snuggle down together under the rhododendron-bushes bordering the 2nd lawn out the back, watching as the sky turned green then black before becoming inexorably blacker and blacker until the first flicker of lightening lit the gardens instead of the burning sun that had been out strongly but a short time before and they would have to rush for the back-door through the rapidly cooling air, the smell of rain and roses, as the afternoon skies threatened to burst.

They would scramble up the stairs, dodging past the maids' bedrooms where the women slept heavily between duties for one hour precisely in the heat of the day, along landing after landing, up more and more stairways until they reached the top of the house and were able to flop down on to one of the beds under the eaves, re-arranging the eiderdown around them to give the maximum feeling of animal or cave-like warmth as they gazed out of the window flat on their stomachs, chins in their hands, to watch the skies boil and crack right over Dolfan in the distance – straight in front – and the

Black Mountains towards Abergavenny running down South, to their left.

TyCanol was in a dip between them and Dolfan but the farm-house was out of sight from this angle. They could only see the top of the Pathfield with the clanging, iron, swing-gate leading into Mr. Morris's field, where the pale mauve and white milkmaids grew in early summer and came down the slope this side as far as the Electric-Lightworks.

They were too big to play these games now, her father had told Mary-Ellen, when he came upon them the last time playfully wres-tling beneath the eiderdown, so of course M.E. had informed Ida ..... and 'Nuff said' as Tom would have it with a significant sniff, Eloise chuckled to herself.

She couldn't be bothered to understand half of these senseless instructions: to hell with them. Anyway, the 'garden-bits' were out as well because they were told they could get <u>struck by lightning</u> sitting under the rhododendrons – so in a way she could see the sense of <u>that</u> but as regards the rest: complete mystification. At least she had got Maggie Price's party to look forward to. She could hardly wait.

They are full up with 'guests' at Mainstone and the bathrooms much in demand so "FHB" Mary-Ellen pronounces; "Family Hold Back" - sending Nellie Davies and Ida Owen scurrying into Tom and Bernard's rooms with the long zinc baths and into Eloise's with the hip-bath while Rosa and Thin Annie led by Big Annie come clambering upstairs with hot water jugs, leaving Hannah to refill the urns and kettles in the scullery before stoking the fires almost to white heat so that the children may be bathed and dressed in time to go out.

They have to be there at 6 o'clock, <u>prompt</u>. It is now nearly 4 in the afternoon so there is no big hurry.

"Top her up Rosa!" Tom laughs cheekily towards the tall, dark-haired, panting woman when she comes up the second time …. "then get out of here. Don't want you eyeing my nuts when I'm stripped off."

"Cheeky young <u>hound</u> –" she shrieks and grabs his tortoiseshell, hard-backed hairbrush off the dressing table. "Take THAT! – you little bugger – and THAT!" she yells and gives him such a couple of whacks across the backside that it sends him howling into the corner, both hands clutching the seat of his pants.

"Oh Rosa!" he laughs – "that hurt gel. You'll ruin me. Can't you take a joke?"

"Not that kind Tom Edwards. Now behave – or else! …..get yourself washed and dressed decently mind you – your clothes are laid out on the bed ….look! – nice clean shirt and socks, best suit, white cotton under –."

"All right Rosa …. No need for the full inventory…. I'm coming up for manhood now. I know what's what …… not a baby anymore. Want a quick look? -----"

"BEHAVE YOURSELF – before I send Arthur in to -------- --".

The door creaks open. "What?" Arthur asks half-humorously from his position behind the planks, his eyes swivelling to Tom in the corner. He must have come home early.

" 'er …… been telling him to behave hisself, Mr. Edwards, that's all." Rosa lifts her chin defiantly.

"Quite right too!" Arthur beams and goes out again releasing the latch. How Tom loves him. So cool. As a cucumber.

"Thanks Rosa", he grins.

"Young varmint," she grins back and picking up the dirty clothes he has shed and folding them over her arm goes back downstairs leaving him to divest himself of the rest before getting himself ready for the party.

He will be 10 in October, all being well.

F I V E

The whole evening seems to be full of roses. They decide to walk down to Price's even though it looks as if it might rain at any moment.

"Better let Bran-Mash get out the gig" kind Hannah suggests. "Don't want to spoil that finery" (to Eloise) "and arrive looking like a hen that's dragged itself out of a puddle."

"I'll be all right thankyou", Eloise replies smiling and so they set off, herself looking 'absolutely splendid' as Tom tells her and the two boys brushed and combed to perfection.

"Bread and butter FIRST!" Ida yells just as they think they have got clear. She has come out of the stables and stands in the drive, one hand under the other elbow holding the skinny arm aloft to emphasise her instructions.

"Mind your own business!" Tom yells back even making Bernard grin, but Ida is not to be ignored quite so easily. "It's manners! She shrieks. "Don't you dare go starting on no jelly before you've done the bread an' ------"

Tom has had enough. He drops Eloise's arm and rushes back towards her .....

"Will you shut that TRAP!" he says quietly "do you think we want all our friends to think we're BABIES who don't know how to behave in public? For Heaven's sake Owen – give mother some credit – she taught us all this years ago – now just go and make yourself a nice steaming compote of stinging-nettles – then" – (and running back laughing) ...... "SIT in it!"

"Or shit in it" Eloise whispers "hem, hem" – and they cross the road and head towards Middleton Street before turning right into Spa road, crossing the grey stone bridge over the line leading to Swansea in one direction, Shrewsbury in the other (more roses) then over the steep slope left into Park Crescent. The Prices are halfway down.

The shop is shut so they ring the bell at the narrow doorway leading into the private premises beside the shop front.

"Quite a decent pair of paddlers, those black 'uns," Tom murmurs to Eloise – "look well on old Mrs. Price-Right..... I'll warr'n" - he says indicating some galoshes piled up behind the dainty heels towards the front of the window and sticking on the Radnor accent to make Eloise laugh.

"That's done it!" she crumples round the mouth, desperate not to loose control of herself. "Tom – don't you dare! Look - I'm supposed to be a YOUNG LADY .. please Tom, PLEASE, don't make me laugh – not in front of my friends -------".

The door opens. Unfortunately, it is not Maggie Price but Mrs. Price herself who stands bow-fronted towards them, filling the narrow aperture.

"Ah – good afternoon, children", she smiles down at them delightedly.

"So glad you could come. How's Mary-Ellen? Is the baby all right? Going to rain d'you think? How's Arthur? O-o-o-h – don't you all look nice! Eloise – like the hairstyle. Had it cut? Yes. Beautiful. Mary Pickford dear, to the Tee-ee. We're going to play all kinds of games – 'HUSTLEMEE' – heard of that one? Has Mary-Ellen got it for you all yet? - 'BLOW-FOOTBALL' – we've bought that – 'er 'SCOUTING' ……. You joining the Scouts Tom? No? Bernard ……? Maybe eh? …. Well, well, come in; come in –". She squeezes herself aside for them to do so.

Tom digs a long finger into Eloise's back as she tries to slip past the enormous dark-blue, lace-collared figure now backed into a recess to the right of the doorway.

"Ah the entry into Valhalla!" he pronounces wickedly and Eloise stifles an explosion of giggling as best she can – bringing the soft parcel she is carrying as a present for Maggie Price, in her gloved hands up to her face, to hide any unseemly mirth.

Bernard follows on, smiling comfortably as usual. They proceed along the narrow hallway, where Mr. Price's face appears like a balloon bobbing around the corner where it leads out of the shop for one moment only. His face is red as if it is has been raked with a garden fork, very white in the stripes, his hair black but sparse, his smile almost apologetic. They have been told to be careful how they use the lavatorial arrangements. He has VD whatever that might be. "So here is the man who's caught a disease from doing things to women that he shouldn't". Tom feels quite astounded suddenly 'Have to ask Chinny?' he thinks to himself before they all mount the stairs, Mrs. Price bringing up the rear.

Maggie Price is on the landing but drops what she is doing as soon as their heads come into view.

"Eloise!" – she shrieks. "Tom! Bernard!" and runs to embrace each one in turn.

They hand over their gifts and she drops them on to a walnut chest until she has helped Eloise off with her coat. "Oh – thanks, thanks", she gasps - "I'll open them now in a minute ..... but ELOISE – what a lovely dress ..... Oh – I do love the way it clings – then all those heavenly pleats in line down the hem ...... the buttons ...... such an unusual green. Pearl buttons – and your HAIR! You've had it cut ..... who did it Crimes? Thought so. He's an artist, isn't he? Now – my presents boys – wait a minute. What do you think of my frock? Eloise? Tom? Bernard?"

"Best I've seen you in Maggie Price." Eloise's eyes shine back at her friend. "Like those bows over the old bosoms, kid ..... and the cut of the collar – just wonderful. 'ain't we a pair?"

"Go-getters!" Tom grins. "That colour suits your hair Maggie Price. Ginger and Lilac...... just the ticket."

"Auburn boy! – not ginger" she laughs good naturedly..... "and what about young master Bernie here. What d'you think of me dress boy?".

"Simply SUPURB, Maggie Price!" he says in all seriousness, blinking his great brown eyes – so that the others can't help but laugh even at the risk of hurting her feelings.

"Young charmer you". Maggie Price bends down, knees together and pinches his chin at which he simpers more than ever. Even Tom feels a moment of tolerance towards the little 'bugger' as he usually describes him to his friends: a moment of pride in his young brother's affability.

"Well let's see what I've got", Maggie Price turns and pounces on the packages they have brought and starts slipping the string off the corners of first Eloise's then Tom's and lastly Bernard's.

"Oh Eloise", she exclaims as the most beautiful scarf comes tumbling out of the brown-paper wrapping. "It is beautiful!" And it is.

The scarf is like spun gold – it is that delicate and the most gorgeous tint of orange to the softest wool Maggie Price has ever seen. It is so soft that it almost springs out of her hands and beaded at the ends with small blue and lilac glass baubles; also with small pieces of metal that glitter almost red in the electric light that Mrs. Price has managed to get the old man to have installed in the family quarters.

"Evidently, outraged feminine-sensibilities can be turned to good account", Tom finds himself conjecturing - for they have not yet had the Electric Light put in at Mainstone even though they were the first small hotel in town to have hot water (guest bedrooms only) linked to the little boiler in the cellar.

He, himself has brought Maggie Price a book of Greek myths while Bernard has chosen a novelty pack of bath-salts done up as a 'Thumbs Up' doll modelled on the American 'Kewpie'.

Maggie Price is delighted. "Come on in," she urges them, "the others are in the front – then turning to Eloise – she half whispers as if slightly shocked ….. "Rosalind Hamer's in a HAREM SKIRT".

They move along the banister-rail towards the open door where all the noise seems to be coming from and are ushered into a room overlooking the street. From the size of it, it must have been two rooms knocked into one at some time in the past and is situated immediately over the shop, on one side, the living-quarters downstairs on the other.

The late evening sun is shining directly in from the west and the room looks golden. It will always be golden in Tom's memory.

Rosalind Hamer is sitting on the floor in the middle of a little group of other girls and boys directly in the sun's rays. She is alight. Her eyes come up and for a moment her forehead wrinkles in a puzzled yet quite cheeky way as they look towards this tall young boy as he comes further into the room; then astonishingly she winks one wicked eye before smiling and dropping back into conversation with her friends. Her eyes are the palest green he has yet to see. Not sea-green nor hazel-green as are his own and Eloise's, not emerald nor sap green – but pale, pale green as glass marbles you might find them putting in the tops of bottles down at the lemonade-bottle factory – no ….. fairy-green – that's what it is …. She is magic – no getting away from it. He is not one to hang back.

"Like your outfit", he says quietly, leaning over the backs of some of Rosalind's evident admirers on the floor. "Stand up ….. let's have a look gel."

"Impudence won't get you anywhere" Rosalind shoots back at him – "and anyway – who are you, you young whippersnapper?". Tom laughs. "Tom Edwards: TyCanol – that's me – and if you don't mind me asking – where'd you get it?"

"Get what?"

"The pyjama-set" he grins – I particularly like the bags."

"Bags!"

"Harem pants then …. Bit like my old man's long-johns, Miss Powell – but yours suit you better than his would – get what I mean?"

Rosalind giggles and stands up, twirling round as she does so, holding out the skirt away from the satin harem-trousers. She looks a treat. The dress is watered green silk split up the sides to reveal cycla-men-pink satin trousers, drawn in at the bottoms under that a pair of silk-clad ankles are revealed before small feet encased in patent black shoes with silver buckles and slim, spiked 2-inch heels adding height to an already quite tall girl. The dress has a matching pink floppy tie securing a wide cream lace collar described as 'crash' and Rosalind's hair hangs from a centre-parting, barely brushing the collar at the front but ascending to the nape of her neck at the back: a kind of bob. Her hair is corn-coloured, as when the sun has been on it for a few days: rich silken gold with barely perceptible streaks of red one minute – then of almost violet the next. Unforgettable.

He leans closer. "Who cut your hair?" he asks politely. "It suits you".

"Oh, do you think so Tom", her hand comes up and prods at the side of her head for a moment – "well, if you can keep a secret – and I can tell you CAN, can't I?"

"Sure thing!" Tom assures her, taking off one of Jim Corp's expressions in the process ….. "Shoot Rosalind!"

"Do it myself boy", she grins.

"Never"

"Do too. Just get Ma's dressmaking sheers – and <u>thumbs up!</u> – you know."

"But it looks wonderful. How'd you reach the back?"

"Oh it's not all my own work Tom – Dada shears that. I tell you, EVERYBODY will be wearing theirs like this soon – you'll see."

"What does he do, your Dad?"

"He's the Arbor ….. well, (can't say it) ….. he looks after all the trees and parkland round the area. He's got some kind of named position in the county – but I can't pronounce him."

Tom likes the way she laughs.

"How old are you?" he asks

"Thirteen" she answers proudly pointing her foot and admiring the way the trouser-leg falls in lines down her leg.

"How about you Tom? You look a fine upstanding young fellah – how old yourself? Come on, tell me?"

"Be ten in October, Rosalind".

"O-o-h – too young for me then."

"I wouldn't have thought so."

Tom bravely catches hold of her fingers.

"Wait for me Rosalind" he grins conspiratorially and she grins back.

"Have to see young Edwards – won't we?"

"Look – what school do you go to Miss Powell?"

"County".

"Oh".

"You?"

"Nats".

"National?"

"Yep …. Though I did spend a spell in Cardiff this year."

"Sent away?"

"Yes ….. but it didn't work".

"You taking the Scholarship then?"

"Don't know yet. S'pose so and if you're in the County ….. better have a shot at it I suppose. Did you pass?"

"No."

"How d'you get in then?"

"They PAY – of course. I'm no scholar I'm afraid. I'm a dunce Tom."

"Oh good. Me too. Can't be bothered me – and they're always ON so. Mustn't use my left hand and all that. We had an exam last week and I got it in the neck once again."

"Why?"

"One of the questions was: if it takes 6 balls of string at so long a stretch to go round the gas-works, then how many balls would it take to go round three gas-works of the same circumference, the circumference being 100 yards?"

"So …. What did you put?"

"I just put: Balls and balls and balls."

"Oh Tom, you are a caution."

"Will you come and see Charlie Chaplin with me – at the Kino – next week?"

"Tom! Get on with you, you young hound …. You're much too young for –".

Suddenly an older boy, taller than Tom, gangly and wearing glasses has elbowed his way through the others and comes to stand, half in front of him, blocking his access to Rosalind.

"Oh Rosalind," he says in a public-school accent "<u>there</u> you are. Look they're going to eat in a minute – so come on – you're with me on this one – especially if you want me to teach you the Tango afterwards – do come now."

Rosalind excuses herself and trots off on her high heels in the direction of the dining room. Tom can hear everyone clanking downstairs but although he follows on and enjoys the food, although he even attempts the Tango later and plays game after game with Lionel Beard and Haydn Black, two of the gang from their den above Humphries-The-Pony-King's place, his mind is clouded with thoughts of Rosalind Hamer. Dead straight hair – not caring. Turned up nose. Trousers. Breasts forming under the silk. He thinks of her and how his prick had stiffened while he was talking to her. It had bloody hurt. What has happened now? He must seek his councillor Chinny's much needed guidance here. Thank Heavens for Chinny! He goes in search of Eloise and Bernard.

They walk back through the late evening, through the air warming up for another fine day tomorrow, the summer dust, the scent of roses.

Saturday evening. They are all there: Chinny, Lionel, Morley, Lance, Stan and Tom.

"Anything to report, boys?" Chinny puts on his mock Justice-Lloyd impression. They all laugh. They discuss many things: the suffragettes, the workers' riots down South, Gus's latest in The Gem, that lot trying to bring an AIR-CIRCUS to Llandrindod: how fascinating that would be. Would they dare fly? Would they go up? What! – Try and stop them. They laugh at something Tom has heard at home: one of the would-be councillors looking for election had promised solemnly if he was chosen – to bring in trams to the area 'running like greased lightening out to Llanbadarn Fawr Bridge'.

The boys <u>howl</u> with laughter. "Th-then ..... what about old Pritchard ... ha ha .... 'member when Jehu the coach-driver found the saline spring down the Rock. – an' Old Pritch was trying to get the Board to buy the land? Ha ha ha ... S – said – Ha Ha – 'If we don't seize this opportunity NOW – it'll be like killing the fatted calf that lays the golden-eggs!' Oh by heck it's funny 'ain't it?" Stan can hardly constrain himself. Then it's – "Now Tom, how'd the party go boy? Morley here was saying you were sizing up a promising young wench. What's this Tom eh? Eh?"

"Well true enough Stan, I suppose. Chinny's probably told you – had to ask him about – certain 'er .... Alterations in the lower regions. Needed a bit of explaining."

"You got it now"..

"Oh ah! – Know what to do all right for temporary-relief".

"Dr. Lloyd officiating".

"Splendidly thank you."

"Well lets all compare sizes – now we're getting down to the nitty-gritty – shall we? Out with it Tom – you first."

"Hell's bells! Tom – where the hell d'you get that one. No bother for you boy – look at this – nothing compared to what you've got there".

–   and one after the other they solemnly bring out their equipment, sit together in the circle as long as necessary before adjourning 'till their next' with Chinny's muted admonitions ringing in their ears. "Whatever you do lads, never allow any buggers near your arse-end. They'll RUIN you."

Sometimes Tom feels an immeasurable gulf separating him from the purity of his mother's profile: the stern dignity of his dear father. He remembers Ivor's hands wandering over him that time beneath the blanket. He had not minded – then in Cardiff he had called round to Cathedral Road to see him once, when he had felt so cloistered at Uncle Zac's – but Ivor had been in a strange mood. He had somehow looked like Mary Ellen for a fleeting moment, chilling, feminine, before Tom had taken the hint and left. There had been an older boy with him in the house. Just as well. According to Chinny's 'observations', Ivor was one if ever one was and remembering his mentor's dire warnings about Buggers Proper he grins, grimacing as he clutches both hands round the seat of his cords and makes for his room where at least now he can let his mind wonder over the beauties that are ROSALIND, ROSALIND, ROSALIND. He can never live up to the standards of this house – but to hell with it. He is mightily glad of his friends.

S I X

Grandmother Anne is dead. 1910 comes in on an icy-blast. There is black ice. The roads are treacherous. Frozen spears hang from the eaves, the doorframes: anywhere water has collected and run down. It is raw weather and the burial party has serious problems getting to Pen-y-Bont for the final internment, the roads being too slick under the covering of snow that drifts down intermittently even though it is too cold now for another downfall.

The horses keep slipping and sliding sideways and they don't like this at all. Bran-Mash and Billy Mills the groom are hard put to hold them upright while their heads keep throwing back, snorting from the nostrils, plumes and horse-brasses bobbing and jingling through the white silences along the way. They will be glad to get back into the stables tonight: to be rubbed-down with hay-wisps, fed warm oats, chill taken off their drinking water – but now!

Tom is handling the 14 ½ hands-high cob, backing mutinously between the shafts of his mother's gig. He stands quietly to the side, a firm yet gentle hand on the rein, speaking to the fiery beast quietly the whole time as it keeps stepping knee over knee, back, back – in danger of kicking it's way out of the harness and trying to bolt.

"Hold on Mother", he says in an agony of concentration. "If he goes now – he'll break his knees halfway down this pitch. Hold him steady. That's right boy – what the hell is all the fuss about then? Come on … come on .. that's it – forward …. forward . Right Mother take him on – take him".

"Thank you Tom …. Oh .. and less of the 'what the hell' in future (hem hem). See to the others, will you?" She flicks softly over the cob's quarters with her long driving whip – and they are back on the way.

It is a nightmare journey but at last accomplished and after they have returned from the consecrated field where all their dead are buried beside the roadway leading up over Pen-y-Bont Common, the family and close friends and neighbours gather together in the function rooms of the Severn Arms Hotel for the funeral-tea.

Again they are amongst relatives, for the Collards, who keep the place are directly related to Lewis the Llanerch who are cousins to Tom, Eloise, Bernard and Billy.

"How be boy?" one of them winks at Tom who answers quietly (in the Redner) as they call it, showing not only a solidarity but an almost intangible sense of humour that marks you down as 'local' and yet …. and yet …. What?

"I be a bit. How bist ee?" he answers and they grin into each other's faces before this relative stoops down to the boy from the breadth of his massive shoulders, bull-like.

"Going to be changes now Tom, boy. How're you going to like that?"

"What changes Bob?"

"Well, Arthur will be moving down to TyCanol himself now, I'll warr'n … taking the lot of you with him, won't he?"

"Oh that. Oh aye!" Tom puts on his half-soaked expression. They are not supposed to divulge too many details of their family business to others. Have to stay cool. He will not let on how confused he feels. He loves TyCanol, of course: has always loved going down there and helping out at harvest time, taking the ponies over to Newbridge horse fairs in the autumn – wonderful …. but he loves Mainstone more. It is good to be right in the heart of town. His friends!

"Have something to eat now Tom". Thank heavens Mrs. Collard has come over to see him. "My – what a big boy you've become too. So good-looking. You're going to break a few hearts young man – can tell that. Come on … there are some nice pieces of ham on the table, pork pies, egg and cress sandwiches – don't ask me how … salmon! That's right Tom! Tuck in now … there's not a lot of time left before you have to go. Mary-Ellen wants to be back for a prayer-meeting at 7.30 – and Arthur means to be home before dusk".

They fade into the brown panels bordering the rooms, the heavy oak, the slow shine of pewter plaques and ale-mugs decorating the corners, the snow-light through the open doors, the steam from the great tea-urns, the spotless linen table-cloths, the gleam from silver soup-spoons, great leaping flames on the walk-in hearths, black crêpe dresses and bonnets, ice jagged at the windows. Like bayonets.

SEVEN

Good threshing weather. Up the road he had noticed the colours: stubble, pale-blood and gold under this fresh, clear-blue sky. Touch of frost in the air. Trees heavy, their leaves not yet fully turned but orange-red in the main. Some would go yellow later on if they clung to the branches long enough but today there was still a lot of dark-green with blue in the shadows as in that French artist's paintings ... what on earth was his name? Can't remember.

He and Rosalind were talking about him the other evening: last Sunday after the sacred-concert in the Rock Park Hotel where they had sat for nearly an hour lost in Zigmund Steovsky's 1st Piano Concerto. Not Pisarro? No, though he himself paints in the same manner, according to Rosalind's art-master at the County; in fact he was the instigator.... But it was that other one. Mt. Victoire ... all angles .... He will think of him later – begins with a C, he thinks.

He wishes he could paint but feels shut off from anything like that – as if he has no talent. Barred. Why? He seems to remember something; but what an evening that was with Rosalind. She doesn't want him to go – begged him not to – yet he must. They have almost reached an understanding: an arrangement. She is definitely his girl.

He grins to himself but suddenly feels sorry for his poor sister, Eloise. For the first time ever, he is really angry with his parents. They have all grown up doing their very best to please them, to do as they say …. But this! THIS IS TOO BAD.

Eloise is being 'heavily encouraged' to marry Raymond Cox, the Botany-Master at the County. Tom hates him and suspects Eloise feels the same only has been too brainwashed into obedience to say anything. She has lost a lot of sparkle since two months ago when her so-innocent meetings and conversations with that wounded soldier billeted at the Pump House, now become a military hospital, was cut short abruptly – by Mary-Ellen via Ida Owen.

How she has changed. He has a brief recollection of Eloise descending the ladder into the Little Barn, Ivor Novello-Davies behind her, taking Ida to bits – IF SHE DARED! How things have changed. Ivor now famous. 'Keep the Home Fires Burning' the most popular song of the war so far, and Eloise losing it. Losing it.

She and her friends had taken to perambulating round the lake in the afternoons, when all the visitors to the town would be out and about and the others had kindly turned a blind eye to her dropping behind for a brief moment now and then to talk to this pale young man in the bandages who had taken such a shine to her glossy black hair, trim figure and bright, laughing eyes.

She liked him, Tom could tell even though she had not yet confided in him. She kept bringing his name into the conversation though – sometimes even in a slightly disparaging manner – but had to mention him nevertheless … so Tom guessed. Eloise had fallen for the boy in blue all right.

But then there was Ida-The-Chaperone. Somehow, wind of Eloise's 'transgressions' had filtered down back to the farm. Eloise was to be accompanied now when out. Ida was to take over.

"If it wasn't such a damned disgrace it could be almost funny" he had told Chinny and Co. at one of their meetings.

"Why – what happened boy?" he was asked.

"Damned if they weren't out strolling by the swans – when along comes Eloise's sweetheart – not suspecting anything: never DREAMING anyone could act in such an uncivilized manner."

"Huh-huh … not coming from the AREA, you mean?"

"Um- quite! ….. but anyway, be buggered - he takes his hat off, just says "Good afternoon Miss Edwards" and about to CONVERSE pleasantly – when before Eloise can even guess what's happening, Ida Owen springs round, gnashing her teeth like a demon, arm up and smashes him over the head with her umbrella!"

"Pu – huh …!" Lionel Beard splutters in an attempt to stop himself laughing but cannot.

"Ah, Tom – they're like that out Rhayader-way – where she comes from."

"Yes – but hard luck on Eloise isn't it?"

"She seen him since?"

"Not that I know of … I hope she HAS – but there's all this talk of marrying her to that arsehole from Birmingham now – I'd give 'em what for if I was her!"

"No wonder these women who chain themselves to the railings, want the vote, eh?"

"I doubt if it would make much difference our end ……..".

"Anyway – how's things going with – Miss Hamer?"

"Splendidly".

"She doesn't mind the age-difference?"

"Doesn't notice it now".

"You met her old man/lady?"

"We've met."

"Sounds ominous."

"I think, they think, my brother Bernard and I are far too popular with the <u>maidens</u>".

"And could be right at that Tom."

"She's got nothing to worry about on that score. It's Rosalind Hamer for me – she knows that."

"But her parents don't. You'd better hurry up and tell them boy. That long, stuck-up Evans-Evans' boy's round there a lot. Nice steady lad, Father's rolling in it, been to university, going into local politics – ".

"- not the war, I'll bet!"

"Exempt".

"What does his father do then?"

"Big farmers out Llanbadarn way."

"I'll get out there and sink him in the mixen then – if he lays a finger on my girl."

"Who says she's your girl Tom?"

"She does", he says shortly.

He comes out of his reverie. Yes – good threshing weather. Father will be up and out in the Pathfield with the men now, if they've finished the milking. Eloise might be there too. She loves these Autumn mornings.

He feels strange, sitting here on a station-seat at this hour, waiting for the train. Huh! – Bernard will have to do the milk-round for a time now – that is until they get another man to do his (Tom's) own former work. Bet Mary-Ellen won't allow her darling to suffer too long, not with Bernard coming up for his School Certificate year. Oh no. Different to his lot, isn't it?"

A year ago, almost to the day, he sat here before. There were 3 other lads from the town with him then. Big boys. Rough – but kindly. 1915 and Tom had just turned sixteen – and as far as he was concerned – was off to the War.

They got out at Knighton, 'attested' for the army and Tom had drunk beer with the others for the first time in his life. There was a pub near the station. All he can remember properly now is that afterwards they had rolled down a bank laughing and laughing like hell before making for the train to Shrewsbury – and on; but it was not to be for Tom.

The stationmaster had recognised him and 'phoned through to Bill Whitford his OPPO. in Llandrindod who had contacted Arthur at TyCanol to the effect that Tom was running away to join up, who had then rung the police-station, now in Llandrindod Wells, who had contacted the 'Force' in Knighton – one of whom was waiting on the platform to put young Edwards back on the train home.

Now having turned seventeen on the Second and it now being the Third, he was on his way again – but this time he was not bothering with Knighton, he had saved up the necessary eight shillings and ten-pence halfpenny and was going straight to Liverpool. No messing. He would 'attest' and this time make sure it stuck.

"What decided you?" they had asked (last year after he had been brought back unceremoniously from Knighton) at The War Office, (the new name for their club-den since hostilities had got underway) and he had told them how, the afternoon before, two ladies had come sauntering past the farm, done up in tailored suits, feathers in their hats, carrying rolled umbrellas. He had been in the Rick-Yard, raking up bits of straw when one of them had turned and pointed at him with hers.

"Think a great lout like that would be at the FRONT", she had cried and that is when he had thrown down the pickel and deter-mined to go the next day: it had decided him. "But it's not RIGHT!"

Chinny had expostulated and Tom, though agreeing deep down, could not ignore all the messages to enlist, enlist, ENLIST : from the 'Gem', from the 'Magnet', 'Boys Own Paper', posters, recruiting officers; even women were being encouraged to tell their men to "GO!" unlike Rosalind who was adamant he should stay.

Also, he had this overnurtured sense of honour. Not to be denied. Justice. The country had to be defended. Look at the Belgians – And dear old Stan had enlisted with the South Wales Borderers. Neale, that nice little, black-headed fellow from out Pen-y-Bont way had been killed. Careless's the Solicitor's son. <u>Dead.</u> He had to go. He was quite tall. He was strong. Wiry. He too was adamant.

It was in all the magazines, all the papers. Men were wanted. <u>He</u> was wanted.

May 15th, 1915 (it had been in The Boy's Friend Published every Monday)

'IF you want the BEST, buy only your Editor's papers. They contain the BEST reading-matter for boys that can be obtained.

The First Chapters Of Our Stirring

Army Life Story

With

Bugle

And

Bayonet

By

Beverly Kent.'

Then in The Boys Own. June 17th. 7d Net.

"Killed: - Brown 9106J"

Does it dim your sun awhile

When you read that brief line through?

Just a number and a name

Both of them unknown to you.

Do you think that there are some

Wounded to the heart through this?

How it means a life to mourne?

How it means a face to miss.

Do you spare a moment's thought

Musing on his Fight and Fall?

For your safety he replied

When he heard his country call!

For your life he gave his own.

For your peace he laid him low –

What of your response to this?

What about the debt you owe?

Are you stronger, humbler that

He has paid the last dread price?

Are you spurred to noble deeds

Through this stranger's sacrifice?

If by his example you

Stand serene and fortified

In life's battle, not in vain

J. Brown lived and J. Brown died!

'This magazine can be sent free to our Troops abroad by leaving it at the Post Office."

Our Companion Papers:
The Magnet Library, Every Monday
The Gem Library, Every Wednesday <u>wartime price 1 ½ d</u>
The Dreadnought, Every Thursday
The Penny Popular, Every Friday
Chuckles, Every Saturday
The Boys' Friend

Tom remembered a story about Canada: 'The Ghost Bear' in the Boys' Own right at the beginning of the War in 1914 when it was still priced 6d and how it had made him think of Jim. Had he gone back out there? (Tom missed him terribly at times, Jim's tales of adventure told beneath the rhododendrons, his listening ear, his slow smiles, his <u>acceptance)</u> – or was he in France? Would he maybe meet him – somewhere? Or was his massive torso up-ended skyways over a foreign furrow, eyes cold and staring straight through to a heaven he had never met on earth? A bullet through his chest?

Tom loved the station: the carved overhangs, Bill Whitford's flower-tubs full of nasturtiums and petunias, pansies in troughs, an old bath painted cream and full of marigolds, the hanging baskets of fuchsias and freesias, pale gold begonias like globes lit from within. And the ornate iron balustrade going up and over the line.

How exciting it had been when they were children, he, Eloise and Bernard – all dressed up with the others from the Chapel and going on the Sunday school outing to New Brighton. Waiting for the train. Waiting for the train – then the rumble on the rails from a distance, the smoke appearing from way down the line as the engine came fussing under the grey stone bridge (they had crossed that evening in 1909 on the way to the Price's), before it came clanging and steaming into the station.

He loved getting ON. The dark brown varnished paintwork, the sashed windows. Banging the door shut when they were aboard and walking down the thin corridors until they found their carriage. The smells of smoke and steam.

Jim Corp had gone this way, just before they left Mainstone. Sat on this very seat – more than likely. Where was he now? He had never returned. Oh Jim.

Tom stretches out his legs into the sunlight striking down over the canopy and reaching his feet if he sticks them out far enough. He has a small leather holdall placed discreetly beside the iron legs of the station bench with his few personal effects stuffed inside. He packed it last night after getting in from the War Office. And now, only hopes Arthur won't come looking for him as he hasn't shown up for the milking, the threshing. He thrusts his brown hands, burned by the sun into his trouser pockets and relaxes. Hell – if he comes, he DOES – but it won't make any difference. He suspects they will know that he has gone anyway – or they would be here by now. Another quarter of an hour. He yawns. He remembers the years and cannot believe they have gone.

EIGHT

It was quite horrible leaving Mainstone in 1910. There were no visitors staying, so they each had their own room and were allowed to use the hot water in the bathrooms but it was a different story once they arrived at TyCanol.

Jim had cleared off because he know there would not now be room for him but even so, it meant the boys had to double-up in one of the small bedrooms (so small in fact that Bernard and Tom were forced to even share the double bed as there was certainly no room for two beds of any kind in there if they wanted the use of a dressing-table) – so it was Mother and Father in the main bedroom with the small fireplace, then the boys, along the corridor to the maid's room (i.e. Ida Owen, the only one Mary-Ellen kept on) then Eloise in the end bedroom facing the road.

Billy spent his time sleeping either in with his parents, Ida Owen's room or as a special treat – with Eloise.

It was very cramped and extremely cold once all the heaving and sorting of furniture and luggage had finished.

Tom hoped never to have to go through anything like the 'move' again. Hope's Removal Firm had been hired but even so it was a hell of a job. The great Welsh dressers had to be unplugged from the dining-room walls at Mainstone, then replugged back in at TyCanol: one in the Big Kitchen and the smaller black oak one – in the Parlour. There was an enormous heavily-carved sideboard to be dismantled and set up facing the Big Kitchen window, its long, oblong mirror reflecting the North light at the large, flat ¼-pained window, the cold, desolate-in-winter aspect of snow-covered hills and fields, its back to the black oak banister leading starkly up to the 'bed-chambers' as Tom would laughingly describe them to Chinny and Co.: no delicately curving handrails here, slender and somehow sensual to the touch, easing your way from one floor to another, one excitement leading to another – as there had been at Mainstone – and now beds to be carried in, huge, goose-feather mattresses, eiderdowns, sheets, mangles and carpets, rugs, curtains – what a shambles especially with Ida Owen yapping like a Yorkshire Terrier at his heels.

One evening he had come in from the cowsheds exhausted with muck on his boots and before he even had a chance to take them off, she was screaming at him – "Great LOUT! What about my clean floor? Get out and leave yer boots by the scraper can't yer …. Get on OUT!"

He snapped. He shoved her out of sight over the back of the uncut-moquette settee. A fitting landing-place, he thought, it was grey, patterned with small black diamond shapes, framing further grey pockets of non-colour.

"Shut UP!" – he had cried. "Shut up! – you're only the skivvy!"

She had never forgotten – but also never bothered him further to his face. The muttering, the murmuring was all done behind closed doors in future. She and Mary-Ellen (Mam she called her) in the scullery, in the dairy, the back-kitchen – over the boiling jams, the hams cooking in the great ovens, amongst the scalding milk-bottles – out of sight, out of hearing she would be more of a daughter-companion to Mary Ellen than any of them ever could be – and she had Billy. He was her little love, her favourite now. To hell with the others.

Tom and Bernard had become more friendly than before. Maybe it was the close proximity in the sleeping-quarters, but they shared more information, laughed themselves silly over some of the local happenings, swapped tales and of course had to practice for their singing duets.

There was singing practice at the Chapel every Sunday for half an hour before Sunday School at two-fifteen and then a further quarter of an hour from five-forty-five until six p.m. when the evening-service commenced and from there they were sometimes chosen to sing for the congregation or advised as to the Eisteddfodau all around the county, where they could compete. They often did – and won prize-money in little velvet bags, but these were special occasions.

Now, as a rule, Tom's days had become full of drudgery. In the beginning of his new existence, he couldn't believe it: that this was to be his life.

He was expected to attend school and to apply himself to studying for the 'Scholarship' that, if passed, would gain him admittance to the County School where Rosalind spent her days, but he had no time at all to think about Rosalind or anything much else beside Chapel and his singing-episodes with Bernard (maybe very occasionally, Bernard and Eloise) because of the work.

The work took precedence and would not have been so bad if it could have been one or the other – but no. He was expected to do both, and as it was impossible to actually accomplish both, it meant he was always in trouble, both at school and at home.

He was to be up at 6 o'clock each morning to help, first of all with the milking, then to come in with the men for breakfast before washing himself in the back-kitchen sink, doing his teeth and accompanying Billy Mills or Bran-Mash to help deliver the first milk-round. His job was to jump down out of the float with bottles, place them on the customer's step or, more often than not, run up and down countless stairs in apartment houses but also to take a can of milk under his arm with a pint or quart measure, depending on the establishment, and splash it out accordingly. This was no easy ticket for they delivered to most of the big hotels that had mushroomed throughout the town and he wouldn't have minded at all: could have driven the cob, delivered all the milk going --but he had to be in school by nine o'clock and how could he be?

Their last delivery was always at the Gwalia Hotel, that meant he had to throw all the equipment at Billy or Bran-Mash, jump down, run right up the hill into town or along High Street before thundering up and over the Station bridge, up Station Crescent, past Mainstone, down Spa Road nearly to the crossing, fling himself right through the black-iron school gates, into the hated yellow-brick building, only to be at least five minutes late for Assembly, most days; so it meant getting the cane. Then when enough canings had accrued for his parents to be informed as to his 'bad behaviour' a note would be sent to Arthur and Tom could look forward to another thrashing at home.

It was totally unfair and most probably might have sent a weaker mind into madness but although no excuses were accepted, Mary Ellen hinting in between disapproving asides to Ida Owen concerning the wisdom of ever giving birth to such a rebellious fellow, the general effect on the boy was an almost exaggerated desire for justice. He learned, with his fists and his wit, how to look after himself in situations that he felt he could handle. Those that were insoluble, he thought it best to shrug of. As for his feelings for Mary Ellen and Arthur, they never altered. He defended them in his mind and would kill himself in the effort to win their approval by working himself to death if necessary, his only unspoken and unconscious demands being: that they would learn to accept him as himself. They could not but this he refused to recognise.

Over the next three years, he learned many things at TyCanol: how to milk cows properly, stripping out the udders and getting the cow to relax when his head was resting in the hollow of her flank, how to plough, chain-harrow the land and plant seed with two great cart-horses swaying ahead of him across the open fields, the jo-ho lines in his strengthening hands, how to harvest the hay using mowing-machines, swathe-turners, hay-rakes and then maintain the machines for next year with grease, oil and bits of sacking tied round the teeth to stop them rusting. He learned how to dig ditches, stake hedges, bill-hook the thistles, keep down the rabbits, shoot if one was wanted for dinner, bring down pigeons by firing just that hair's breadth in front as they were in flight but best of all – how to tell a horse. How to look one over and appreciate its lines. To feel its hocks and fetlocks, to tug up heavy feet and inspect the hoofs. He became an expert – as had been Thomas his grandfather, as was Arthur. He was allowed to ride. Was given his own cob: Flash. This freed him.

Once on Coronation Day in 1911, he thought he caught a glimpse of Rosalind in the crowd viewing the illumination of the County Buildings, then again when he and Bernard were half-way through a duet out at St. Harmon's chapel, he felt compelled suddenly to look up as if someone was watching him and there she was over in the shadows beyond the swinging Aladdin-lamp but she had gone when they finally managed to get to the door.

Girls in the crowds who usually surrounded the two boys when they had sung were forever trying to seek their attention. One big, busty, County-School girl from Builth Wells even grabbed at Tom's heather-mixture, tweed-suited arm one evening, luckily while the harmonium was still squeezing out its notes so that she was not overheard by others and told him straight out that Bernard was the best-looking youngster she had ever seen but he Tom Edwards had more sex-appeal than anyone in the vicinity and – "How about it?".

"How about what?" he had laughed and she said "You know" but he didn't so luckily the crowd pressing soon separated them (or unluckily) he thought.

At home, the boys did their best to try and persuade the parents to buy a motorcar …. Or even to get delivery vans for the milk-round – after all, Tom Norton had got the Colonel Bogey a kind of Charabang running up and down to the Golf Club now.

"Via the Ridgebourne!" Bernard smiled sarcastically – "it's only DESIGNATED stop!"

"Yes 9d up and 6d down too" – Tom added laughing but good moods or bad, they couldn't get the Old Man to budge.

"Contraptions!" Ida spat out but they were not going to take any notice of her. They would keep on.

Then in 1913, Tom Norton envisaged an Aerodrome on the Rock Park Ddol. TyCanol's big field. It never officially became one but on 6th October, four days after Tom's fourteenth birthday, Gustav Hamel, a wealthy Swede, landed. It was one of the most exiting events Tom could ever remember. He longed to fly but would have to wait another year before Tom Norton could promote the first air-pageant when a certain Vivian Hewitt would organise displays and for a certain payment, one could go 'up'.

Tom Norton was a real character. In 1906 he purchased the land on which the Automobile Palace still stands today. But when he first went into business with his bicycle and sports depot in the High Street, was one of the first Raleigh dealers and maintained a stock of some 200 bicycles. He even offered to pay the train fare to any buyers travelling up to a certain number of miles! Tom loved to stop and talk to Mr. Norton whenever he had a free moment in town. They had the same hustling nature and he also loved the smell of petrol where it had spilled under the Colonel Bogey: it smelt of a future. Exciting.

Nine days after Gustav Hamel had been and gone came the day Tom had waited for most of the time after the summer holidays. October 15th was always the day of the first Newbridge Horse Fair. The next one came in November but this was the one he had been looking forward to for so long. He would officially be allowed the day off school to attend, as most of the farmers' sons in the vicinity were for they had to ride ponies that needed to be sold over there, then come back on the new- if any were bought.

Flash was getting too small for Tom now he was growing so quickly and as Bernard was not particularly interested, he was to be sold, Tom being allowed to choose another one and if Arthur and Mary Ellen approved his choice – then they would buy it there and then.

Mary Ellen was riding over to Newbridge side-saddle on her pretty, thin-legged riding-mare with Arthur accompanying her on his great, sorrel saddle-horse: Fire.

Tom couldn't wait to get home from school. He was told not to bother with his usual chores so made straight for the wain-house where he had left all the tackle that morning so that he could soft-soap then polish the leather, shine up the irons, the bit, the buckles. When that was done, he would start on Flash with the dandy-brush and curry-comb, grooming the cob until he gleamed red under the stable-lantern, leaving the mane and tail until last when he would separate the long hairs through with the short steel comb, spinning it out like thread.

He loved the special dust smell that came off a horse's coat, the way the hair over the fetlocks would brush out white and feathery.

Billy Mills had forked out the stall and laid it bare for Tom to get Flash done up without the straw getting in the way, and now there were only a half-dozen or so round, green, steaming piles of horse-shit to shovel out before he would pitch-fork in a couple of shoulder-fuls of straw to make up the bed. Funny how horseshit had almost a pleasant smell, whereas anything else stunk like a drain. Horses were definitely special, he thought.

He lifted the bits out on to the mixen in the soft, dark country night, and bringing in the straw, distributed it high up on the stall until it came to the level of Flash's hocks.

"Want you to have a good night's sleep Flash and this will keep you warm, draft or not from that blasted shutter. Must tell the Old Man. Now –" and he swung himself, pickel in hand, up into the loft through an aperture above the manger to throw down the sweet-smelling hay from beneath the dusty beams under the roof.

"Here's your fodder then. Have a good feed .... Last but one here boy."

Before jumping back down, he suddenly had a vision of Eloise and Ivor the other side of the loft that ended looking down into the Little Barn, where they used to tunnel through the hay. "Happy days"he murmured before patting Flash, now moving his feet eagerly one after the other towards the manger, munching and munching away, tossing his head, one eye to the light.

" 'night boy. See you in the morning", Tom snuffed the lantern and went out into the late evening, latching the old wooden door. There was a rim of frosty-red simmering right on the edge of Dolfan over the horizon. As if a fire had died down or as if red hot ashes were banked ready to re-conflagrate. But to Tom, that evening, the air was pink and alive, painted on the mole-dark background separating from tomorrow. The excitement of tomorrow.

NINE

He awakes in the dark. The cock is crowing off the roof of the hen house in the Plock. Six o'clock. Silently, so as not to disturb Bernard, he pushes aside the bedclothes his side and rises in one fluid motion at the same time stretching his hand out to the rush-bottomed chair under the window where he arranged his clothes last night, the excitement of this day now in his belly.

He had a good strip-wash down before going to bed so merely has to dress himself until later. He has no need of a light as he can dress by touch: first the long-johns and vest, then the soft, silk-poplin shirt, the faintest tint of pink colouring the otherwise oatmeal colour, before tugging on his new, dark-brown, velveteen-corduroy britches (made for him at the 'Gents Outfitter' in Builth Wells last month) – picking up his good, heather-mixture jacket with his cravat and making for the door.

Downstairs, he places the jacket and tie over the back of one of the chairs in the Back-Kitchen, tugs on an old sweater out of the cupboard behind the door, crosses to the sink and turns on the high tap so that he can splash cold water on to his face to wake himself up properly before quietly depressing his thumb into the spoon-like latch on the back door and stepping outside.

The house is dark and quiet, still full of sleepers. He is up before anyone. Not even Bran-Mash has emerged from the Saddle Room where he sleeps, poor devil, and Billy Mills has yet to come up the road from the Crossing out of the quiet, pearlised dark. He puts on his cleaned boots that are arranged suggestively (by Ida no doubt) against the foot-scraper. He will attach his best leather leggings later on after breakfast. For now he has to see to Flash.

He crosses the yard and enters the stable-door. Flash moves his back legs from side to side in the straw now heavy with horse piss and Tom hears the yank of his head pulling the halter against the chain. Flash snorts and whickers out a greeting while Tom grabs the lantern, lights it and hooks it above the shuttered window.

"Now boy – let's get going" he says quietly to Flash and pushes him over with a hand on his rump. "Bit of hay first so that you can drink before we go. Give it you now – and there'll be colic. Move over. That's it". And he swings himself into the loft again to send a good shower of hay into the manger as he did last night.

Coming down, he takes the fork and shovels Flash's bedstraw into the wheelbarrow and brushes out the stall before tipping it on to the mixen outside.

"That's it Flash – let the dog see the rabbit eh: You eat, I'll brush" and the final grooming takes place, Tom whistling like an ostler between his teeth as Bran-Mash showed him years ago and after the combing and brushing, hoof-inspections, mane and tail arranging, he finishes off the horse's coat with a wisp of hay coiled round in the hand for scrubbing the hairs all one way, giving it just that added lustre.

It is showing signs of getting light when he crosses the yard once more towards the house. The air is frosty and there is a hint of pink in the dark. He can hear Arthur in the far wain-house seeing to Fire and Mary-Ellen's mare and Bran-Mash passes him, going in the opposite direction towards the cow sheds with a couple of milk tins under his arms. Tom is hungry and can't wait for breakfast this morning: bacon off the bone, eggs, mushrooms, tomatoes and thick chunks of Alfords country-made bread with butter and marmalade. His mouth waters.

At last the moment has arrived. Washed, dressed, teeth cleaned, hair-brushed, boots polished once more, leggings strapped over the 'breeks', warm socks beneath, Tom stands smiling at the end of the long kitchen table. He has done well. He looks good. His parents smile down on him. Even Ida pats his shoulder with a smile.

"You'll do boy – come on". His father says and he, Tom and Mary-Ellen prepare to leave. Why can't it always be like this? Happy. Mary Ellen wears her black, riding habit with the tight jacket and long, full skirt, a little hat pulled down over her greying chestnut-curls, Arthur very dignified in britches, a long black woollen jacket over a waistcoat, silk cravat, his gold watch and chain stretched across his stomach, a black bowler hat securely placed on his hair now turning bright silver.

Flash comes out of the stable at a running trot, his shoes clattering sharply over the cobbles. Thirsty. Tom jumps on to his back and adjusts himself in the saddle as the horse heads blindly towards the old bath full of water that the cows drink out of, placed under the wall into the old cowshed. Mary Ellen and Arthur are waiting there, tall on their horses.

Flash sucks down as many gulp-fulls of water as he can before Arthur orders Tom to pull his head up.

"Colic" – he says meaningfully so Tom obeys without question, shortens the reins and they are off. Into the growing light. It is pearly-grey now, pink and misty. The frost nips at their gloves and booted toes but it doesn't matter. It is going to be a lovely day and the sound of three sets of hoofs is wonderful as they clatter up the yard then through the white gate, pegged back against the high stone wall, to turn left down the road towards Newbridge.

When they get to Llanyre Bridge, Tom looks back for a moment as they walk the horses briskly along at a good pace, to see the farm now emerging from the mist into the pink/lilac of morning. The air is sparkling and as they clop over the river, the bridge echoing under their hoofs, he feels the beauty is almost too much. What can he do with it? The place is magic.

Mary-Ellen and Arthur are taking the long way round: up Llanyre Pitches then along the main road. They know that Tom will want to be in Newbridge early to meet friends his own age also to look over the horses so they tell him to turn off down Dol-Llwyn-Hir lane if he wants to – as a short-cut.

"But don't take him above a canter!" Arthur warns. Don't go sweating the horse now boy – and don't blow him!" (Meaning get him out of breath).

Tom agrees to everything ordered until he actually gets out of sight along the lane but the empty expanse ahead is too much. He will gallop Flash one more time – until he gets to Dol-Llwyn-Hir, the farm, then pull him to a trot and go like hell for another half-mile afterwards before wiping down the brisket and the flanks, wherever else he might be sweating and saunter on from there. Any signs of those little astrakhan curls down his chest that heat up into a sweat and he will have to get rid of those with the wisp of hay coiled in his pocket. Arthur gets furious if disobeyed on this one.

There are two people in the yard at Dol-Llwyn-Hir but they have their backs to him. They remain in his eyes: faded blue figures in a landscape like Van Gogh's digging farmers having a rest. Ignoring him on purpose, he supposes, for the lane runs straight through their yard and they probably resent it. "Don't blame 'em" – but "Good morning" he shouts anyway then turns sharp right up the rise before digging in his heels. Good job he had pulled to a trot before getting to the farm. Don't want them reporting him to Arthur. Now. Up higher and deeper into the countryside, not a soul in sight, he gives Flash his head. They career smoothly, madly, through the fish-like ferns still green in the grass and waving either side the cobbles. Pieces of dried mud flinging back in half-circles from Flash's silver shoes. They strike sparks here and there. Tom hates to pull up – but he fears Arthur's disapproval. He jumps off and notes the astrakhan'd, sweating brisket with horror. It will take more than the coil of hay to absorb this. He tugs up handful of grass and massages Flash's chest, stroking the hair down into line before finishing off with the hay-piece. "Have to do," he murmurs eventually before swinging himself back on, one foot in the stirrup, the other curving round and clamping back into the saddle. He taps his toes in, heels down, knees Flash into a jog-trot and they are off once more. He thinks of all the Romans who must have marched up this road for it is one of theirs. Where would they have been going – and why?

It is bright morning light, mist gone, as he comes out of the lane to meet the highway once again. It is Chaucer's Canterbury Tales. All the riders coming out of the sun-blue laughing and talking, a jingling of harness, breath of horses snorting steam as they tug their heads down then throw them back, long shadows still stretching before them.

He is about to turn left and move on into the stream of riders when suddenly someone calls his name and a small bay cob with a black mane and tail seems to unwillingly detach itself from a group to the right on the crest of the road and is steered very inexpertly by its rider, all elbows out and flapping knees, in his direction.

"Tom … Tom!" she laughs, trying desperately to get the pony to advance in a straight line towards him but failing miserably… "It's me, ME … Rosalind!"

He sits where he is, waiting. Wondering how anyone so inexpert has managed to ride this far.

"Rosalind! – What the hell are you doing here? He asks when she has more or less drawn level. "And what on earth are you doing on that horse?"

"He's mine. He's MINE. We're going to sell him."

"Well for Heaven's sake sit up straight, grip with your knees, get your elbows in and shorten the reins! You've got no control like that. Who taught you to ride ever?"

"Oh you! – Edwards. Never mind all that." She is laughing now and kicking at the cob's sides with her heels, the reins long and useless in her hands. "Come on Tom – I'll race you. See who can reach that telephone pole along there first. Off! – ."

And she tries to get away to a running start.

"I can't Rosalind. I'm not to sweat the horse."

"Oh pooh! - Come on."

"But father and mother are - -."

"I know – just met 'em. Your Mam's riding SIDE-saddle …. Didn't approve of my get-up either – I could tell."

"Why? What did she say?"

"Humm.m TROUSERS! …. Thought you were some little gypsy girl coming along Rosalind. Does your father know?"

"I've never seen a girl in overalls – like those before Rosalind. Looking good though. I expect she was just astonished."

"Shocked boy. Shocked. – more like."

"How far back are they – along there?"

"'bought a mile and a half Tom. Come ON."

"Oh – all right." He laughs himself now infected by her insouciance. "As long as they're not just round the corner."

"Oh bugger 'em!" Rosalind squeals and having at last got the old slouch she is sitting astride to move, takes off, legs flapping again like a cowboy, hair flying, green chenille scarf unwinding from her neck, with Tom easily beside her, guiding both horses off the hard concrete road on to the verge from where they bear down on the telephone pole, Rosalind in the lead finally, not noticing the tightness of Tom's reins. "I've won. I've WON." She cries.

Coming into Newbridge there is the same feeling as ever: each year a sense of ages and yet brand new. The new day. Just beginning.

On either side the road into the village, carts are parked, shafts propped on boxes – or merely down, the horses stabled or put out to grass for the day in someone's field.

Piled on some of these wagons are mounds of fruit and vegetables, cakes, loaves, lemonade-bottles, sweets, gingerbread...even sticks of rock; then on others, bits and bridles, head-bands for horses in serge-ribbon: red and blue, horse-collars, car-saddles, harness of all kinds: martingales, fancy belly-bands and then there are striped awnings covering sweet-stalls, electrical appliances – while Daggerfields the gypsy-family from down the Crossing in Llandrindod – are here with beautiful spode-crockery, carpets, brasses, house brooms and brushes, chamois-leathers: anything the housewife needs: towels, face flannels, dish-cloths, floor-mops while skewbald and piebald ponies remain tethered to the back of their LORRY .... For Daggerfields have got one! – Bought a motor. Are mechanised.

Lol Daggerfield smirks as Rosalind and Tom clop past on their ponies.

"Morning <u>Mister</u> Edwards!" he calls cheekily and in a moment of pure envy Tom feels he would like to shove him in the face but won't - unless of course he is rude to Rosalind in any way – but Lol is not such an idiot. He touches his cap to Rosalind, who smiles. Tom answers. "Morning Lol!" and they progress down to the hitching rail overlooking the rushing river, narrow at this point, tumbling on to grey rocks, the grey, granite backs of houses looming over.

Already there are a lot of ponies and cobs in the streets, some being trotted up and down showing their paces in front of the rugged-faced men standing around in their long, fawn macs, beneath battered caps: down from the hills for the day and hoping for a sale or a bargain.

There are horses under the trees and tucked away behind corners but soon the town will be full and that is when Tom will start touting for a customer.

"You still in school Tom? Thought you were taking the scholarship and coming on to the County."

"Expelled last year."

"Expelled!"

"Yep."

"What did you do Tom?"

"Hit the Duck".

"What or who is the Duck."

"We call him that because his arse is too close to the ground.... Duck's disease ... you know."

"One of the teachers, d'you mean?"

"Yes. Always hitting me – and I had this boil on my back – so when he hit me on THAT: phew! – I tell you, I nearly saw red. I got him down between the desks, had a hell of a fight – but of course had to be pulled off. Got another whack of the Old Man too, when I arrived home."

"Why was he hitting you – the teacher?"

"I was late."

"Why were – ."

"Oh never mind. Expelled from Sunday School too …. This Summer."

"Tom!"

"Hypocrisy."

"What?"

"Some things get me down."

"Such as?"

"This chap – he was our Sunday school Superintendent but – oh heck Rosalind … don't laugh. He'd been had up for poaching baby salmon: SAMLETS out of the Ithon. Jack, the River-Watcher had caught him red-handed."

"How do you know?"

"Heard. Anyway this Sunday I was told 'never to darken the doors again'.…. He was giving us a lesson on the five loaves and four fishes – or whatever and I just couldn't help it.

"What?"

"Well, when he asked us all to put up our hands and repeat how many loaves, how many fishes –?"

"What did you do?"

"Put mine up – and he CHOSE me to answer so I said "Five loaves Sir and four b-e-a-u-t-i-f-u-l little SAMLETS!"

"-A-a-a-ah! Oh Tom … you devil – and that is –."

" 'nuff said, Rosalind. Look it's getting busier now. Do you want to come with me and look for Mother and Father – or do you want to go and find your people? Don't forget, we've got to sell these two."

"I'll pop off for a time – but tell me Tom – how do you like this outfit? Is it a bit too risky – or not?"

"I love it. Suits you Rosalind. Where did you get those green-cord overalls."

"Mamma made them."

"What?"

"Yes – bought a pattern. Walden's Illustrated Dressmaker series. She's priceless my Mam – isn't she?"

"I'll say. That warm blouse underneath looks nice too. Like the collar and the way the whole thing kind of flops …. You know."

"Thank you Tom. Look … when you've sold your horse and bought another, ditto me …. Let's meet up at that pub on the corner for a cup of tea, eh?"

"About half-past two."

"If I haven't arrived – hang on".

"I'll do that. And if I'm not there – wait for me Rosalind."

They grin, remembering. She unhitches the cob and walks him up the street, soon disappearing into the throng.

They sell Flash very early on. Arthur is with Tom when one of the hill farmers makes his approach.

"'morning Arthur."

"'morning Seth."

"Going to sell 'im Arthur?"

"Ask Tom"

"Selling Tom?"

"If the price is right Mr. Preece."

"How much yer asking."

"Seventy-five pounds."

Seth makes a great show of turning away as if not interested but Tom punctures the wind out of his sails by taking the bridle and moving off up the hill.

"Fifty five," Seth turns and shouts. Tom returns.

"Now Arthur, you know he's not worth more than that –," Seth starts but Arthur cuts him off.

"Look at his action boy. This horse is a thoroughbred. We don't mess with any old horse-buying at TyCanol – you know that Seth."

"I know that Arthur – but …. Get up on him Tom and trot him up and down! – Let's have a look at him moving."

Tom knows he has won. He vaults on and pulls the reins in sharp causing Flash to arch his neck. He digs in his heels and guides the horse sideways with his knees, leg over leg, neck arched then trots him sharply up the hill and back urging Flash to pick up his feet and fling them back down as much resembling a Hackney as possible. This is why Arthur doesn't like him galloping the cobs. It ruins their stride. Still he hasn't done it often enough for that. He's pretty sure they've got a sale.

"Sixty-Five!" Seth offers, grimly.

"Seventy!" Arthur replies.

"Sixty –SEVEN! Not a penny more". Seth half-turns away.

"Sixty-Nine. My last offer." Arthur states quietly, eyes green in his good-natured face.

"Split the difference then Arthur!" Seth demands, high-pitched with emotion.

"Sixty-Eight it is then", Arthur concedes.

"Done!" says Seth. "Spit on it boy". He and Arthur both spit on their palms before slapping their hands together, Tom slips off the horse's back, unbuckles the saddle, takes it off gently and lays it on the grass, exchanges the bridle for Seth's halter (miraculously appeared in his horny, weather-beaten hands) and taking out his coiled piece of hay, rubs Flash down to take up some of the sweat from under the saddle. The money changes hands between Arthur and Seth then the new owner takes the halter and leads Flash off into the crowd.

"Bye Flash," Tom murmurs and for a moment feels bereft but seeing how pleased Arthur is with the swift termination of the sale, asks for and is given permission to go looking for the replacement.

"Where's mother?" he enquires.

"In having tea and biscuits with the Prices. They're all over in that teahouse up the street; you'll know where to find us if you want us. We're having lunch with Jim Rowlands: the end house, by the school." "Right", says Tom, who is no waster of words – and is gone.

It was there for an instant, flung up and back above the flat caps, beyond a wall of fawn and grey macs, tweed overcoats and thumb-sticks raised and lowered. This gorgeous head. Buckskin with a black-lashed blue-eye, flaxen mane tumbling into a forelock and down it's arched neck. He must see. Yes – he pushes through the crowd and the stallion is there before him. Powerful, thin legs well turned hocks bouncing the great body up into a rear, the tail a splendid wave of blond: blond wheat colour.

But someone is on his back, clinging for dear life, arms secured round the horse's neck: a man. Tom can't see his face, it is buried in the far side but … a tall, scholarly looking, older man is trying to control the horse from right in front! – The very worst position. My stars – it's Rosalind's father and there's Rosalind, hands to mouth, on the pavement.

Tom ducks beneath one of the farmers in front's extended thumb-stick. "Probably knows the horse is going to loose it at any moment," he thinks as he approaches the great rearing beast, quietly crossing past its head to take the reins out of Mr. Hamer's willing hands as he does so and slightly pushing him towards Rosalind.

"I'll <u>officiate</u>, shall I Mr. Hamer – with this one," he murmurs and then starts talking quietly to the horse, standing well out of line of any forward striking hoof but close into the neck, a firm hand on the rein right by the bit.

At first the horse keeps jumping up and back, up and back, snorting and furious but soon he quietens down enough for Tom to look at the fellow on his back, slipped almost round his neck by now.

"Get off", Tom whispers, "and let go of the rein."

The young man does so and drops to the ground ignominiously before righting himself into the tall, gangling youth of 1909 at Maggie Price's party, teaching Rosalind to tango – now fully-grown into 'that long, stuck-up Evans-Evans boy' to be described by Chinny later on: Jenkin Evans-Evans.

"Thinking of buying him" he says in as off-hand a manner as he can manage to Tom, before stepping out of reach up on to the pavement beside Rosalind.

"I shouldn't, if I were you" Tom replies smiling.

"Doesn't suit you – and anyway – he's mine." He swings himself up easily into the saddle vacated by Jenkin Evans-Evans, the horse turning its head to give him a friendly nip of his teeth as he does so, then Tom gathers the reins and perfectly in control, backs the horse before taking him up the road to fetch Arthur. He knows what his Father will think of his choice so the next thing is – to find the owner and to beat him down to a reasonable price.

At half-past two he is outside the grey stone public house where he and Rosalind have arranged to meet for a cup of tea. He dare not let go of his new horse's bridle for it is far too lively, so hopes Rosalind will understand when he asks if they can meet elsewhere. The glass in the windows of the old building is tinted green: bottle-glass. The colour of Rosalind's eyes – and here she is, hurrying round the corner, her fair hair still straight and hanging to her collar. How he loves her appearance. How comfortable he feels talking to her. She understands things, he can tell – and she is so good-humoured. Surely she won't be angry he has to break their arrangement. The buckskin is already pawing the ground, anxious to be gone.

"Rosalind I can't stay. Got to get this one home." He apologises. "Please don't mind – but you can see – I've got a handful here."

"Oh Tom – of course. Look Dad's about to clinch the deal on a black mare for me: a beaut. - We'll meet again, eh?"

"Next week Rosalind. Come to the pictures – please. Monday".

"You don't hang around Edwards- do you?" she laughs

"- but look Tom. I'm older than you …. It's going to seem a bit funny, someone of my age –"

"I know all about that, Miss Hamer. You might be a trifle older …. But I'm more than a trifle bigger than you are – so we're quits – come on. Monday night outside the Kino. Six o'clock."

"Done!"

"Spit on it then".

They laugh, spit on their palms and slap hands and as she runs back into the crowd he sings to himself "You Made Me Love You….. I Didn't Want To Do It …. I didn't Want To Do It," as he springs back up into the saddle and urges his beautiful, sixteen and a half hands high horse into action. He sings all the way home.

And so it begins. They meet often, at least once a week. Sometimes they go to the pictures and she will allow him to put his arm around her now, in the dark – though shrugging him off when the lights go on.

He took her up the Golf-Links on their first day out together – in the Colonel Bogey, Tom Norton's green miniature charabang like a lead toy-model replica you might find wrapped up in a cereal packet, delightfully odd with little Mr. Price driving at the high wheel having to reach up, even sitting on a pile of magazines because of his small stature. So enamoured was he of his links with the motor-industry that later he was to sire four sons and name them after different makes of cars. Of course Rosalind and Tom where not to know this otherwise they would have been more amused by the whole thing than they were but even so they laughed nearly all the way and loved the time they spent together that day.

The heather was out. They lay on the turf and gazed down at the town spread before them, the feeling between them making everything new: beyond what had so far been.

Then one day they climbed all the way up Castle Hill, leaving their horses hitched to the slender boles of trees by Shaky Bridge. Arthur had insisted on the buckskin being gelded by the local practitioner so he was much more manageable than the day he was bought.

It was a strange place. You would climb up the first humpy rise thinking you had reached the summit, only to be met by the next, then the next, then the next – in a series of humps and rises until at last you could claw your way to the top. But the view was magnificent. "Happy Valley," Rosalind told him and there was the river meandering below and you could see for miles in either direction, West to Dolfan and the hills thumping the skyline all the way to the Sugar Loaf outside Abergavenny, the Black Mountains and beyond, then Eastward into unfamiliar territory: gentler, yellow and green fields towards other hills: yellow. Maelienydd. Land of the Lord of the Yellow Hills.

They walked back across the summit now facing the Radnor Forest but lay down on the short turf for a time to take in the view. Rosalind was wearing a voile blouse, white with a blue and mauve pattern of flowers over it, that had a green silk collar, cut low and secured with three green buttons sewn in a diagonal line across the swell of her breasts, tucked into her brother's corduroy trews that she had clinched round the waist with a leather belt. She didn't seem to care what she wore – and anyway, had to wear something suitable for riding her new black pony.

But she did care, when Tom, lying beside her became too familiar, suddenly taking her in his arms and even lying half-on top of her as he kissed her firmly on the lips. It was nice. There was a smell or was it a feeling, half-turned into a scent … something primitive. She wanted him to continue kissing her, holding her but – it had to be wrong. Remember the warnings. Never let them -.

She pushed him off and aside. "Tom Edwards – don't you EVER. Get off! Get off! I'm going."

He was startled, ashamed, puzzled – relieved?

"I'm sorry Rosalind – honestly I just – Hell…. I'll behave myself, I promise. Anything you want Rosalind is OK with me. I just like you – that's all … I thought …."

"As long as you understand Tom. None of that … I'm … I mean – I shall want to get married one day. People are supposed to wait 'till their married for all that – aren't they?"

"Oh well. Anything you say Rosalind is all right with me … I don't know, I'm just –".

But she allowed him to hold her hand going down the hill and as time went on, she would lean against him and he would kiss her when he saw her home – and now, now – it was always accepted – they would find somewhere quiet where they could lie together, fully-clothed but as lovers in all but deed. He knew the feel of her naked breasts, he lay in the hollow of her open thighs. One day Rosalind. One day.

Their parents never gave any signs that they knew they met so often. There were always excuses to shore up their absences in the evenings or Saturday afternoons off and anyway, Mary-Ellen and Arthur had plenty to think about with their own affairs, her almost ceaseless work in the farm kitchens and Arthur's' Council-meetings, Chapel-Deaconite activities, accompanying Mrs. Gibson-Watt to London sometimes on County matters when he would stay at what was to become the Regent Palace and once though accosted by a young street walker, to the delight of all back home, had murmured sweetly "Oh no, my dear, no – run along now, run along," when he had related his adventures in the privacy of family gatherings.

What did it all <u>mean</u>? And now here; seventeen years old and sitting on this bench, waiting for the train to take him – where?

Ah – at last … there is steam rising along the track under the grey stone bridge, the chuff and clang of the approaching engine, a whistle.

He stands, picking up the holdall with his few possessions, keeping well back under the station canopy for he hates to be seen by people wondering where he is off to always: can't bear nosiness or carrying a suitcase for that very reason.

The train pulls to a stop. He is going. He climbs aboard and clangs the door shut behind him, unbuttoning the leather strap and letting down the narrow window so that he can put his head out to watch the town disappear, see if he can catch a glimpse of TyCanol's chimneys as they head towards Pen-y-Bont.

Later, when they are further along the line, he will find an empty carriage where he can sit alone. He hates having to make conversation with any buggers who, in the main, bore him to death; in fact, the only people he can stand at all are Chinny and co. and of course Rosalind.

He will have a long think until Shrewsbury where he will have to change for Crewe before going on. 'Goodybe Dolly – I Must Leave You.' Yes – it's a case of that. 'Kitchener Needs You'. 'FORWARD! Forward to Victory! ENLIST NOW'. 'You are Wanted At the Front. ENLIST TODAY', 'Your King and Country need you: a call to Arms', 'Step into your place', '….. we're both needed to serve the guns! Fill up the ranks! Pile up the munitions!' 'Step into your place!' 'Women of Britain say – <u>GO!</u>'

Rosalind hadn't.

TEN

They come with me, the ancestors, as far as Liverpool. I started thinking about Aunty Luce. Whether I would go across and see her and Charlie when I get there – and her friend who we call Aunty Dora. Aunty Luce's husband died not long after Charlie was born. I don't know whether Dora is a relative or one of Luce's in-laws. They live close by each other anyway.

They all started pouring through my head then: Grandfather digging up the gorse bushes and starting the milkround in 1872, then in 1891 when the Local Board was petitioned, getting elected with 135 votes while John Heighway's Grandpa was in with 115. Huh – didn't we have it drummed into us? 1894 Local Boards were constituted Urban District Councils, Thomas Edwards re-elected with 95 votes … (Slipping Gramps!) Later election, some members retired then after a few more years had gone by, town divided into wards.

That's where Father comes into it. '– the following candidates became early members of the Council. Arthur Edwards, WC Harper, Thomas Pritchard, Joseph Coombs and J. Louis Wilding.' Can see the old boys now: the worthies. Shops and businesses. Go-getters.

I've always liked going into Coombs' shop especially. Smell of paraffin oil, brown cardboard boxes full of nails, hinges, brackets, brake linings. All those fittings: brass knobs and draw handles, shelf on shelf, floor on floor. Upstairs, china and glass, wood panelling, trelliswork, garden implements, zinc buckets, rubber hoses, bits of furniture, overalls, socks, deckchairs. The smell gets at the back of the throat. Pleasantly.

It must have been one of those early elections when one of them told voters his policy to include – the running of trams 'like greased lightening' to Llanbadarn Bridge and outlying places. Ha! Greased lightening! Damn – they make me laugh, some of 'em.

I never told them at home that I'd been in the County Buildings and looked up facts in Records. The Census of 1891 and 'Thomas Edwards 53, (previously) Farmer of 36 achres, Llanbadarn Fawr Road. Ann, 45. Born Llandegley.' Then all those children. I hadn't known before. The family doesn't <u>discuss</u>. Not enough. So:

William, (Uncle Willie) written in there, no messing. Twenty years' old son, born Llanbadarn Fawr. <u>Idiot from Birth.</u> My stars! And he was the oldest. Never have thought it.

Thomas 10. Son. (Uncle Tom, Three Wells).

Elizabeth 16. Daughter (and died when Father was 19. Never even knew about her!)

Agnes 13. Daughter.

Alice 11. Daughter

Arthur 9. Son. Born Cefnllys – (ah – they were in Llandrindod by then, I Expect.).

Margaret J. 5. Daughter. Scholar. Cefnllys. (Why <u>Scholar?</u> – and who was she anyway? Perhaps the 'Nats' had started up by then …).

Lucy A. 4. Daughter.

No, I wouldn't have wanted them to know or to go and dig in the Records themselves. Not with Uncle Willie written down 'Idiot from Birth', - but I forgot to tell Chinny that the 'Nats' was at one time the Middleton Arms: Thomas Watkins Licensed Victualler. Appreciated that. National School now.

Mainstone. I used to love the sun quite high up before 9 o'clock in the morning, shining from over the hills at the back. Used to be strong shadows coming forward from buildings, hedges, posts – yes and the sunlight striking the right hand side, back of the house, looking at it from a side window high up on the top floor. The backs of chimneys were deep in shadow as well, so was the stable yard. Remember Hector? Bringing him out and up on to the Back Lawn? Hell, we didn't know. Kids. Yes, deep shadows except for flowers in the borders around the back door ……… and I missed it when we left. Still do. There is a depression at TyCanol. Something sad sings in the silences. That terrible silence in the Parlour. Might as well say it. It's a bloody dump after town. Love the fields but don't like being stuck down there full time. Miss my pals. Ha! – Those damn crab-apples. Ha Ha. Still makes me ache laughing even thinking about old Stan, or was it Chinny? Sliding down nearly into that crap-can and landing practically on the old gel's shanks.

Yes …. And none of us would have been there either, most probably, if old Jehu, the stagecoach driver from Newtown, hadn't discovered the sulphurous spring when he was driving that tent peg into the ground down the Rock. 1865 and a marquee being raised for an auction after the Park was made the greater part of Rock House Estate, being offered for sale. Chance – or Divine Inspiration? It was the smell of sulphur I suppose. Attracted. Unless old Jehu thought it was the Devil. Rising. Anyway the 'worthies' had it tested and Whoopee! Strong saline. A Spa is born!

Wonder what they think now I've gone? I won't write till I've joined-up. No – I'd better not call on Aunty Luce either yet. You never know. Probably try and talk me out of it anyway. Like Rosalind. Wonder what she's doing? Didn't she cry last night when I met her before going to the Llanerch? It was awful. "I can't stay, Rosalind," I told her. "I can't S-T-A-Y." I've never seen anyone that upset before. As soon as I'm settled, I'll write to her. Hate writing letters – but I will. I'll write to Rosalind. I'll write to Mother.

Down we go. Tunnels before ferns waving like those green fish again at the side of the track. Must be coming to Pen-y-Bont - over there. Oh yes – I know this country. Cefnllys on my right. Maelielyn: Land Of The Lord Of The Yellow Hills. Fortress hills.

Radnor Forest. Pale blue above the green. Wide. You can breathe. Bits of gorse sticking up in the middle distance. Sheep tracks up through the common land, through the heather. You only get that colour in Radnorshire, I'll bet. Blue/mauve. No – beyond blue. Violet – blue, right in the distance ...... fading .... Gone like a blink.

Early Summer, there's a lot of yellow broom round here. Lot more broom now. A Radnorian wearing a cap in the garden is looking towards this train. Elbows up. Hands hanging like buckets. Droll. Somewhat annoyed. The definite <u>look</u> about him. You can never mistake them.

What's this? Is it my old Grandmother's place – on Father's side before she married Grandad: the Widow Anne's? Llandegley? Dolau? Gone – e – e . Oh Hell - that was unexpected and the old black tarred farm buildings falling to pot by the look of it.

Going fast now: down through cuttings of green and granite. I see a red May Tree, white May (at least they would be those colours in Summer). A ginger sheep on a hill. Sheep. Sheep. Pointed hills. Pointed fir trees. Larches. Feel the ancestors. Feel Radnor Forest and Pen-y-Bont Common pulling back on the horizon. What am I doing? Cows very fat and contented looking, knee deep in golden pollen off some late flowering -- shoving through. Munching. Gone – e – e.

Llanbister Road. May trees shaped like those in fairy book il-lustrations. Or Aubrey Beardsley drawings. Three crows flap left. A black bull is lying like a log in a sunken bog-like field surrounded by waterweeds – and more yellow flowers. What are they? KingCups? Too late surely. I expect Bernard will deal with hundreds of bulls like that if he's going in for the veterinary business. And sheep. He loves it..... huh! - So would I if I could get away from the farm more often. It's the mixing with all the farming-chronies. Radnorians from the hills. The humour. The chat. County gossip. Belonging and being seen to belong. Acceptance.

Bernard will be going to the University if he gets his C.W.B. They'll see to that at home. Mother will, anyway. He's a little bug-ger with girls though. Chinney says Collette Arrowsmith, the vet's daughter has the hots for him. Fat chance. Lardy type. Private schooling: the <u>Misses</u> Vaughan-Williams or <u>Miss</u> Mary Powell up Broadway. Yes 'Ivanhoe' where I had to leave half a pint. Can feel the metal measure in my hand now. Sort of whitened-grey alloy of something. The Arrowsmith girl. Thick thighs and ankles. Those heavy brown woollen stockings. The downturned mouth. Hates me. Would Bernard be smarmy enough to get in there - marry into the business say? You bet. I couldn't. Too fastidious. Like shagging a brick shithouse, four square to the wind. Built up solid. Gor-r-r- wish Jim was here. He'd like that – 'too fastidious'. BernARD won't be volunteering, that's a cert. "Oh no, NO! – Dad" (Mary-Ellen). "Too young." TOO precious. Far, far too young. (Like me?). Bullshit.

Llanbister now and I'm laughing. Can see Eloise, as she used to be, eyes crossing and rolling, pulling the most awful faces as she pretended to be one of the hicks from here performing at an eisteddfod, hands consciously clasped low in front, elbows out and up, Eloise pronouncing it with a local exaggeration: CLANbister! Can't stop laughing now. Anyone watching will have me down as a solitary madman on this train. Llanbister Road.

More pointed hills, fields where masses of buttercups grow in the spring, hawthorns, hawthorns, broom back there. Sheep. Laughing again at Llangunllo. Eloise returns and a very 'knowing' way of pronouncing this one – as if one of their yokels nodding and becking, amazed (for incomprehensible reasons) eyes popping. Cruel buggers, us. At times. Llangunllo!

Approaching Knighton. There's that old pub listing at a crazy angle just up the road from the station. Yes, the trees – seem to remember them. That's the pub all right. I look for the bank we rolled down. Is that it on my left now? Yes. My first taste of ale – ever. Tight as a drum. Wonder where those others ended up? A year ago. A YEAR!

We are heading for a gap in the hills. I remember pink wild roses all along this line from here to Craven Arms. Sunday School outings. Who to tell what the sight of wild roses does to me? Eloise maybe? Ivor? Never Chinny and Co. Or even Rosalind. Would have to be someone known almost from birth. Who wouldn't sneer. Who wouldn't think 'what's up with him?' I tried to write it into a composition in Standard Two once, before the bloody Duck took to hitting my boils with the ruler. But it got cleared away by Ida in the morning before I could get it to school.

"Done yer homework, Edwards?" he said

"Yes" I said

"Where is it then?"

"Lost" I said

He didn't like that.

The pointed hills are coming up again all round now. Radnorshire impressing like new birth behind a larch tree. No county like Radnorshire. It looms bright through fog. Light as elves. Joyful. Real: the only real place on earth probably. Tied up with the wild rose and farms emerging or disappearing through morning mists. It contains my mother, my grandmother and her mother, my father, my grandfather and probably his father and grandfather for all I know. Got to be kept in the family. Bugger the Germans. Look what they're doing in Belgium. Bayoneting. Taking over if they can get away with it. Not bloody likely.

Huge herds of black and white Fresian cattle outside Wenlock like a rash of measles. Good milkers. When I get back I'll try and persuade the old man to buy a herd for TyCanol. I love the look of them. I'll be older then. He might take more notice – whatever Mother might say. Tricky with Mary Ellen. Very cautious always. Watches me like a hawk. Doesn't altogether trust me. Doesn't like my friends or the football. Frigging BERNARD I 'spect. Afraid of undue and wrong influence. To hell with it.

Lot of sheep dotting the fields now. Lot of them this year. White, newly shorn bodies. Bits of blue dye marking. Black heads and feet. Smaller heads. Intelligent. Light-footed.

Swoop of broom: masses of it flying past. No yellow on it now; but not turning yet. Have to wait for next Spring. For the wild roses, the dog daisies, the cow parsley. Hopton Heath. The sun has come out from behind the spot of mist. No – that was Bucknell!

Two youngish men got on back there. There is a stink. Vodka drinkers, I think. People think they can drink it undetected but it leaks through the pores. One of them looks moist and puffy as if saturated in it. Smells like a poultice. Perhaps he has shit himself. It is the sour smell of the long-term unwashed. "Keep off the spirits" Chinny advised. He's right. I like a drop of ale, though. Mary-Ellen would go crazy if she knew. Probably does know. Nothing could get past Ida. Maybe that's why ----. Yes, the Llanerch is the place. Les. Doesn't let on. He and Archie like having the boys in. The swapped tales. The laughs. Clandestine. They know all about disapproval and would never say anything about the adjournments from the War Office to the Back Bar. Family. The moment of entry. Through the old front door, down the step and into the gloom. The overpowering smell of ale. Les sitting smoking by the blackened fireplace. Small window behind looking out over Morris's fields, then up, up to our Plantation outlined against the three hills. Last night. The farewell gathering. The stipulation; If by any chance Yours Truly should buy one – any funeral arrangements would be appreciated if the cortege would kindly make a brief curtsey halt at the entry to the Llanerch Drive….. by the old rotting gate sagging into the nettles and wires down against the Court-House.

So many times the feet, accompanied by the feet of friends have entered through and supported (steadily in the main) many pleasant interludes. But for Pete's sake don't let on to Mary-Ellen and Arthur. Ida must have smelled ale on my breath that time. She was accidentally getting herself a drink of water when I crept in late. Blast! Never mind. Good, the vodka boys have got off now.

It was nice to see Aunty Corys last night too. Came all the way from Rhayder just to see me off. Loves the boys of the family always. Especially me! I made the mistake telling her Rosalind and Eloise had on occasions nearly wet themselves laughing. Corys was standing against a painted plate of blue and rust-red picked out with gold leaf. "Never mention anything like that again in here, dear," she said firmly. Base-bodily-functions of no interest whatsoever so we must abide by her local rules. The smile hardly faltered. She merely swept busily along into her next enquiry before stepping, toes out, to oversee things in the kitchen. I won't forget this lesson. She was right, I suppose. I had no need to mention peeing as a source of amusement. Lavatorial humour. Childish. Bit inhibiting though: Base Bodily Functions. HA! Good old Corys.

It has been overcast for the last fifteen miles or so but now the train slides past the Butter Market at Shrewsbury and there is a glimmer of light here. Gold. Just a shaft. Maybe it is going to clear up and be fine again as it was before we crossed the county boundary. There is a gull on the roof, white against the prune-coloured slates. No it is raining.

A big man in a light tweed jacket and dark trousers is staring over two sets of lines, two platforms, at me as I sit here in this carriage that is to take me on to Crew before I change for Liverpool. I don't mind. Have just returned from the Gents and am quite pleased with my appearance after all. I don't look too bad I suppose. Funny how we want to look our best. What is 'Our Best'? Why should we think we look better with hair brushed this way or that? Quite tidy anyway. Teeth clean and very white.

As the man stares, I wonder idly, what he does for a living. He has a small, neat attaché case with him so I surmise he is still employed as a civvy: not in the army. Unless he's on leave. He doesn't look as if he's on leave. Perhaps he could be connected with the entertainment-business. There is something vaguely hinting at the older syncopationist (Come to Me My Melancholy Baby or Rosalind's favourite: Chinatown). Or then he might be a journalist.

Thinking of the music has brought Rosalind back into my head. Wonder what it is about her when there are all those others who are always hanging around Bernard and me at the concerts? At the chapel functions. At the races, the shows, the dances. Don't know. Can't define it. Won't have any messing will she? Strong. Good pal, too – though – a-a-h.

The man in his light jacket departs before me. His train slides in and as far as I can tell, he moves towards the first class carriages. Perhaps he's in the Government. You never know. Probably best to be polite. You never really can tell who people are. Might be angels ––as it says in the Bible.

Getting back to Rosalind. Do I really know who she is? Does she know me entirely? Would I, for example, want her at the War Office, sitting in on our sessions? If she wanted me to give up my friends – would I? No damn fear ……. But thank heavens I don't think she would ever ask that.

Wish we could get to hell out of here now. I want to arrive. Want to sign up. Get on. This rate I'll be here all day. Just as well I'm not calling on Aunty Luce.

S'truth, I remember when she used to arrive on holiday with Uncle Will and tread around Llandrindod Wells in polished, pointed shoes: brogues. Used to look like the Countess-Of-Somewhere-Or-Other: little sable cloaks hooked over her shoulders. Silk dresses. Looked lovely: peach-coloured face with gold - striped eyes like mischievous little animals shining out at you from under a hedge. She would smell of expensive colognes and always the lace-edged handkerchief ready to stuff in her mouth if she were in danger of laughing at something she ought to be taking seriously.

A likely occurrence for she too has the family's over-developed sense of the ridiculous to cope with. I loved her. Still do – but can't risk going out her way – have to find the Recruiting Office anyway. Seems ages since I was a kid saying 'Hello' to the aunts Agnes and Lucy in the milkshed at TyCanol. The morning haze. Milk churns with bits of polished brass on copper stating Edwards TyCanol Dairy. Est. 1872. Clanging as they were set down in cool corners and the hens moodily clucking and pecking about the black-tarred and white-washed farm buildings. We have all stolen away. Are stealing now. I find it painful to mull over the passage of time. Changes … Good. We're off.

Approaching Liverpool a dead sheep on a grass incline in a field, four black legs sticking up in rigor mortis above a collapsed woolly carcass. My stars! Is it an omen, a sign of some kind, (ah – here comes the Welsh bit now: the morbidity.) How awful to fall like that sheep back there and not be found until after the stiffening process has set in. Imagine for a minute or two the horror of undertakers having to fit the dead into boxes with arms and legs raised like sticks against their efforts. I give full rein to these meditations. It is an attempt to overcome past fears (Mr. Pugh, leaking brown fluid out of a dropsicle carcass as they were carrying him to his grave etc.). No, grown-ups ought not to expose children to facts they are unable to cope with. And anyway – are they facts …. Or merely tarted-up half-truths to gristle over, chew and spit out like old bitches with half-chewed bones? Gossip. Horror-gossip. The swapping of bloody old wives' tales. Ach-y-fi!

ELEVEN

Well now for it. I have entered and am in front of their counter.
Three enormous soldiers are the other side. They are so tall, I wonder if they are standing on boxes. No. They are not. Right through I
will wonder why most of the NCO's and officers, sergeants, sergeant
-majors plus most of the men look and are so tall. Won't realise, will
I, that of course I haven't finished growing?

Kitchener's likeness is on the wall even though he was drowned
in June. The room is low. Is brown. Wood floor. Boards. The light,
in some of the windows, is filtered through semi-opaque glass. Grey/
lemon. Dust-motes floating.

"Well young man – what can we do for you?"

They are pleasant. Eager. Glad I am here to volunteer. Am I <u>sure</u>
I am eighteen. Oh yes. They don't push it. I sign. Attest. I am passed
A1 by the MO. I am in the army. Tomorrow I will be sent to Bury
for the initial training. They will kit me out there. I will spend the
night here in barracks. It is quite late afternoon now so they will show
me where I am to sleep, where I can eat. Then I must go to the room
and stay there until morning. They will give me a pass for the train.
I am to be up at 6 a.m. Got that? Yes. YES SIR. Yes sir.

In the room there are three bunk beds. There is a black coal-burning stove. Two men are in here, grinning affably. Fondling a white cat. Their army-jackets are off and they sit in their shirtsleeves, relaxed by the fire. They are not old but they look like old soldiers. Experienced but dissolute.

It is 8 o'clock. The room is not big. Narrow.

"That's your bed, dear ..... over there."

What the hell is this? Dear! They indicate the bunk against the far wall facing the door. Thank Heavens, their two are together, the other side. Got to watch this. They fondle the cat, smiling towards me the whole time.

"Do you want to stroke pussy, dear?" one asks.

He has a slight lisp now. Thank goodness for Chinny. It exists then. The condition. Chinny's dire warnings. Watch Your Arse. Ruin yer! I feel a kind of sick rage rising. I don't deign to answer this question. Am I not a Radnorian? A farmer's son. Radnorshire farmers don't go fondling bloody cats. Cats are for catching mice.

I sit on my bunk as far away from them as possible and start tugging off my boots. The one nearest the stove rises and goes poncing off towards some shelves before sashaying back to his seat with a box containing shoe-cleaning brushes, polish and duster. Look at the stupid bugger. He flounces, gets up knock-kneed from the hips and swivels over towards me with polish and dusters in his white, effeminate hands. Must be a desk clerk. Office-worker.

"Would you like us to clean your boots for you dear?" he asks ingratiatingly, holding out the stuff as if for inspection. The other one gets up and drapes himself over his partner's shoulder. They both stand there looking down. They are much bigger than me. Huge. I am so angry I must now be white with temper. The flush has gone from my cheeks. No longer hot. Feel the steel bite. I know roughly how to kill and will attempt to if necessary. I tug off my remaining boot left-handed. Pick the other one up off the floor.

"You want my boots, well then HAVE 'EM."

I throw them full force right into their faces. One each. They fall back. Hell's bells, here it comes. Get ready Edwards – on your feet stance. What was it Jim taught you? Get 'em off-balance then swing across and back from the elbow. Get 'em in the wind-pipe or a jab to the temple. Side of the neck ... swift chop must immobilise the arm. Get their right arm first – then kick in their balls. Can't – no shoes – but never mind. Ah – not necessary. They are falling further back. Retiring. Smiling still. Must have seen it in my face. They pick up the cat again. Through my teeth now: "And keep away from me", I warn. They sprawl. They caress the cat. I climb on the bunk and stretch out fully clothed. I will not be taking anything off tonight.. I pull the rough grey blanket up over my shoulders and doze, arse to the wall. Be glad to see the morning.

T W E L V E

BURY.

I had this idea of Bury in my mind: the red canyons of Manchester. Towering brick buildings: endless; but after mile on mile of mill-workers' back-to-backs smoking under purple slate rooves, belching factory-chimneys, hills and valleys covered seam to seam with industry going like mad, viewed now from below then from above: ridged, stretched out mile on mile again against the hope of hills untainted in far, far distances that pigmyfy you, giving you that feeling you had once on the train to New Brighton, on that particular outing. Lost. Lost. Young boy alone and walking through wide, alien landscape (if by any chance the lid was taken off the life you knew: if Mother disappeared off the seat where she sits erect over the gold-knobbed cane, black band round the stretched neck, skirts tucked round the ankle-buttoned boots and you.... flung out to make it alone), alone and searching. But searching for what? A journey into chaos. Silent. Empty. <u>Dreamlike</u>: that's it. Just a glimpse of that feeling. England.

But here you can come down the hill near the small river round the corner and along into the town. Placed above it all. Away from all that: the overkill of smoke. Yes, there are the old Crossland Mills but tastefully out of the way. Victorian red brick, squared off with young Crossland having a hell of a good time on the proceeds – (and by damned I don't blame him) – so they say; and other factories, of course there are but there's a hump in the town, a swelling up for carnival, a brass-band feeling, a flags and bunting and happy atmosphere. The air is fresh like home: a good wind blowing little round trees near a large central building from where the business of the town is run. Plenty of tended grass areas and here and there, in off the roads, the streets, little squares and rectangles of shadowed lawn. Very tidy.

I arrive in the centre of all this downwind from Peel's statue. The train pulls out. There were other recruits on the train. We are met and herded into a lorry, conveyed to the Barracks. Out of town. Down round corners, sight of mills, sight of ordnance-factories, up the long road past the Wellington Hotel (1898), past the quarter-master's Stores to the billets.

We are the lucky little bastards, they say. The others are over there (waving huge hands towards the road leading back to town) in tents, up to their backsides in mud while the alterations are done. Temporary quarters. Just as well we arrived when we did. Volunteered especially. Comfortable little sods, us. Twenty-four to thirty per room. Twelve or fifteen up one side and down the other. Wooden stands at the bottom of each bed. Locker to dump your civvies. Won't be taking those overseas – so turfed in later. Place to be kept IMMACULATE. Got that? Yes. Yes SIR. Yes SIR. Right. Get down the stores.

"Fuck me!" says the tall youth who has taken the end bed. Sounds funny because he has a look of perpetual surprise on a shovel-shaped face. White as a ghost. Eyebrows up, eyes popping then the laugh as if infinitely surprised before – "Fuck me!". He is taller than the rest of us and comes from somewhere between Chester and Liverpool. Doesn't say exactly where. Probably wanted by the Force. I like him. Don't hear many 'fucks' in Radnorshire – 'cos of the Chapels. He doesn't mean anything. Just an expression.

Some of us start down the road at the back of the Barracks. More like a lane really. Like something out of Swan's Way. Trees hanging over. Grass shooting from the sides. Cart-ruts. Dust. Smell of late summer.

We lope across open concrete space to a small double door under a porch at the very end of almost an innocuous-looking building painted cream. Red and military-markings somewhere.

Fuck-me gives a laugh and a huge bang on the door. It opens and we are viewed by a pair of suspicious eyes above a twitching moustache. Who had the damn cheek to bang like that? We stare straight at him giving nothing away. We are told to enter and turn left through another door. We are in an incredibly tall room, lined with shelves and divided by partitions into sections. There are brown cardboard boxes in row after row.

The Quarter-Master looms behind a desk on the right as we enter. Corporal and Lance-Corporal with him. There is a door open behind them letting in a greenish- filtered light. This room has no windows and electric-lightbulbs hang in celluloid cones from the high ceilings.

We are not measured so much as assessed. True there is a tape measure round the Corporal's neck in case the Q.M. should deign to reach out for verification but in the main it's "How tall? What inch chest? Collar? Shoe size?". Though they seem quite fussy on cap and helmet-dimensions.

The kakhi comes out. Is pulled and yanked from appropriately labelled boxes. We are dancing from one foot to the other, tugging off boots and breeks. Jackets, shirts, ties are folded away. Packaged. We are given handfuls of badges and insignia to be sewn on. 2nd Battalion Lancashire Fusiliers. We are given all the necessary and told to get back to the barracks, fix up the uniforms properly and report back within the hour. At The Double.

Been here three weeks now. There's that excitement in the mornings. It's nothing to me having to get up early. Same goes for the training. I don't mind stamping around a bit, forming fours: all that. And they think I'm a good shot. Where d'you learn to shoot? They wanted to know. Shoulder arms! Present arms! STAND AT EASE. Like a game.

The excitement is fleeting but perpetual at the same time. It's being away from home and not knowing what's going to happen. The sequences. It's the feeling sometimes in the lane out the back when we are walking down. Something to do with young girls smiling in the town. Young people – and you one of them. The flowers growing. Red-hot pokers and Love Lies Bleeding around the Town Hall. The smell of the leaves at evening. The rough serge against your body. Looking good.

We march down to the Castle Armoury every day for physical jerks. A lot of officers down there in doors off a wrought-iron balcony that goes all the way round the drill-hall, high up. They come out and watch sometimes. Stand there assessing us. Can't help showing off then. We all do it. Shoulders back, stomachs in. We toss the medicine ball. We head footballs. They think my co-ordination is excellent. I tell Serg. I've been playing on the quiet for years. He laughs.

There is to be a dance in the drill hall down at Castle Armoury. So many weeks and a slight relaxing of rules and prohibitions.

The girls are great. Everything about them comes forward: they way they are made. Breasts like pigeons, noses, mouths, even their faces – all seem to have been fashioned <u>forwards.</u> And they smile and welcome you. Their arms come forward. They reach out for you. They are genuinely friendly: not after anything. They come forward to give. They are givers, not takers. They smile. Their lips are puckered ready to kiss. We have noticed that most of the populace we observe in our passings have these characteristics, the body inclined forwards, heads moulded towards the face. Pulled. Smiles – but all the good things emphasised in these beautiful girls.

"Hope they've got forward-facing fannies!" Fuck-Me laughs. "Makes for easier access!" We laugh as if we know what he means.

Jim Fairhurst is going to the dance, next bed to me. So is J. W. - . (I won't mention his name because the poor bugger is shit-scared the whole time). He comes from the hills round our way. I've met him at horse-fairs and once at an Eisteddfod in the back-of-beyond. He is a bit older than me and I've told him to keep his mouth shut about my being under-age. I've never seen anyone so glad to see anybody else, as he was to see me. He thinks I can tell him what to do if he doesn't get it first time. He's willing enough but there's something missing somewhere. He's not quite all there. I've told him that when we go over, to stick close to me and I'll see he's all right. I can't tell you how sorry I feel for people sometimes. It must be damned awful to be like that. So helpless in a way. It's when he whimpers. Can't stand it – this feeling of almost sick-worry for another person. What if it was Billy, my little brother? What would I do then? Well, can't do any more now.

Halfway through the dance and this girl, Esme, is not holding anything back. She is one of the best-looking women under the balconies. Her hair shines black beneath the lights. Black eyes. Very intense look boring into me if I say anything: anything at all. She seems ready to pounce. Makes me chuckle. Feel a bit condescending, almost like the Old Man sometimes. Can feel how he feels. Slight brushing of the moustache if I had one. Slight adjustment of the gold watch-chain across the belly. I laugh. A) because I can't dance – just steer straight ahead like pushing the wheelbarrow, B) at the ridiculousness of me as the Old Man.

"What yer laughing at?" she asks eagerly, ready to laugh along at the drop of a hat, so I tell her out of pure cussedness. She actually drops her hands to her knees and laughs too. Genuinely.

"Well – thee's a case and no mistake", she tells me, wiping her eyes. "Never had n'aught said like that to me before, I can tell thee. They're usually all over me to <u>please</u> in everything the beggars have to say".

She wears brown silk with grey insets. A bit of mauve. Some blue. Tight waist. Those blackberry eyes. Intense.

"Yes an' I'm ready to pounce as you so tidily put it. Come on. Come wi' me soldier-lad."

Her accent is strange to me but pleasant, warm. No side. Don't have to be careful of your P's and Q's as you do with the town elite at home. Pure Cambridge there. 'Pess the gless you silly ess' – dampens you rather. Rosalind and I used to laugh like drains watching some of her friends putting it on. But Rosalind is something else.

Esme and I leave the hall for a breather and walk along the cobbles through the lane before coming out in front of the Town Hall. There is a breeze but the air is still warm with flowers and leaves not yet turning. Late this year. Must be all the rain up here.

There is no moon. Starlight. We are under the Big Dipper pointing to the North Star then we walk downhill to the right again, cross over and further on down to the Waterloo Inn. I shouldn't enter but take Esme into the old bar. The landlord is clued-up to the 'boys' and our plight and kindly nods us into their Function Room through double-oak doors at the end of the passage. I buy a small port and brandy for Esme and a pint for myself.

Fuck-Me is in the function room with a girl. "Meet Julie", he grins. "Esme", I reply. We all laugh.

Not much later Esme takes me over the road where there is one of those little shrub and tree-enclosed lawns. Very dark and quiet in the shadows. She laughs indulgently for she knows I've never actually been with a woman. She is most kind and practised. We stay out of the dance for almost a further hour. "Most enjoyable", I murmur on the way back in. Again, she collapses laughing, hands to knee. "You'll do lad. More than a bit! -'ee will you come to tea next Sunday? I'd love that".

"So would I, but I'm afraid I have to decline my dear. It would coincide with too many duties. However, if you and my friend's Julie could arrange to be here at approximately midnight next Wednesday – we'll do our best to come and see you".

Sundays we have Church Parade (compulsory) then have to scrub our Barrack-Room from top to bottom; even the planks under the bloody mattresses. Only a few hours off after that – and I have to write to Rosalind, also to Eloise. I haven't written to Mother and Father yet and have written to Eloise via Chinny in case they stop me going to France. I didn't think they could once I was in, but then I read about that kid Dall, fifteen years and ten months. 'A letter from Mum put paid to his service in France'. Hum.m. Anyway, I don't want any of this 'getting my feet under tables' kind of thing. No, Fuck-Me and I will have to use the drainpipes at the back. The lane is dark at night and if I can climb those ropes at the gym, should be able to shin up a drainpipe hand over hand, knees scissoring – using the same principle to get out then back in again. Great.

Our days are increasingly frenetic. We are issued with all kinds of weaponry: revolvers, rifles, Mills Bombs. We have to learn the drill. Cleaning …. Endless cleaning, the extraction of firing pins, how long to wait before throwing. How to throw.

Bayonet practice is the most revealing. We are to harden ourselves. We are to realise it is either him or me. We are to detest the enemy and spill his guts. Lunge! In! Twist! Retract! Lunge! In! Twist! Retract!

We carry enormous weights and at the double. We drill. We march. We run, full combat-gear up and down hills and slopes, we <u>learn</u> the theory. There is not much time. We are needed in France. Who'll go boys, I will. I will.

I write to Eloise 'Tell the folks I'm fine but will write later when more settled'. I don't tell her that I have to scoot off for a couple of days or where. I ask her if she can get hold of some 'Soldiers' Friend' and 'Blanco' – before the next kit-inspection as I find it hard to afford out of my bob a day. Also, for heavens' sake, some Players Medium Cut.

I write to Rosalind. Wait for me etc. I try to mean it but it's hard. I know if I saw her it would be the same but things have got blurred.

If I'm honest, it is an effort to write at all. I don't want to write to anybody. The thought of writing letters or even postcards depresses me with a kind of guilt-feeling. Why? The feeling is situated in the rib-cavity. Heart. Lungs. Lower, into the Solar Plexus. What – just the thought of writing? Having to take up sheets of paper and stuff them in an envelope? Buy stamps? Buy postcards? Have to address them? Lick the stamps even? CAN'T BE BOTHERED. But I write to Rosalind all the same and she comes back: that glow when I have seen her walking down Middleton Street and I know we are going to see each other again in the evening. She's not like the girls here. She's saving it: Rosalind. Just as well. There's the glow. The shine. The constriction in the throat, restraint on the tongue sometimes (not always) but also the separation: a kind of splitting-off, this glamour, from …. The other thing.

It's so much easier when you're not in awe of them. As when I was Billy's age at home and would almost prefer the company of those in the kitchens and sculleries, the stables, to the sacred precincts of drawing-room or parlour; for instance – some time last week they had me in upstairs to ask if I'd like to put in for a commission. 'Officer-material', they said. I said no. No SIR! (prefer to be with the boys).

Pity Rosalind couldn't have been a bit more generous with it all the same. It could have focussed her in place to a certain extent. Given a hold on things. Would I have written more often then? She doesn't say much in her letters. Says her parents keep on at her. Hope it's not a case of 'the-same-as-mine-are' with Eloise. She's going to have to marry that bugger Cox now. Pressure. But surely the Hamers haven't got anyone like that in mind for Rosalind? The Rosalind I know would soon tell them to get the hell out of it! Though …… remember Eloise. The change that occurred.

Fuck-Me and I were going to Ireland tomorrow. Detached – to find and bring back a couple of squaddies who went AWOL last weekend but he's been confined to Barracks. (C.B.) Went down the drainpipe, night before last and on a massive pub-crawl. Ended up right out at Haywood in the Wagon and Horses where they told us that other time that the rhododendrons are cyclamen-coloured in summer. We have masses of dark-red rhododendrons round the lake in Llandrindrod. I must have mentioned them when I recognised the leaves. Homesick!

Bell Lane, leading out of town is lined with pubs. The Grapes, Golden Fleece, New Inn, Old Bluebell, George and Dragon, Gamecock, Browncow Inn, Thwaites Fairfield. Fuck-Me was going to have a pint in every one – and did. Thank heavens I didn't go. Couldn't. I was roped in by the boys in the pontoon-school. We rig up blankets under the tables down the centre of the barrack-room after Lights Out. Candles then. The Orderly-Sergeant will some-times douse the lights then jump under the blanket with us. Never made much out of it – but what the hell. Mary-Ellen would be more outraged than ever. Gambling – and for money! Peanuts. Sometimes we harmonise sotto-vocce: 'Keep the Home Fires Burning'. It's the favourite in the canteen at the moment. I don't let on that I knew Ivor. They would think I was swinging the lead.

It's to be Jim Fairhurst and me going to Dublin.

A mad place this. We get off the ferry down the Quays. Everything seems to be heaving about. Horse-drawn drays, carriages, traps, motorcars all whirling around and breaking out into side-streets and market-places. Sticks wave and voices call over other voices. There doesn't seem to be any order to the traffic-flow either direction, yet there must be for it doesn't come to a permanent halt.

Jim and I decide to have a look round before heading towards the address we were given by Serg. "Don't hang around", he told us. "Not in those uniforms." Red rags to bulls were mentioned. We carry rifles. Revolvers. We get stared at. Couldn't care less. We stare back. Straight in the eyes, shoulders back, chin up. Politics don't bother me. Have to do a job. "Keep buggering on, Jim". I grin. We saunter down to Trinity and have a look through the arch into the inner courtyard. Some beautiful, tall, black-haired girls come out. They do a double take where they catch sight of our uniforms. One smiles or attempts to smile from beneath arched brows. I look as threatening as possible without laughing outright. I feel taller than I used to when I joined-up but if she did but know it, she's probably about three years older than me.

The traffic is really chaotic here, circling round as if on some crazy roundabout. We shove off left and cross O'Connell Bridge to have a good look up and down the Liffey before turning back and battling the crowds in Grafton Street. There are tinkers wrapped in shawls squatting against the balustrades either side of the bridge. Begging. With babies in their arms. Never seen anything like it. "Don't!" Jim says as I try as surreptitiously as possible to drop a coin into the up-turned palm of one young girl, pale and in the last gasp of some terrible disease. "Probably – got stacks more than us in the bogs," he goes on. I drop the coin anyway. "God Bless You My Darling." She says.

There's a café half way up the street. A smell of buns and coffee wafting out. "Come on" I say. We enter. It has a feel of school about it. High windows. Overall brown wood. Polish. Block floors. Pews at the side in alcoves. Brown polished tables. Serious men sit talking, talking, talking on church-hall chairs. Professionals of some sort: dentists? politicians? newspapermen? Jawing and jabbering away in the pews, some, heads bent clandestinely towards one another, swapping state-secrets – Ha – Ha. Leaded lights to some of the windows. Bits of stained glass. Green glass too filtering green air in beams striking down. Dust motes.

Hospital-matrons masquerading as high-class, snooty, no-nonsense waitresses – hurry to and fro with silver coffee pots on silver trays, brown, half-glazed coffee-cups, cream jugs and sugar-basins stacked expertly alongside, attired in brown and cream checked gingham dresses reaching the top of brown ankle-boots and crisp white aprons, strings tied in enormous bows at the back, completing the uniform. On their heads they wear tiara-shaped headbands.

"Nice and clean in here Tom, let's eat."

I'm all for it. We've been given a small allowance for rations. I like the smell of coffee, the look of the food, the professionalism. Can't eat in some places. But this is Bewleys.

It's raining when we come out. A strange thing. Businessmen in suits run in the streets with newspapers folded and held above their heads. They smile. They run from one office to another, one shop to another. Their neatly trousered legs go like scissors snapping. Snap, snap, snap. They run, smiling, down the streets. It must rain a lot here. They seem very practised. Taking it in their stride. Running through the rain. Can't see the elders back home doing that. The Old Man. Mr. Coombes. Ha Ha. Hell!

We put on our ground-sheets and instead of going for a stroll round Stephens Green, as advised by a well-meaning character near us in the café, decide to hot-foot it down to 21 a) Camden Street to pick up the defaulters and bring them back to Barracks.

The house is next door but one to Camden Stores whose façade reminds me of certain shop-fronts in Llandrindod. J.O. Davies: High-Class-Provisions, for instance. Classically-designed under the first and second floor though Georgian windows here.

Next door has only the ground floor, that is – a massive front door plus a Georgian window with a tree that appears to be growing out of the <u>roof</u> but 21 a) on the other hand is tall and narrow, shooting up four floors of single Georgian windows though only a massive door and fan-light over it, ground floor, yet no room for a window at all. A peculiar sort of tottering street, leaning at crazy angles. Irregular. Uncoordinated. I like it but it is pissing down and the rain runs off us relentlessly.

Our boots crash on the cobbles as we run for the doorway. Jim raps on one of the panels with the butt of his rifle. No use hanging around because there is no width to the overhang and we are anxious to get out of the rain. We wait. I use the great iron knocker. Bang. Bang. Bang. The door opens.

A young, plump woman with red hair stands before us dressed in shiny, artificial-silk bloomers and a liberty-bodice with purple lace round the scoop neck and sleeves. She has perfect skin.

"For the sake of all that's holy – come the hell in," she says and drags the door wider. It grates at the bottom.

"Boys!" - She calls over her shoulder… "they're here. Come to get you." Then to us, "Go in. Go in. – That's right … Take off them sheets – just drop 'em on the floor. Right. Them things loaded? Good. Dump 'em in here against the hallstand and come on up. We'll get youse some tea." We drop the sheets but not the hardware.

She is not in the least perturbed, either by us surprising her in her bloomers – or by the situation – us with rifles etc.

"Cool under fire." I murmur to Jim as we mount through the dark stairwell. The house smells pleasantly of bran and vanilla mixed with something else. Machine-oil? Pins? Maybe there are dressmakers in the house.

They are all in a back room extending over a garden. Though narrow, the house is quite large this side. The window is huge and what light there is spills down on to the oak table beneath it, around which they sit: our two recalcitrants, each with a girl at his side. There is another young woman with her back to us, this end, with a huge dressmaking shears in her hand and a pile of dark bottle-green silk spread out on the table in front of her. I was right about the smell. Have smelled it at Rosalind's mother's place many times when she's been using the sewing machine.

There are bottles of Guinness on the table and full glasses. Black with white collars. The boys are easy. Elbows on. Smoking. No excuses.

"Found us then?"

"No bother ..... come on."

The dressmaker is now pinning some of the striped material on to the girl in the bloomers.

"Ah sure – you can go in a minute," she says over her shoulder.

"For the love of Pete sit down can't yer, take the weight off your feet and have a Guinness. Sheilagh – up and get two glasses for our visitors. Shove up boys. Let your man see the space."

Never known such friendly informality. Nothing matters. No tensions. Be idiots to argue. We sit. We drink Guinness. The girl in the silkish bloomers comes and sits on my knee. The dressmaker closes up to Jim Fairhurst. The rain lashes and pours down the windows.

"Sure they'll be taking off the auld ferry if the wind increases anyway", she says.

"Where's the hurry? Come on up. Up. Up.... Soldier boy, can tell you like me by the look in your green, green eyes."

She tugs at my non-resisting hand and we ascend two floors. I had never known, would never have guessed that women can be completely without inhibitions. Completely disinhibited. She spread-eagles herself on the bed and I am lost. A new academy of learning.

We do not descend until mid-morning the next day. We re-join the drinking-school, the card players, the smokers, the fornicators, the recalcitrants, the lone escort now himself AWOL – same as me. We laugh, we shout, we sing and thump things: we carouse.

"I love you. I LOVE you!" she swears. They bring out an old guitar. Jim offers to play. I sit, feet under a black-lacquered piano, fag in mouth.

"Sing, sing, Taffy-boy. Sing our Taff from over the ocean," she says.

I take out the cigarette and place it butt-in on the edge of the piano. I sing 'Danny Boy'. I sing 'Keep the Homefires Burning' I sing 'Long Way to Tipperrary'.

"I love you. I LOVE you!" she cries. I replace the dippy in my mouth and vamp out 'Marcheta', Marcheta, I Still Hear You Calling'. …. And 'You Made Me Love You …. I didn't want to do it, I didn't wanna do it.'

"Stay. Stay!" she cries. We all shout. I thump the keys. Jim wizzes up and down the frets of the guitar. They think we are accomplished mush … mush … mushishians. Hell yes. The recalcitrants grin appreciatively and smoke on. Now and then they slap the table, one-handed. The material is pinned on to Marcheta yet again. It is taking shape as a dress. We chorus on like cats wailing now. I stamp the pedals. Stamp the floor. Head back, throat exposed. Roaring. Jim screams on in a high-pitched syncopated rhythm, unknown hitherto. We raise merry hell. The place is jumping. One of Jim's guitar strings breaks with a loud PING. We stumble a bit at their point. Hard to keep upright. Shouldn't have drunk so much Guinness. Marcheta and I bow out, my arm hooked round her plump shoulders. She supports me. My l-little darr-ling. (Hick). Oh yesh. Upstairs.

We ascend. We descend. Up and down those narrow, threadbare carpeted stairs to the attic. The black-iron frame with brass knobs. The huge feather-mattress. Jerry under the bed. She pisses like a horse. Knees out from the squat. Dead straight aim. The yellow pee fizzes into the bottom of the china. Doesn't care a damn. She climbs all over me.

Goodness knows how many days pass. Time is no longer relevant. "Your man's at the door", she shouts.

Four of them. Big blokes. No nonsense. Red Caps. Boots fill the hallway, thunder on the stairs. We are rousted out like fowls from their bedding. The straw flies.

"Fall in. Fall IN. Where's yer rifles? Shave. Shit and kit-up. AT the double!"

It has stopped raining. Days ago.

THIRTEEN

Captain ---- gives us a lecture that would take the enamel off the bottom of a saucepan with no bother at all. The Guardroom quivers with his rage. It pulsates. We are a disgrace to the British Army. Have allowed our carnal-instincts to interfere with proper duties. We will be Confined to Barracks. That's Christmas taken care of. He doesn't realise I don't mind that. Can't bear the thought of having to appear in uniform back home. Embarrassment at being grilled by family and townspeople. Conspicuous – merely by appearing. The civvies too small now. No longer suitable. The thought of being taken to Vaughany-Jones in the High Street to be re-fitted, measured – unthinkable. No … leave all that until I return for good. But Rosalind? Rosalind will wait. I can rely on Rosalind. She understands these things.

Jankers. From the moment of sentence I am in the hands of the police-sergeant. Reveille. Then the bugler blasting out 'You can be a defaulter as long as you like, as long as you answer your name.' – Then run like hell for the police-hut, answer my name and get told off to my fatigue. Late, and it's another dose of Jankers on top of this one, so watch it.

Right. Empty the urinal-tubs and crap-cans. That's the first. Supposed to be no-end of a carry-on, this. Used to it, me. Been emptying the damn things for years. Both at Mainstone and TyCanol. Chores. Don't let on though. Got to be thought to suffer. True – more of the bloody stuff here. Mounds. Get on with it! Right. Spud-bashing up in the Officers' Mess. Big dinner. AT the double. Rattle off down the lane, across the concrete, through the narrow doorway, stairs on the left, eyes right, round the corner, on to the polish now: polished wood blocks under the oak table with a massive silver monolith on it: 2nd Battalion Lancashire Fusiliers: South African Centrepiece. A silver soldier each point of the compass. North, South, East, West. No time to look, past that, up the oak – but richly carpeted stairs. Under the portraits, the battle-scenes (2nd Battalion Lancashire's.... More casualties next year, 1917, than any other regiment in the British army) – along a few feet and there they all are jawing away in the dining room.... Hell – not that way! Back and through into the serving-quarters..... get down to it! More potatoes, more potatoes, ... then the washing up and a kind of false bonhomie. It is relief that the dinner has gone well on the part of the mess-caterer-supremo and his staff, the mess-waiters etcetera. It filters down to us at the sinks. We are offered tasty leftovers. The staff swap exaggerated accounts of innocuous incidents that have occurred at table, blown into almost major events. Ha Ha Ha they laugh. They are all good-humoured now. The pressure is off. They tease me as I am the youngest in the Battalion. They even allude to certain functions I have to perform in mock Irish accents. "Will ye get Your Man to put a move on with the dishes. There. Pity there's no little Coleen hovering – to maybe lighten the load of it – so it is!"

Christmas was best. Skeleton staff – and me. True they had me running up and down, in and out and around practically every corner but not all the good spirits were fuelled by alcohol. I was given plenty to eat and reasonable time to re-read Erskine Childeris's, 'The Riddle of the Sands' and 'The Invasion of 1910' by William W. E. Queux. I had loved reading all this spy and adventure stuff when I was a kid so shoved these two in my holdall to read on the train. Now, of course, I can see what a load of crap they are in the main – although, I don't know, could have been based on some kind of fact, I suppose – and I like reading them. Bring back smells and feelings of when I was ten or eleven, dreaming in haylofts or under the eaves at Mainstone, flat on my belly, chewing an apple, relatively innocent. Relatively unfettered.

FOURTEEN

The year is passing. Passing. The red, green and gold baubles strung over the Christmas trees in the Officers Mess, the tinsel and crêpe paper subdued lights (DON'T PUT THE PAPER ACTUALLY ROUND THE SHADES! NOT TOO NEAR THE BULBS, PTE. EDWARDS!) disintegrates in my mind gradually as January progresses. The boys come back off leave but the snow had descended starting Christmas Eve. By the time they got to Bury the roads were already unpassable. Eloise wrote and told me it was the same in Llandrindod – and to ask why, oh why hadn't I come home for Christmas? Her wedding-date was fixed. She did not say much about that. She had seen Rosalind and Maggie Price walking up Beaufort Road the other day. Only their back view. It was snowy and they were clutching hold of each other so as not to slip on the ice. Rosalind was wearing a deep sax-blue coat with a fur collar. They both had muffs.

This vision of Rosalind set me off wondering why I hadn't written. I would write again soon. She had sent me quite a snotty letter. Why the HELL hadn't I come home for the holiday? Wanted so to see me. Was it that I didn't have the money?

How could I tell her I was confined to Barracks, having gone Absent Without Official Leave – over a young girl in Dublin? No need to even ask that. More to the point – how could I explain my aversion to appearing on the streets, maybe coming and going however essential my sallying-forth, as if parading my altered status? 'Look at me – I'm in The Army' kind of embarrassment. No. And I can't stand the mechanics of arrivals and departures either. Luggage. To be seen (or observed from behind net-curtains) carrying a suitcase! Never. Just managed to conceal everything last time in that small holdall – but to manifest at the station with a kit-bag, legs wrapped in puttees, cap on – anathema to me. I write. She gets the gist. I will return <u>afterwards.</u>

Meanwhile it was icy up on the tops. The silver slice of shovels cutting into half-frozen snow, clanging as they hit the pebbles underneath was a daily accompaniment to our activities. The lane at the back had to be cleared again, the road out the front. We had to dig out paths to the stores, dig along the intersections though, thank Heavens, Bury Council took care of main roads. The snow kept falling and it was hard to remember how it was in late summer: the first hint of autumn when there was a sudden gold, a sudden age-old feeling of antiquity in the air. Venetian. How can I say that? I've never been to Venice. Zinnias and dahlias spun in the Town Hall borders and front-gardens opposite and then the chrysanthemums came looming through mists and there was that half-smoky, half-crushed apple smell on the air as the leaves turned red, turned yellow, orange, ginger, brown and fell crackling to the ground.

Autumn is going to be earlier this year. I was almost astonished, walking down the lane last week, to just catch that glimpse of a patch of red and gold amongst the dull, late-Summer green on one of the branches overhanging the hedge. And it's barely August! I've noticed since though that the 'collapse' has occurred. It happens every year if you look carefully. One day, there they are – all the trees spread out, not unlike cats when contented, stretched to their very limit: stretching over their deep shadows on the fields in their absolute prime – and then one day you might just happen to glance up and there is a sag to the branches. The spokes to an umbrella have slackened. There is disarray: an alteration in the symmetry. A fuse has blown. The leaves have become cooked-spinach green and leathery as the lips of ancient vaginas, the twigs stringy. Yet the year is exiting with change.

They have picked me out for the Machine-Gun-Corps; also Fuck-Me, Jim and J.W -. I think J.W. is in because of his need to be with those of us who he knows. We are to go to Grantham for six weeks training. I should be eighteen at the end of it but they think I will be nineteen – so (hopefully) will be sent to France. You have to be nineteen according to the War Office. I'm saying nothing about the course even in my letters to Eloise. Just in case the Old Man decides to intervene.

FIFTEEN

Rosalind

That evening we said goodybe and he turned and went down the Llanerch for a farewell drink with his friends. I can't tell you how I felt. Bereft. Scraped inside as if with a garden-trowel. All down the red bits glistening and banging and thumping away in there.

I walked home somehow. Everything was passing at speed. My thoughts mainly. Going so quickly I couldn't think properly at all. He had abandoned me. I was a lumpish creature suddenly in the late-summer dusk where before I had seemed beautiful and got-together. Cow-like now. Bovine. That's the word: a great abandoned hump against the sunset, hurrying home. Had to get in, shelter from the sky and the roses starring from brick walls over the dusty pavements. Had to get IN, sit quiet at the long, wooden, kitchen table, back to the fire that is kept alight summer and winter. I needed the comfort of its heat, coals spurting. I needed to support my head in my hands, to think straight. To let my feelings settle. Just hoped they'd gone to bed. Mam is usually asleep by 9 o'clock. Dada not long afterwards. Sleeping the sleep of the just.

I would light up, I thought. One of those Players Medium Cut
he likes. Sit there and smoke and think it all out – if I could think at
all. The lid had come off everything: the fields, the sky, the familiar
streets beneath my buckled, pointed-evening shoes … Yes stumbling
down by the courthouse heading west, I notice the terrible unreality.
Everything grey. Lid come off and emptiness, emptiness, emptiness
underneath. No green. Dust and decaying late-summer roses and
me, some awful, lumpy, country-bumpkin not knowing A from B,
not knowing a damn thing about what to do, how to be against the
sophisticates.

Some girls can smirk and smile so confidently with pseudo-in-
nocence plastered on the pink and cherubic. They are upsides. They
know. They know. While I knowing nothing, am abandoned to
dressing-up only and the heckling of Mam's constant advice.

But for a time, she laid off after he had gone. She knew I was sick.
I had always loved the farm and walking through the fields; been
conscious of the insects buzzing and murmuring in the hedgerows,
the bursting sound coming from the wet nostrils of great brown-and-
white-splodged cows as they come, one foot after the other, heads
down and chewing, chewing, chewing on the short meadow grasses.
Had loved flinging myself back on to the yellow-ochre river bank under its fringe of green, a long juicy stem of grass in my mouth, grinding the butt between my teeth as I listened to the river and watched
it surging by over the round blue-grey pebbles, polished smooth since
long before the Romans were here. And then, in my head, I darted
with the minnows in the shallows, imagining what it must be like
to live beneath the clear, blue-green, Ithon water where in the heat
of summer and we had picnics down here, white cloth on the bank,
plates full of sandwiches and cakes, jams and pickles hawked down

in baskets by the maids, the air became yellow: amber – as if we were looking through the glass of a lemonade bottle.

I loved all that: but now --. Now there is a Friesian, all udders, up high on the bank, reaching and chewing under the falling branches before the white balustrade of the bridge crossing the river – but I can't take it in at all. The cow is unreal and useless. What does it mean all this? - The river running by, the trees above the yellow-clay bank, the shallows with hoof-marks cut into the ruts where the cows come down to drink, where we splashed and paddled so happily as children – then explored further up-stream as if wading through a green tunnel until we could swim but were then warned of the whirlpool under the far bank. Will suck you down! Suck you down! They would cry. They would admonish. Oh yes.

But Tom has never been here to swim. Never sat on this bank. I am so alone. He is gone. With others. They all laugh at jokes between themselves. Of course they do. I am outside. I get up from the bank and go down to the river. It chatters in my ears, never ending. The unreality is everywhere.

I pick a perfectly flat, perfectly round blue-grey pebble out of the water and scratch "I Love Tom" on its surface with a long, thin piece of rust-red rock. I am afraid of this. I am not supposed to feel this way. They would tell me off at home and scorn my emotions. I bury the pebble deep among others above the water line. It will get washed away anyway with the next flood.

She is concerned. Yes. At first. She brings me food on a tray when I am awake in the mornings and stops the others singing any other sentimental modern songs, especially Marcheta, in case it starts me crying. I am white-faced and thin. I must eat – and anyway, ANYWAY "- these Edwards boys are no damn use to anybody!" They scream at me. "Look at that Bernard. Only sixteen and here's his father having to buy off some of the outraged parents when he's got their darling daughters into trouble. Eh? – what about that – and that poor girl from Newbridge chucking herself in the river over him! Eh? EH?"   "But that's not TOM. Tom's different."

"Is he, eh? Eh? All the same if you ask me girl. Arthur's no saint either. Not him. Never has been. Oh yes – respectable as hell now he's a J.P. on the Bench – all that …. But I could tell you tales all right. It's HIM they get it from, those boys. Too damn cocky and good-looking for their own well-being. Yes HIM plus Mary Ellen's beauty ….. what can we say? Leave 'em alone girl. They'll only bring you pain."

"I don't want all of them. I just want Tom. He's different – and it's probably all lies about Bernard anyway."

"He's NO different. They're all the same. Why they say even that little bugger Billy is hung like a donkey and PROUD OF IT. At His Age! – Hardly more than a baby."

"What has that got to do with anything?"

"Well – er 'um …. Never MIND. Look here now, your mother and I are getting fed up with this Madam. You need to get yourself a nice, steady and RELIABLE young man with PROSPECTS --".

"Tom's got prospects, as you call them. When he comes back he'll be with his father at TyCanol. One day he'll -- ."

"ONE DAY! When he COMES BACK! One day – if I know anything about Mary-Ellen and her Bernard … probably means NEVER, girl – and WHEN HE COMES BACK! – you say. No it's IF he comes back, Rosalind. IF!"

I cry out "What do you mean? He's coming back. He IS coming back – for ME".

"Read the LISTS," they hiss, eyes bulging. "Read the bloody lists."

"I HATE you! I HATE you!" I scream, out of control. "You're cruel beyond comprehension. CRUEL, CRUEL, - and heartless."

I am told to get out of their sight, go to my room. It is made obvious that from now on I am to pull myself together. My poor, dear mother is unable to cope with my grief. She has had enough of my awkward behaviour. The breakfast-tray is a thing of the past and they have arranged for Jenkin Evan-Evans to drive me over to Llandrindod to visit Maggie Price and to go boating on the lake.

As a matter of fact, Jenkin and I become quite good friends. I tell him exactly as it is following that awful evening we were sitting in a café down Park Crescent after he had taken me to the pictures and Eloise Edwards came in with one of the girls from the Limes: Ben Davies' oldest daughter who used to play golf with Tom sometimes, then entertain him for drinks in the Club-House at the top of the Links.

I had been jealous as hell of her when Tom was about. Hated the way she would simper up to him when she was being flirtatious, then at other times, stride along, cigarette in mouth, like a man, quacking in Cambridge tones out of the side of her mouth, making him laugh. Fascinating she was: IS. Even though Tom always laughed and said there was nothing in it 'Just a friend'. 'Hell of a case'. Then when he could see I was upset – 'No … he didn't like her at all. Couldn't stand the sight etcetera'. But they always take on like that, don't they, when they're really smitten? Pretend not to be. Run 'em down – if only just to say their name. "What – NESTA? …Never!" kind of thing before that slow grin, quiet intake of breath as he leaned back and inhaled smoke from his cigarette.

But then that awful evening and she came in with Eloise and I thought 'Oh no! she's going to get him!' and they left her gloves on our table for they were going to join us after they'd been to the counter and I felt like taking up one of them and dunking it in my coffee, then wringing it out and flinging it on the floor. But I didn't do that for both she and Eloise had been smiling so sweetly and I like Eloise, I really do – but I couldn't bear that – Couldn't BEAR IT. I was going to have to sit and listen and watch Nesta's attractive face going through all its different expressions: so <u>like</u> Tom in a way and then look straight at Eloise who was going to so remind me, remind me; but they were returning now, slowly, cups in their hands – for this is an unusual, casual place – unlike Morgan Morris's or the Penn or the Marina where there are waitresses in caps and frilly aprons – not like those and –– oh! My nose spouts blood: both nostrils. What is happening?

Jenkin is really amazing. He stands, already extracting a hand-kerchief from his trouser-pocket. He claps it over my nose. "Up!" He commands. "Out!"

He doesn't bother to excuse our exit. No time. We are outside, him with his handkerchief still clapped to my face. The blood is pouring out of my nose. There is a storm going on out here. Thunder cracking and booming overhead and lightning flashes very quick, very fast. A wind has arisen and is flattening the branches at the entrance to the Park as Jenkin half-drags me down by the Gwallia Hotel into Ithon Road and we career like clowns in the wind on the long walk home. The rain starts hissing down with such intensity that we are soaked before reaching the Ddol entrance.

We can't speak because of the rate we cover the couple of miles to our place. But then I shove my mouth out of the blood-soaked rag long enough to gasp "Round the back." Jenkin flings open the unlocked door and strides into the back-kitchen. My nose bleeds on and on. I don't care. He seems far more worried than I am. No, I don't feel ANYTHING. I am zombied.

"Is your mother up?" he asks abruptly.

"No – she's in bed." I manage, "she goes to bed at nine".

Good old Jenkin. He doesn't care about this. He bangs open the middle door leading to the other rooms and the stairs. It is tinny, this door, and makes a noise when you open it.

"Mrs. Hamer!" he shouts up the stairs. Good HEAVENS! How dare he?

"Mrs. Hamer. Get up please. Rosalind is ill."

He returns and inspects my condition. Asks if I have a cloth as the handkerchief is saturated. I can't be bothered to direct him to the linen cupboard. I am wondering why he had me up and out of the café so quickly – without wasting time explaining to Eloise and Nesta ..... as if he knew. As if he appreciated my situation..

My mother enters the room quietly. She assesses the situation, brings a clean cloth out of a drawer, sits me down, takes the huge iron key out of the back door lock and pushes it down the back of my neck. The iron is cold against my flesh. The bleeding stops after a time. She thanks Jenkin and tells him that when my father gets in he will run him home in the trap. Jenkin declines and leaves after asking me if I'm now all right. He is not particularly friendly towards my mother.

Had he noticed she did her duty towards me, couldn't fault her, but picked up on the lack of warmth? Her desire to be rid of me goes before her like a breath. She wants to be free to dream dreams, sew them up on her sewing-machine without me interrupting her fantasies with worries that she is sick to death having to put up with. She has done her duty as a mother. Can't we all see – it is TIME for me to go? Only two more left at home then and she can please herself again.

Incongruously, I imagine a china head nid-nodding over bolts of material as they are directed beneath the foot of the Singer with coloured dreams like vapours wafting in and out its emptiness. Impermanent. I am appalled at my thoughts.

Jenkin phones me the next day to ask how I am now. I say I have recovered. He suggests that we meet for a cup of coffee in town. I say that would be pleasant as long as we avoid that dump in Park Terrace. No, we will go to the Penn, he assures me. He is very serious.

We meet outside and he ushers me through the cake-shop and up the dark-oak stairway to the café above. Mrs. Black is packaging cakes for a customer as we pass.

"Hello Rosalind," she smiles as we make for the steps, "Jenkin". She frowns for a moment when she sees us together. Doesn't like this. The Blacks are big friends of the Edwards' – and in a small town things can be assessed or sized-up, to be more precise, with not very much to go on. Wrong conclusions drawn. To hell with it. Jenkin means nothing to me except as a friend.

Mrs. Black is not a great talker anyway. She is too busy and into running the bakery plus shop and café to have much time for idle speculation. She is small and efficient beneath tight, pale-auburn curls. Clean as a pin. No nonsense. Sharp-tongued if offended and straight as a die with the staff. Sacked on the spot if not up to it. The small ginger-freckled hand in the till, out with the necessary for wages owed and leave the premises.

The Blacks are one of the few Welsh-speaking families in the area since the time it was deemed a disgrace for locals to continue using the old language and The Board was hung around the neck of anybody found speaking it in school. Tom's mother can recite the Lord's Prayer and count up to ten but the only time Tom persuaded her to do so, we soon got short shrift when we tried to find out how much more she really knew afterwards. I must say though, I used to feel somehow dispossessed and inadequate hearing Mrs. Black talking to the Breton onion-sellers when they came over before the war. Breton and Welsh are very similar and little Mrs. Black and these brown-skinned, tanned-by-the-weather-on-their-travels men, used to go at it hammer and tongs. How I would love to have done that. Shown off, me; but Tom always told me he got fed up: listening to the visitors in the summer when they were at Mainstone. 'Talking too fast' - he called it. Probably got that off Mary-Ellen; but really, I suppose it was because he couldn't understand more than a word here and there and was resentful. My Tom – all over.

Mrs. Black is from down South. I like her rapid accent and the lilt of her voice when she speaks. She keeps things going. The café is a picture, all oak beams and polished oak tables spread with red and white gingham cloths, silver saltcellars and pepper pots gleaming. Sugar-tongs in silver sugar bowls.

Hadyn, her husband, appears behind the counter as we ascend. He comes forward slowly, thoughtfully, pipe in mouth but the usual slow smile in his eyes. Sweet, sweet nature. He emanates a ginger glow. His hair is pale, pale almost orange. Going bald but no matter. Faultlessly dressed: canary-yellow waistcoat beneath good tweed. Pale cream shirt. Paisley-patterned tie.

Slowly, slowly he emerges from a dark doorway into strong sunlight beating through his windows, through the glass shelves and twirling cake-stands. He doesn't say anything but his eyes smile. A sweet, quiet man. There is depression in his family. Already there have been suicides. It's a crying shame.

"What are you thinking about Rosalind?" Jenkin asked me. We are sitting at the back of the café in a space half-encircled by black-oak banisters where the stairs lead up. A crowd of girl-guides are across from us, taking up most of the space the other side in front of the windows looking down on the street. The sun has gone in. It is beginning to get quite cold out.

So I tell him – and then I tell him about the other night and how I really feel about Tom and my jealousy of Nesta and any other girls I think might be a threat to my relationship with him. And I tell him how I used to love scrambling about the farm so, seeing to the animals, learning to ride. And I even find myself telling him all sorts of daft thoughts and instances from my childhood – while all the time he listens and absorbs and comments in all the right places. Says all the right things.

"No-one … but NO-ONE Rosalind could ever hold a candle up to you" and that "Edwards is bloody lucky to have you carrying a torch for him, you know" and then ….oh dear how I must bore him but I can't stop myself, I start giving him my ridiculous theories on life in general and how I hate the thought of having kids to look after and WHAT IS LIFE if it's all copulating like goats and forever chasing after love, love, - of that sort but once you've been ensnared in it anyway – nothing else seems worthwhile?

"Totally agree", he murmurs. "Totally".

The guides are being led out by Miss Holman, Brown Owl. I feel nauseous at the pointlessness of it all. The guides, all bubbly and rosy-faced clumping down the stares, Miss Holman humping a kind of rucksack up up on to a bony shoulder, smiling, smiling, and what for? What for? Yes, it gives them all motive and something to aim for – but why? Oh I just feel sick of it all. Everything is so empty.

"Don't cry Rosalind". Jenkin says softly. And then Maggie Price comes up the well of the stairs with Colette Arrowsmith, Bernard's admirer.

A metamorphosis has occurred. Collette has thinned down. Has grown up; grown – beautiful. Her hair is drawn back and pinned. Her black/brown eyes are alive and happy in a perfect oval face. She is exquisitely dressed in pale beige, light wool and fur. My stars! As Tom would say. And I wouldn't want her anywhere near him now. It might run in the family – for they say that things are quite serious between Bernard and herself. He's so young..... but will go to Aberystwyth next year anyway. Forward for his age. He won't be going to the Army like Tom, that's a cert. He's for the university.

They pass with a kind of greeting that means they have lots to talk over between themselves. I don't mind. Jenkin asks me more and more questions about myself but gives very little away regarding his own affairs. Yes – he has finished his studies now – and when all this is over .... will be going in with a firm of solicitors to start with, leading to his own business eventually, of course. Meanwhile he is doing his bit at home on father's property as the old man is no-longer up to running the place by himself..... so he is in what he (Jenkin) believes is termed 'a reserved occupation' for the Duration. I am too wrapped up in my own misery to question this. Why should I? It is nothing to me what Jenkin Evans-Evans does or does not do.

We arrange to meet again – and I'm glad that we have, for something has occurred: a necessity, on my part, to continue our conversation in case I have given the wrong impression over things. I <u>must</u> clarify them and I need also to tell this friend, the like of whom I have never spoken to about such intimate matters before, more and more of my true feelings, my true self.

Jenkin becomes my best friend ever. He could be my brother, no – my SISTER for I even tell him when I have my periods.

We meet in pubs, in cafés. Sometimes, when I am feeling particularly low – I might come out of a shop maybe, or the office, and he is there leaning against the wall, smoking and smiling quietly when I appear. He was there on that day I felt so dreadful because Tom hadn't come home for Christmas.

He must get sick of the sound of Tom, Tom, Tom – because I'm always on about him but although Jenkin doesn't often comment, I can tell he hates Tom. After the Christmas incident, for example, we were sitting in the Metropole, on a settle under the window and he leaned down towards me and said quite forcibly: "It's the waste of a good woman, Rosalind."

Things changed after that. I wrote and told Tom off for not coming home and then he wrote and explained it all – in one of his rare letters.

I didn't see Jenkin for weeks I must confess. Didn't want to. Didn't want to see anybody – or care about anybody. All my theories went flying. I imagined Tom and me married and together forever. I even started peering sweetly into prams. So what if it's all so obvious and mundane. The FEELING: the WHAT-EVER-IT-IS – makes up for it. It has to be sustained though. And that horrible long silence afterwards was searing once I realised his letter was not going to be immediately followed by another – if at all.

Then there was Mother, of course and when she needed it, Father backing her up. Dada had become a nonplussed silence crossing the yard with milk-tins under his arms or shovelling manure out of the bull-shed. Not speaking his disapproval but it was there all the same.

Why had I stopped seeing that Jenkin? Such a good, reliable young man.

Every opportunity, she would let me know I had not yet realised which side my bread was buttered on: that is – I wasn't getting any younger, that girls younger than me were already married with a couple of children and <u>doing quite nicely</u>, thank you very much; that Tom Edwards was unlikely to fulfil these same requirements, why – it was rumoured that Colette Arrowsmith's father (Arrowsmith now accepting the fact of Colette's devotion to Bernard) was insisting that later on if any engagement was in the offing, the young bugger should be circumcised in order to quiet him down. Why only last month Edwards had had to buy off another irate – no? Well then – could I, Rosalind, imagine Tom acquiescing to such a demand? Could I? Could I?

"No, I protested," because in Tom's case these circumstances do not apply.

"Pshaw! ... we'll see about that, my lady. Why hasn't he written then? Why hasn't he been home to see you? They get passes for train-fares, don't they? No. No. You're barking up the wrong tree. Where's your <u>pride?</u> You'll be a laughing-stock. Do you want to be left on the shelf? ... An old maid?"

It didn't help, when after I had bumped into Jenkin again at Maggie Price's and missing someone to talk to who I could spill it all out with, we arranged to meet one evening in Morgan Morris' café above the Emporium.

It was a relief to relay the gist of Mam's manipulative propaganda on behalf of a proper mate for yours truly i.e. himself – Jenkin. We even laughed at the ridiciouslness of this but it hurt so – oh it hurt, when in his role as frank and honest recipient and interpreter of my confidences, after a brief moment of puzzlement with his face creased in what was supposed to be a half-concealed frown (as if wondering whether he ought properly to say anything or not) he spoke hesitantly from above his long, white, bony-knuckled hands locked beneath his long, white chin. He is very tall and thin, Jenkin. He loomed over me like a monolith. White marble – I thought. I nearly giggled. For the last time ever.

"Just caught sight of him once …." He pondered, his eyes sliding towards the gold-flocked wallpaper. "St. Harmons Eisteddfod. You were there Rosalind – at the back. They won the duet … huh – he h-he and Bernard."

"Oh yes?" I couldn't see where this was leading.

"It was afterwards. In that passage behind the vestry and that room where all the cakes and jellies were laid out."

"Um.m. There's always that smell isn't there Jenkin? - Coming off the food and the plates and the –."

"Yes, well ANYWAY –."

"Almost like a Christmas party smell. The lights seemed to shine brighter. I wonder what it is. Do you think it's the tea-urns plus sponge cake with icing? – jam? Trifle?"

"As I was saying – ."

"In fact, Jenkin, … I even think the jellies and trifles give off a kind of light! Tom put it in a poem once. 'Trifle-light', he called it. But he never handed it in. Been expelled by then."

"Caught sight of him, Rosalind – in the passage with that maid from the Bell. He was feeling her up Rosalind. She was pinned against the wall and Edwards had his knee between her legs."

"What – what do you mean?"

"I mean, you were there at the back – and there was Edwards in that dark passage – with a maid from the Bell."

"You must have had a damn good look to see –."

"I was …. I was looking for the W.C. It's outside there. I – ."

"I hardly knew him then anyway."

"Hm.m. Just thought you ought to know, Rosalind. Not all of us go getting up to fumbling girls about in passages, I can tell you."

"Huh! – Probably aren't given the opportunity, Jenkin, if the truth was only known."

"Rosalind, there is such a thing as self-restraint as – "

"Oh. ALL RIGHT. Let's go now. I have to get back."

"But …. But, I thought we were out for the evening. That concert in the Rock. Bruce Dargoville is singing".

"I've told you and told you Jenkin, I can't go to concerts. Not since Tom and I -- . I would cry. I don't want to cry. I don't want to go. No – I must get home."

But it went in – the thing he had said. It was none of my business what had gone on before – but as I pictured the scene: his head bent to kiss the brown-eyed girl, her plump, white arms encircling his neck, his frame leaning into hers, his knee --. I was sick. I vomited all down the window of my room. I felt like throwing myself out and down on to the concrete path beneath the beds of chrysanthemums, now pinched by frost. Blooms long gone. I cleaned the window. I changed my clothes: grey alpaca, buttoned from throat to hem.

Jenkin phoned the following Tuesday. I was cool. I was different. Yes of course we could meet. He was a true friend. A trusted friend. We would make a foursome with Nesta Davies and a friend of hers called Angus down from Scotland. We often went out together from then on. The evenings lacked some essential ingredient but at least we were doing something: not stuck out in the wilds twiddling our thumbs. Waiting. For what – now? I was sure Tom didn't love me. He had gone off me. He did not write. I didn't know where to write. Not even Eloise knew now – so who could I ask?

In July Jenkin kissed me. I did not resist. It didn't mean a lot to me. He was a loving, kind, honest and decent fellow with enormous potential once all this business in Flanders was over according to Mam and Dada.

They were well pleased with me. Couldn't do enough. Jenkin was the blue-eyed boy (grey-eyed really) son of the family already. His kiss lacks that indescribable smell. Maybe it only occurs once: first love and all that. Is it a smell or a taste? The taste of an excitement so primitive it can only be experienced but never described. Apples? Green or duck-egg blue streaks at the back of the throat, the nose? Something leading on to something else – but what? A boat on the lake, gliding at dusk, the oars plash-plashing quietly? Sudden plops in the dark-eddies? Rhododendrons blooming: paper flowers, crimson-subdued by twilight over their fresh, thick, dark-green leaves trailing into the evening waters from the island? Yes and a white-spotted voile dress with one small hand making a Vee as <u>that other</u> pulls on the oars: dark-suited, hair brushed down. Cigar smoke drifting lazily behind. Over. Over.

And now -- ?

SIXTEEN

J.W. – nearly didn't make it through Grantham. Harrowby Camp was the main training base of the Machine Gun Corps and most of the instructors were from the Guards. What they lacked in actual fighting-experience themselves they made up for with near-insane tyranny on the parade-ground. Sergeant-Major – was the worst as far as I was concerned. A real bastard.

Stiff training started as soon as, on the edge of town, we shoved open an old creaking gate and saw the three huts, one for medical inspection, one a blanket store and one the office.

After the M.O. had passed us – as A.1. we were issued with a blanket each and told to bed down in a field – if and unless we had no money for lodgings in Grantham. "Fuck-me!" was heard for the first time in the environs. The only amenity was one cold water tap.

We went into Grantham all right but not to spend what small amount of money we had on lodgings. What? Sit for the evening in some old dutch's back-parlour – horse-hair couch under the nets, smell of cabbage-water as some old guy in tennis-shoes (mine host) boils up something unspeakable on a chapped, grey - enamel stove behind a grubby curtain while his missus comes at us dishing out the rules of the establishment, dyed-black hair crimped beyond repair with tongs that have most probably just been used for tugging kittens out of the cat. No. No. Seen too many of these places, delivering the milk back home. Can only ever eat, me, if I either know who has prepared the food or if it's completely impersonal as in the barracks – or funnily enough, big hotels. But boarding houses – where the proprietors are right there before you and you know, you KNOW they are going to shed dandruff, maybe flick bits of snot into the sticky carpets, hawk over the soup. The thought of chewing a long white hair entangled into the shredded-wheat with milk! A-a-a-h!

No. We imbibed pint after pint in The Wheelwright, then it was down past some grocery emporium to The Royal Oak where we fell in with some local girls who told us where to go for fish and chips on Friday night, that we were supposed to have off – and which church-institutes would supply us with a damned good meal and entertainment – if we felt like it. The town was heaving, they said. Men pouring in by rail – but a big, fair-headed girl or woman really came to sit beside me and started taking over the conversation then. Her name was Beatrice. Fuck-Me kept grinning behind his eyes at me and making great shovel-like gestures with his lower jaw. I spotted her wedding ring and trying to be polite asked if her husband was overseas. "No, he keeps the grocery." She said shortly.

"'appen you passed it on yer way down." "Oh," I said. Didn't know what else to say. "Yer all great lads. Great lads. You especially." Her large left-hand came down on my khaki – just above the knee. She squeezed gently. I couldn't stop staring at it but without moving the angle of my head slowly raised my eyes to Fuck-Me sitting opposite. Now grinning enormously.

"Wilt do us a favour, lad?" she leaned closer and I felt almost threatened by the size of her. Moon-like face. Yellow curls. Big powerful shoulders. Arms massive out of blue puff-sleeves. Slightly pink. Porcine. I thought of the bacon-slicer in her old man's grocery emporium. Shivered.

I was not au fait with the terminology of invitation yet.

"Certainly," I said, "what can I do for you Maam?"

"Beatrice will do." She was now almost archly business-like. "Come outside lad an' I'll show thee". She glared at me significantly for a long moment. Against my will, I got the message. I stiffened at such a rate that I had to bend, hurrying behind her to the door. No longer against my will. No longer anything only the blood pounding in my ears. We crashed into the wall round the back of the pub, beneath trees and shadows and she took me or I took her up against the bricks without let or hindrance – as I was obliged to relate to the others when we eventually retrieved our blankets and bedded down in the field for what was left of the night.

"Don't know what you've got, Edwards, that the rest of us 'ain't". Fuck-Me grumbled pleasantly and then J.W. chuckled from his corner under the hedge and spoke for once. "All like that in his bloody family. No holding the girls when they're about. Buggers."

"Take that as a compliment J.W." I said magnanimously but wondered on the quiet, how many great people might have conceivably been brought into being after a mere encounter such as that – in the dark, yet shuddering again at the thought of marriage to a powerful female licensed to boss, to use, to discard or cheat on as she might see fit. Her old man was at a very important council meeting she had confided on the way back in.

Next morning, we stuck our heads under the cold-water tap, smartened up and reported for duty in the office and were given our MGC numbers (mine is 154059) then a batch of us were marched to Belton Park and put into wooden huts. There was to be no Squad

Drill or Infantry training now – only machine-gun work. Sunday would not be a day of rest. The whole Depot paraded at 9 a.m. for Church Parade when we would march behind the band to a nearby church. After divine service the barrack-accommodation had to be scrubbed (as usual) top to bottom including bed-planks. There was, of course, a long line of men waiting outside the stores for cleaning equipment so it took longer to draw brushes and soap than to scrub the perishing hut. When we had completed the job and the hut was inspected and found to be satisfactory we were free until Lights Out, 9 p.m.

You have to be fit to be a machine-gunner. The all-round standard (general-physique) is far higher than that necessary for an infantry soldier for we have to be well-developed and sufficiently strongly built to work with and carry a machine-gun or similar weight under adverse conditions and if necessary to double or crawl with it. We must have no physical defects that could interfere with this work.

We are not supposed to be less than 19 years ('nuff said) nor over 35 years though evidently the actual age is not so important as the general physical condition of whoever.

Not less than 5 ft. 3 in. (except in exceptional cases). Chest measurement counts. Range of expansion not be less than 3 ins., 'but 3 ins. sufficient for untrained recruits'. Eyesight. Without glasses V = 6/9 with at least one eye. We have our teeth, inoculations and vaccinations attended to in Bury, before leaving.

In comparison to Grantham, Bury was more or less a holiday-camp; yes – even in spite of the jankers.

Here it's all spit and polish almost without end since they re-instated the shining-up instead of the dulling-down that some far-sighted official had ordered in 1915.

They had thought it better that highly-polished bayonets, buttons, badges etcetera should be made harmless to the wearers and bearers by dulling to gun-metal hue so bottles of acid were issued for the purpose and howls of delight went up as 'Soldiers Friend' was flung away by the hundredweight but one of the veterans back in Belton Park for further training has told us that in the following August of that year the luxury of not having to waste time and energy – was to end. Probably the top brass were afraid of loosing control of the troops if 'Bull' was not reimposed: even if, even IF polished brass gear in the trenches can be the undoing of the superb camouflage of a khaki uniform and the means of almost deliberately discarding a natural protection. Gone are the days, I think.

For life in the huts is miserable. Plagued by kit inspections every week. Kit to be laid out in proper order: knife, fork, spoon, razor, comb, lather-brush etcetera. If someone has pinched anything of yours, pity help you. A lot of pinching goes on. Fuck-Me has said he will kill 'em if he can find 'em. You have to make up the losses from your pay. I am always broke. And that bloody Sergeant Major -.

I keep wondering where I have seen him before and believe me I have had ample opportunity to study his face because it is usually a mere foot or two in front of mine, contorted with animosity and shouting when we are inspected on parade or when kit inspection takes place.

The first time he found fault was with my puttees. There was a bulge in the windings, he said. I was a lazy little bugger who probably missed his mummy, he said and in future I would make sure I came on parade PROPERLY DRESSED – or should he ask the C.O. if I could wear a nappy? I think in pictures sometimes so had to fight myself not to grin. Had I done so, it would have been all over. I could tell he was dying to get me thrown in the guardroom.

The second time he said my rifle hadn't been cleaned properly. It was immaculate but he wasn't going to admit that. I rattled back the bolts and broke the barrel from the stock for him to peer in. "Dust!" He screamed, "Get it cleaned up. Understand?"

Oh I understood all right. "Yes Sir!" I complied.

Now it is every time we have a parade or inspection of any kind. I am called all the names going. It is hard to keep my head. I long to lash out. To hit and hit and keep on hitting. His face approaching, is a face I have seen before definitely. Impossible to tell once he starts yelling. Red then. Veins standing out. Eyes bulging with fury. Spit round his mouth. On his chin. Frothing. Mad. Stupid shitting swine.

The boys heard it on the grapevine. He has been 'coping' with the wife of some grocer in town. Local bigwig. Hm.m.m.

And suddenly I remember where it is I have seen him in the past. Last year. Waiting for the train in Crewe. In civvies. Carrying an attaché case. Wondered whether he was an actor. Some actor. Probably escaping from the local lunatic asylum.

He had it in for J.W. too. That's where we really had to watch ourselves: Fuck-Me, Jim and me for we know if he broke J.W. we would attack and then it would be all up for all of us. Luckily for J.W., Sgt. Maj. Bugger has been far worse towards me than he has to him. "Just let it roll over you" we tell him. And he can take the advice coming from one getting it worse than himself.

Apart from these very real annoyances and obstacles in our way, life is hectic at the school. There is a shortage of guns on which to train so the Sergeant Instructors use mess tins as tripods with the lid for a gun and metal cover for the belt box. We become perfect in the drills for we learn them all. We learn all the theory. I read the instructions over and over until they go in. There <u>are</u> guns of course that we are able to see, feel, pick-up, take apart, reassemble, learn the drill but not to fire.

We learn that there will be three Gun-Teams to each sub-section now as things have hotted up. As things are in a hurry. No time. No time and men needed at the front. Men out in front of the lines – us. Suicide Squad. Yes – so three Gun-Teams comprising four men in each team. No. 1, who will carry the tripod, throw it down and set up the gun. No. 2, who will carry the barrel and feed in the ammunition. No. 3, to maintain the supply of ammunition to No. 2 and No. 4, to pour water over the mechanism, to be a carrier and be in reserve.

What we will do: we will gain our position, usually at the double and set up in diamond-formation: the middle Gun-Team out in front with the other two teams, one on either side and slightly back. We will set up. We will fire.

Whoever is allotted No. 1 will carry the tripod i.e. the heaviest component weighing about 50 lbs.; the gun itself weighs 28 lbs. without water and is carried by No. 2. In good nick, the rate of fire should be well over 600 rounds per minute and when the gun is firmly fixed on the tripod there will be little or no movement to upset its accuracy. Being water-cooled means it can fire continuously for long periods even though heat caused by the rapid fire will soon boil the water and cause a powerful emission of steam but this is condensed by passing it through a pliable tube into a canvas bucket of water so that we can continue to fire without a cloud of steam disclosing our position to the enemy. We are each and every one trained fully in every aspect of dealing with the gun except the actual firing of it. We will learn that soon enough. In France. Yet – six weeks training and never fired a shot!

We are on the Spa in Scarborough. As a rule trains leave Grantham
with reinforcements at 9 a.m. and 9 p.m. Three days later the boys
are on the Somme but we've been here, billeted in a commandeered
girls' school for a fortnight. We are constantly drilled, inspected and
lectured on the gun. They have noticed that I am remarkably quick
with my left hand if anything needs adjusting that side. I decline
details of my past difficulties. "Ambidextrous" I say casually. It's the
truth – now.

I love Scarborough. The billet has been Heaven after the huts.
Halfway up the hill over-looking the North Sea. And what a sea.
I love the storms and the way the waves come surging up and over
the promenades. As rough as Aberystwyth at times. I've been down
there then and let the spray come right up and over me. It sucks
back. Made sure there's something pretty solid to hang on to! It is
very powerful.

Now we're pulling out. It's quite hot again today. Indian summer. We are lined up on the Spa ready for the final inspection before
marching down to the station. The sea rolls in and out. There is a
huge, black, cast-iron lamp-standard on my left with 7 enormous
globes attached. Edward V11th stood under it when he came visiting
as Prince of Wales in 1871. With his Princess. I saw a photograph
in a shop off the Esplanade last week. I thought of sending a couple
home but they have told us not to write from here.

I feel fit and resigned to going though inexplicably, after all our
efforts, after all the hassle to join-up and 'get over there' – there is this
strange nervous feeling. It is not excitement. It is suddenly an aware-
ness of something or <u>things</u> pressing down. A feeling of enormity as

if we are insects beneath an indifferent scientific gaze. The clanking of some frightful machine behind the scenes. <u>Attention</u>!

We bring our feet together as one. We stand tall. Shouldered arms. My eyes are directed straight ahead beneath the peak of my cap. Everything is in order. I am proud of the way we look the boys and I.

He is before me. The Sergeant Major. He will return to Grantham after we have gone. He stops and peers unpleasantly into my face. I keep my glance ahead steady. He demands to see my rifle. There is the rattle of bolts. He squints inside. My rifle could not be cleaner. "FILTHY!" he shouts. "Why you little bleeder, you're a disgrace to the British Army. You might have broken your mother's heart – but you won't break mine!" He goes on and on, his mouth opening and shutting like some horrible, yawning grave. The remark about my mother cuts like a knife. He mentions her again, and throws the rifle back at me. He keeps screaming obscenities. I catch the rifle and am preparing to swing it back into position after thumping it down by my right foot. I am shaken. He keeps mouthing away. I am reminded of the Duck hitting me on the boils, of my Father thrashing the life out of me for being late though forced to do the milk round. He is reaching some kind of crescendo in his cursing. His mouth widens even further into its dragon's cave. I commit the unspeakable with my heart hammering against the sternum, blood rushing to my face then dragging back like the tide until I feel the deadly pallor of ice-cold intention in my face, my hands steel traps around the rifle and I throw it all away: everything - with that smack as the gun crashes into his face, silencing him. I could be shot for this. Death penalty isn't it, for striking a superior officer? I am too enraged to care.

He is shocked for the moment he takes to swipe the blood from his mouth but then comes his moment of triumph.

"Two men fall in!" he barks. "Take the prisoner to the train. He will go to France UNDER ESCORT – for sentencing –."

Fuck-Me and J.W. spring forward before any of S.M.'s cronies have a chance to do the honours. We get back into place, line up, the orders are given. We snap to the right and the parade moves off. We are in the last rank. We march out not speaking. No talking in the ranks. I was going to enjoy this, before. All smartened up and perfectly in time. Swinging along to the band playing Pack Up Your Troubles and It's A Long Way To Tipperary with some of those girls we met on the Esplanade maybe come out to watch and the ladies fluttering handkerchiefs from balconies up the sides of the huge hotel by the castle – working-men having the decency to doff their caps as we march by – but no. I am conscious of having an 'escort'. Hope to High Heaven no one will think I'm being escorted against my will. So what?

The train waits silent and grim. It is blind. That is, all the windows are covered. We are not to see out. Why? The doors are locked, once we are on. Why? Well don't be so bloody daft: so that no one can jump OFF – of course. But would anyone want to? Maybe if they've <u>been</u> there and are going back, I guess.

Fuck-Me, Jim, J.W. and I sit on our kit bags in a huddle at the end of the carriage. J.W. – whimpers quietly "Oh Tom, they won't shoot you will they? Oh Tom –."

"Naa –." I reassure him. "Hope not."

"I'm worried Tom. I'm really worried … what if they make Fuck-Me and the rest of us form the firing-squad?" I grin –

"In that case J.W." I say, "You're not half as worried as I will be, knowing what a bloody crack-shot you are." We all grin quietly and drag on some Klondykes someone's sister had sent when we were still at Grantham.

"We should have done the bugger in before it got this far." Fuck-Me mutters and Jim Fairhurst curses quietly over a mug of Gun-Fire. "He was bloody disgraceful. Bloody sadistic old grandmother in trousers. Letting out the bile. Probably fancies you himself, Edwards ... then finding out you'd knocked off his bint on the side that proved to others he's a real he-man – touched off some fuse-paper he's been trying to conceal in his underpants for years."

"Yea – I like a bit of psychology thrown in", I say but don't want to talk any more. Stub out the cigarette and sit with my hands, grown useless now, dangling between my knees.

The train rushes on. I don't know what will happen when we get the other side – but can no longer enjoy the moment. I feel tarnished as I used to at home when I had dared to defend myself against the real aggressors: the sneaky variety who dart in with their poison, strike then recoil before they can be blamed in any way; for who can ever find the evidence to fault them? Who the hell was able to break my rifle open and peer in – except him? I had spent ages cleaning it. Every part. It was in perfect condition.

"You aroused the Anima- in him", Jim lisps in my ear as if one of those silly buggers in the Peace Movement expounding at one of their lectures. I have to laugh.

The train rattles and shakes from side to side. Wish we could see out. We have only ourselves to look at. A remarkable change has come over some of the battalion. There is quietness, a new thoughtfulness. Sure, some of the boys are forming a card-school here and there but in the main, there is a lot of staring straight ahead. Not so much raucous laughter; hardly any laughter at all. There are silent grins even signs. When they catch my eye some will raise a thumb in approbation before looking away; but we are all contemplating our own capabilities here rushing towards such individual uncertainties after all. Will we be up to it? This hiatus serves its own purpose. I realise there has been no time to think. Until now.

Victoria is heaving with troops and trolleys. Women with huge teapots are standing sweetly smiling behind trestles. We are not allowed to mingle. We are herded with remarkable speed and efficiency from one train to another. The boat train to Folkestone. Again the blinds are down. Again it waits. Quiet. Sinister. Something about it reminds me of the belt on the threshing machine, conveying the oats into the mechanism to be separated from chaff once the engine has been started. Conveyor-belt. Well hell, I volunteered didn't I?

We pull out, we get up steam, we speed, rocking and squeaking down the rails. The carriages are locked, blind. Sometimes the screech coming off the tracks in certain places sounds just like the squealing of pigs when the pig-sticker first sets foot in the yard at TyCanol. They know. They always know – long before he starts getting out his knives.

SEVENTEEN

Tom

On deck coming into Boulogne. I'm not handcuffed. We lean on the rail, smoking Beeswings. Foul. Where on earth did they come from? Fuck-Me and J.W. will have to jump to and look the part when we get ashore. Most of the boys have been puking their guts up crossing. Not me. Just kept thinking 'We're a sea-faring nation' and went with the roll, as when Jim and I crossed to Dublin.

There is a fortification up on a cliff to the right and now we are passing a jagged piece of rock sticking out of the sea. Black. No – it's a piece of an old sea wall, with trees and shrubs growing round the base. History. I wonder how many kings have passed that particular relic going to their wars.

Coming in now. What a horrible looking building on the left. A shed-like structure with roofs at different levels, pipes, galley-ways: one, a long arm-like feeler, running right away back of the dockside. The whole construction is outlined black against the light but now, as we pass beneath, I can see it is a dark, brownish-tan, sandy colour with light brown here and there in patches. A yellow fence in front of it. "Like a hanging-shed" I think morbidly. A place of execution.

My stomach turns over involuntarily as the thought of my impending ordeal looms nearer. Won't be long now. 'Could be shot', as the man said. 'Striking a superior-officer'. I throw the cigarette butt into the dark water. Disgusted. Might as well have killed the bastard if I'm to be shot for the reflex-action he, himself engineered.

There is a white gull on the roof of the nearest part of the huge shed-structure; more fighting and squealing over something round a corner. Is it a fish-processing plant? I wonder. Can smell fish. Real stink. Cranes are sticking up beyond the sinister-looking roofs against a pale-blue sky streaked white. 'Iron-filings factory', someone murmurs. He's been before. Is going back. Doesn't seem too happy about it. I'd be all right if I didn't have the sword hanging over me; would like to have been free to merely gain impressions of my first trip abroad. My depression is somehow matched by the long, long stretch of deserted beach running off to the right where we must have turned in after passing that old piece of wall nearly submerged by the tides. The beach sand is also streaked white, like the sky. There is half a broken pipe embedded in it, near the jetty, a bank of grey-green some way off, then further on again, a long, dense bank of darker green with the city rising above and beyond. We have tied up.

We line up to march through Boulogne, leaving the depressing dock area and its foul smell of rotting fish plus sewage although a strong smell of human shit accompanies us out and under the great trees lining the lower streets before we begin the ascent to St. Michael's camp. They must have a different drainage system to us ... or else it's the muck they eat; snails and such, so they say.

The leaves are still mainly green and massing above our heads in broad patterns against the pale blue. The cathedral looms out of foliage and lesser buildings in terraces halfway up that wretched incline we have to mount, fully loaded as we are. It has a grey roof;

dull, reflecting little light over separated sandstone-coloured pillars, vertical, holding up a high dome. I sniff. Not a patch on Westminster Abbey. Too bold. Too dark.

There are pink Dahlias in the gardens and as we get to the end of another parade of giant trees before turning for the long drag up, up, a beautiful pink flowering shrub is in the corner of my eye. It has hairy fronds as leaves. Very delicate.

Coming out from beneath the leaf-cover, the clouds are all in line, from this new viewpoint. Like puffed up meringues on plates. The sort you can get for parties in the Black's Penn Café. Wonder how Rosalind is? What she's doing.... Right now? We march on.

French women and girls are crowding the streets to see us go by.

"Voulez-vous promenade avec moi, ce soir, Madmoiselle?" we call. We have learned it off by heart on the boat. We laugh. They call 'Tommee! Tommee!' One runs beside Fuck-Me, peering across him to me marching bravely on and up between himself and J.W. Jim Fairhurst is somewhere behind.

"IL est Tommee", Fuck-Me gestures with one hooked thumb towards me, speaking out of the side of his mouth. The girl squeals and signals her friends. They scream, they peer, they sigh .... We suddenly burst into song, the whole parade. 'Keep The Home Fires Burning.' Well, I'll be damned. Good old Ivor. We march on.

From the top, the iron-filings factory's black arm has become more like the tail of a scorpion now. The sky is a misted over pale, pale aquamarine and there is a ridge inland opposite us with clouds right on the edge, half-emerging on to the sky-line like something in one of Billy's fairy-story illustrations.

We do not have time to appreciate the view down over the docks and back out to sea though, we are lined up and literally shoved into old buses to be conveyed over to Camiers, the base-camp for our future operations. Might as well make the most of what <u>could</u> be my last impressions.

Typical! We have to descend again in order to hit the road to Camiers. "Why the hell did we have to march all that way up? Why didn't they pick us up at the docks?" someone complains. "Fuck-me!" is heard.

Things keep reminding me of Radnorshire. There is a large, mansion-type house on our left now: three huge windows at the top, three below, six panes top and bottom to each window. The place has grey, stone battlements and a dark-grey, sloping roof with two tall chimneys either side. Bit like Doldowlod, the Gibson-Watt's place. It heightens my depression. I can almost see the rain slicing down over the grey, Welsh slate, pouring down the walls, Father gathering the reins and flicking the long yellow whip over the mare's quarters as soaking wet ourselves we leave the steps up to the front-door and head for home, miles away through the grey, grey, grey ... after Father's chuckling communion with his landlords and ladies. It is not that I dislike the Gibson-Watts, far from it, but something about their <u>isolation</u> - ... could it be? Their strange apartness? Could almost feel sorry for them.

Oh – and now there were houses like Myrtle Villa just passed and disappearing amongst trees. To me, Myrtle Villa, on the corner facing the Common at home, always gave me the creeps, as if a murder might have been committed in one of the many rooms lurking under those scalloped eaves: a fleshy-feeling. Unspeakable acts. What? Unhealthy. Death. Victorian red-brick plus sickly ochre bricks in patterns going up the sides with that horrible decaying kind of blue/purple – almost swelling like carbuncles – brick-work here and there. And all crouching somehow under a witch-hat roof.

Back there the structures were grey with round windows, black round frames and black-painted eaves. A lot of black paint with echoes of Sunday School teas where we might end up, after a day crossing meadows, on some old aristocrat's estate for tea in an outhouse.

We are rattling along. Yellow flowers and weeds in a bog on the right but in the distance on the left there is a farm-house, low down, really like something out of Radnorshire, giving me a feeling of childhood in fact; but the only difference is — it has a red, cobbled roof and we don't have those at home.

This is damp country. The bog continues on the right with rushes sticking out of it and a line of willows runs almost continuously alongside as we are conveyed away.

Here's a stone bridge, a bit like Llanyre Bridge joining the road over the Ithon between TyCanol's ground and Dol-llwyn-Hir's, except this one is without the white, rounded uprights and fresh, green paint. Without — oh — on our left, bright yellow weed of some sort, never seen that before. Spiky, tall stem, greeny/yellow. Pont de Briques … it says on a wall.

There is a railway-line in view, high up on our left, leaving Boulogne. It is way over. This is almost golf-links country. I can't help comparing. The line sweeps high inland over ravines and drops. There goes a train now. Creeping along over a gorge. Blimey. Can't it get up steam — or what?

A singead, ginger - coloured tree here on this corner, it's leaves half-consumed with bronze and yet it is a willow, I think. Or is it dead … for they don't turn colour like that, do they?

I wonder if Jim Corp. came this way? Wouldn't mind betting. Yes — old Jim would have joined-up, no doubt about it. If so, would he have noticed the things I'm noticing? Probably not. It's all new to me. Jim's been around. All over. Got used to things. Come to think of it, hundreds and thousands of us … our lot, I mean, must have passed along this very route … to the front. I forgot the <u>lists</u> too. One-way journey for most of them, then.

The boys are singing 'Mademoiselle From Amentieres', each verse with filthier words to the tune than the songwriter intended. I don't join in. Don't feel like singing. Could be a one-way journey for me too. First plus last stop Camiers, never mind getting to the front.

We've hit a straight stretch of road. There's a church on the right near another chateau-type house with a pointed up roof on the side with the chimneys. Odd. Another big chateau on the left. This is rather like the road leading out of Bury towards our old barracks. Don't know what reminds me. Why this perpetual comparison to places I have known? Kind of anchoring myself, I suppose. My past. All eighteen years of it now! I grin. They think I'm nineteen.

We're driving at an angle, negotiating a curve through spindly trees. White cattle, one black and white … no – one, two, three. Hens in a field. Hundreds of them like a fidgeting cloud of deep brown. Pullets. Black and white cows again. Willows, beech, ponies running. Little things almost like baby-Shetlands. Wonder what breed they are? If I ever inherit the farms – I'd like to get rid of the cattle …. Can't bear all that, suckling the calves then seeing the little bulls shunted off to Builth for grading: all the awful, everyday-taking-for-granted thing of getting cows to the bull, then the calving, suckling, separating so that we can latch on to the tits and milk the poor buggers dry – until the next time. No! Get rid of all that, if I take over – and breed horses me. Cross thoroughbred, Welsh mountain-ponies with Arabs! Beautiful. Buckskins with flaxen manes and tails. They'd turn out the very ticket. Fast. Hardy.

Now this stretch could be either a slice of Worcestershire or Radnorshire. ½ and ½.… Right on until a sweep of land leading skyward beyond a round ring of bushes, up, up to an altogether alien horizon after all with trees, going up and down as if on a switchback. Very dark, VERY dark against the distance to the East.

There is a pleasant smell coming off another brilliantly greeny/yellow plant, a kind of vetch, not rape, a smell gentle as gilly-flowers before there is this wide expanse before us, corn on the horizon dead ahead and to the left another huge structure, all angles, gantries and huge chimneys, belching out smoke. Don't know what – and a hill, a ridged hill with fields zigzagging up, up again to the left then this quarry in front: that's what it is, a stone quarry. Yes, you can see the dust rising. Yeah – and a high bank on the right of the road, hiding the view now.

Ah, we are getting towards Camiers, someone says. I feel almost a manic compulsion to record every single detail of this fleeting scene. A ridge above those fields on the left with that awful sinister-looking factory or no, - quarry, nestling in the folds yet black against the pale silver sky. Foreboding; but now on the right again where we can see, having rattled and bounced past the high bank, there are twisted pine trees, yes, and a pine-forest on our left. How quickly the scene changes. We could be heading for Brighton or Bournemouth here. Same sort of territory.

I hear Fuck-Me asking "So we're not far from the coast here? What? … LeTouquet? Um.m.m. Must have a swim." Then the laugh. Good old Fuck-Me. Damn – even if I'm not shot, they're sure to put me on a charge. I'll get Jankers and that means the others will go on without me. Corr-r. What about poor old J.W.? I'll miss those B-s. And THAT'S only looking on the bright side.

There's an alien feel to the country now, even if this road going through pines is a bit like the road to Rhayader, never mind Brighton or Bournemouth. There's something different. The road leads on. Is that a yew-tree in front? Gigantic one? Is it a sort of fir? Firs and pines all around then a mass of golden berries on the left. Oh – it's a mountain ash. Hum .. Not as red as the Radnorshire variety. Rowan tree. Mam's favourite.

Bushes, like curtains, right down to the roadside. Tall trees behind bushes. A narrow corridor. Footpath on right. Paths I've trodden so many times at home. Covered in pine needles. Soft beneath your shoes. So many times – with Rosalind.

Left now to Camiers and a hill facing us. Camiers. Spreading, healthy-looking trees on our left. Sort you get in gardens of the well-to-do at home. Small wood on our right. A white house with a sloping roof at the end of the street. All kinds of flowers. Red, yellow, pink. Are they dahlias, astors or whatever?

A very forceful woman is saying something pleasant to us, looking up from the pavement on our left. She makes magnificent, forceful gestures and if she wasn't speaking French, I would say she talks almost exactly like my old nurse, Nellie Evans. She even looks like her.

We are approaching the T-junction now and I see a terrace of grey houses half round the corner almost like one long building divided into segments. Beautiful round bush on right side of this road before the turn. Dainty leaves again, dainty pink flowers in a circle high on a bank in a garden against the five o'clock sun behind clouds, like an egg spinning threequarters of the way up the sky.

Nearly there. Bound to be. Must record. Must - . Take my mind off it: what is to happen. Round the corner now into the main street. Hotel De Voyageurs. Huh! Hopefully. Even I can understand that. White plaster, dark brown surrounds to the windows, to the eaves. Imposing. Looming out of the past. Waterloo and all that. Very French. Ah oui! Bien sure! Beautiful smell in Camiers of leaves, of flowers, fresh leaves, sweet flowers. Summer. Flowers. Pink. The smell of pink.

There seems to be only one main street with little lanes leading off. Not many people are about. The old soldier on board says, "Wait till later," meaning – when the squaddies are off-duty, I expect.

A very grand little post-office on our right briefly as we get up speed to leave the village. It has a portal with rounded pillars holding up a semi-circular, brown, tiled porch. It is all pointed walls, arched windows, terra cotta tiling. The doorway has an Art-Nouveau design. I must write to Rosalind now and to the parents. Get Eloise to send me some fags. Phew … those Beeswing! Horrible. At least I know where to post - . Forgot.

Hotel du Lac on left just before the last of the houses and over the road on our right, just a glimpse of an expanse of almost black water beneath trees.

Both sides the road I see the tents and huts now. On the left, high up in the dunes, and spread out on the right after the lake. A hive of activity here. White-painted gates. Notices. Barriers. Arrows. Crests. Army lorries with canvas flaps.

A white pole crashes down as we make a sharp turn left to an entrance leading up into the trees. The sergeant in charge of our lot gets up and makes for the front of the bus. "Sorry Edwards" he murmurs as he passes me. Fuck-Me and J.W. stir and sit up, J.W. moans.

"Door!" says the Sergeant to the driver who releases the catch. Serg. goes down the steps and across into the small sentry-hut alongside the barrier. He's a good chap. Fair. They'll probably ring-up for instructions from above.

We don't have long to wait. Two enormous redcaps come marching down the lane. Serg. emerges form the hut, the sentry after him smoking. He soon drops the cigarette and grinds it under his boot when he sees the MPs. He returns into his hut, double time. Have to smile.

They approach the bus.

"PTE. EDWARDS. Attention!"

I jump to my feet and stand, chin up, rigid. Fuck-Me and J.W. stare straight ahead.

"Load up!" I am commanded. I swipe up my kit and rifle.

"Quick march!" I am escorted off the bus and down on to the gravel that has been thrown on the surface of the lane. No time for goodbyes. No space to even wink or grin towards poor old J.W.

We have to manoeuvre about on the gravel for a minute or two, until I am considered suitably clad and got together. Also, they have to fall in with me at the precise angle between them. They tower against the leaves like monoliths. Easter-Island faces. Cut out of rock.

We proceed up the hill to the Guardroom. I am incarcerated for the night on iron rations (some sort of huge dog biscuit, plus water). My 'trial' will take place in the morning. The cell is at the back of the Nisson-Hut.

I wake to the sound of a cock crowing. In fact it has woken me up with its raucous cry – well before dawn. There is not a glimmer of light through the close-set steel bars at the two-foot square aperture in the wall facing uphill. Must be about 3.00 a.m.

It wakes me again at 10 past 5. "Qua QuA qua qua. Qua QuA qua qua." Foreign. They don't have the same squawk as ours. Different language – even the bloody cocks. Strange.

I am up, shit, shaved and ready as I will ever be when they come for me. It is early.

"Attention! Right wheel! Quick march!" Along clanging corridors, up steps, down steps, outside, along a bit, right turn, in again through an open doorway, bang, bang, bang, boots along another echoing wooden corridor. "Right turn! Forward MARCH! HALT! OFF CAP!"

The young officer looks half-asleep behind his desk. He is exceedingly pale. He must have been in action because he has a ribbon up. Don't know what.

I am delivered to him. The two redcaps ascend like cliffs. One either side. The young officer has been reading my charge placed in front of him on the polished planks. He appears to be holding in the most terrible wrath. I expect I am for it.

He looks up into my face, head still between his shoulders. My chin is up. I look straight ahead: eyes front, but I can see him in my peripheral-vision zone.

"How old are you, Private Edwards?" he asks softly.

"Eigh … NINEteen Sir!"

"Um.m."

"Did you do it, Private Edwards?

Throw your rifle at the Company Sergeant-Major?"

"Yes Sir."

"Excuses Private Edwards?"

"No Sir."

"Case dismissed."

(Gasp), "Thankyou Sir."

"On Cap!" from the escort.

"Right wheel! Quick March!"

It is our last evening in the Hotel du Lac. We are in the bar, a lofty room with a high, dark, wooden counter opposite the open door. It is still warm. Probably the end of this long Indian summer. A late wasp buzzes up and down, up and down the big, brown-framed window behind us and there are red and gold, yellow and brown Nasturtiums in huge terra-cotta pots outside the open door. The sun is going down and the trees around the lake are dark against the gold. We are going up the line tomorrow. Our interval in Camiers is over for now.

Since being here we have put the theory into practice regarding the firing of the gun. The standard drill for going into action is complicated and we have had to practice and practice to get into shape. They rely on us a lot in the lines. We have to be first-class.

On the blow of a whistle, Number One dashes forward with the tripod, releases the ratchet-held front legs so that they swing forward, both pointing out and secures them fast by tightening the ratchet handles. Have to sit down then and remove two metal pins from the head of the tripod, at which point Number Two shoves the gun into position on the legs etcetera, Number One whips in the pins – and we are ready for loading. Number Three dashes up now with an ammunition-box (bloody heavy), containing an ammunition-belt, pocketed to hold 250 rounds. Number Two inserts the brass tag end of the belt into the feed-block on the right-hand side of the gun. Number One (usually me for some reason, even though I'm not even a lance-corporal) has to grab the tag-end and jerk it through, at the same time as pulling back the crank handle <u>twice</u> … to complete the loading operation.

To sight it you have to flick your finger to spring the stem of the rear sight upright. You can get a quick-fire selection of ranges by turning up or down a spring-loaded wheel as necessary. Practising at the butts – over in the dunes above the road, well out of sight, we are supposed to knock over steel target plates and expected to do this by accuracy of aim and not by watching the dirt flying and using this as a guide to the target.

We have practised for hours and hours, day after day. They are pleased with our progress. We have come up to scratch in record time. They don't bother with 'Slope-Arms', 'Present-Arms', here. It is all concentrated on firing the guns. I have even been congratulated on my 'dead-eyed shots' at times and must say was quite pleased at that because they only seemed satisfied, up to those moments of sparse congratulations, when our hands were bleeding. The more bits of skin knocked off – the better they seemed to like it, we thought.

I can now strip down the gun, change the barrel, replace broken parts and re-assemble at speed. This is supposed to be of prime importance. Several hours of our training have actually been spent doing some of the jobs blindfolded, so that we get to be absolutely familiar with the various parts and functions of the gun; for instance, different types of stoppage are shown by the position of the crank handle when you stop firing; all of us are trained to remove the cause of a stoppage in a matter of seconds. Our C.O. was not given to fulsome compliments but he is pretty satisfied with his new company after ten days hard work.

I like Captain - . I suppose he is a bit of a hero to us. He doesn't seem to care a damn about Jerry, as such, even though he has been up and down the front like a yo-yo. He won't have any nonsense. We have to learn and learn fast. We have to be proficient for not only our own lives are at stake, he says, but scores, hundreds, tens of thousands of others. He is coming back up with us. Thank Heavens. He is fair.... Like the one who let me off that B- charge. Aristocrats, in the proper sense.

This evening we are with Judith and Maybelle for the last time until we come back down here for delousing and a rest from the lines. We are supposed to come after so many weeks at the front but the girls grimace mirthlessly at this above their cigarettes and blowing out blue smoke into the yellowish atmosphere in the already nicotine-stained, barn-like room, they say quietly that it doesn't always work out quite like that.

They are nurses from one of the military hospitals outside Etaples. Between the camp at Camiers and Etaples – are any amount of these hospitals, alongside the estuary, in the dunes. They are supposed to lie in an area almost undetectable by enemy aircraft.

Fuck-Me and myself, after meeting the girls in here for the first time, almost as soon as we were allowed off-duty weeks ago, have sometimes managed to scrounge a lift into Etaples (we call it Eat-Apples) on the back of two dispatch-rider's motor-bikes, to see the girls in town. They are grand girls, although Judith, my particular, is very sad at times. I don't ask her why. She can be quite abrupt if you probe too much.

She and Maybelle are billeted here in a couple of wooden chalet-type annexes round the back of this hotel. Fuck-Me and I have got up at dawn before now, awakened thank goodness, by that wretched "Qua QuA, qua, qua, Qua QuA, qua, qua" .... In time to be back in camp for reveille. Bugle-call and it will be a nice memory: stumbling quietly out through the wooden doors, beneath the vine trailing from the corrugated-iron roofing over the concrete path with all those nodding flowers over the wet, emerald grass against a high, stone-block wall. The flowers trail upwards through the early mist, round, simple shapes, almost like asters, yet not: more delicate. Pink, yellow, white, they star beyond the heavy green overhanging trees outside the cabins, the wet lawns, a sawn-off tree with three separate limbs, right of centre. A ladder leans against a subdued duck-egg blue wall at the end on the right as the morning grows. Reminds me of home. Misty.

Then as we clatter down the concrete towards the side of the Hotel du Lac, a narrow door-way almost coming apart from the white-washed wall at the end of the 'run' up to the chalets, frames the morning sun, new again rising over the lake. Almost orange-gold behind some heavy trunks, fir branches, ivy on a fence, large pink blooms and a sweep of nasturtiums over rocks bordering the path out on to the hotel forecourt. Goodbye for now.

Judith

Yes, I am sad. Full of sadness. I could never have cheered him up but thank Heavens he never seemed to want that. Always teasing me. 'Sober-sides' … things like that. Still, I've been able to give him other things. So young. So YOUNG. I've looked at him sometimes, when they've been sitting down below us, Maybelle and I – if we happen to have come in late … and it's the planes of their faces, Tom's especially, so soft and almost unformed. His beautiful mouth, teeth – and then their necks are too slender for the collars of the uniform. They strain upwards like tender sticks of celery, the necks. The throats.

And the times when I can't bear it. He doesn't ask questions. Leaves me be. "What's going on in your head?" – he never asks that, like the one before who wanted to own everything about me so I had to run off and hide when I saw him coming. Too close. Too close. Anyway, there's Rosalind. Tom has told me about her. Like it or lump it. I like that. He's honest. I don't even envy Maybelle that she and Fuck-Me are even thinking of arranging 'the day'. Good for them, I say. It wouldn't work for Tom and me, that. Too different. Fundamentally. Me – I'm a city girl. 155, Lady Margaret's Road, Southall – and proud of it. My parish. Folks been there for years. Just get on the underground and down to town. Love it. I was never sad. But now.

How could I tell him? That when I'm not with him, how it is ... with him going into it himself?

Why BOY: we are swamped, day and night! The staff are frantic. There are convoys and convoys of casualties pouring in and nearly every case should be on a stretcher.

Did you not know that they come in ragged and dirty, their tin hats still on, wounds just patched together any old how, not even covered? Direct from the line, Tom, and their dear little faces white and drawn, eyes like boiled sweets, hazed over from having hardly any sleep.

Matron asked if Mabelle, Ruth and I were able to clean up five hundred walkers the day before yesterday. We said we thought we could but were each wondering, HOW? We made up a small table for the M.O. and then a large one piled with bandages, splints, boric ointment, sponges and a basinful of Dakins Solution for wet dressings. Only two lanterns in there and a feeble Primus stove to warm them up a bit.

Ruth took the doorway position, scissors in her hand and beckoned the boys into the dressing-station. They were allowed in, two or three at a time. We were so rushed; it was impossible to be too careful taking off the stiff, dried bandages. There was only one way to do it: snatch them off with a desperate tug.

Poor Maybelle. She could hardly cope with this. Could hardly stand it. She would cut the dressings down the middle as we all had to … but it was the look of the lads having to see what was going on, with set jaws and imploring eyes that almost did for her. For all of us. Quick jerk, sharp scream from the boy, sob from us – and he's passed on to the M.O. Then you begin on the next.

They come much too fast you know, you UNDERSTAND? … within fifteen minutes you can be standing twenty deep around the dressing table. You cease to think, my little Tommee-ee-ee, as the hours pass. We usually work through the night until dawn. That's why it has been such a relief to wake up to the cock crowing, in a wooden cabin and an unscathed young man half-whistling, pulling on his britches. Laughing quietly. Leaving. Leaving.

Oh I cry. I cry. It was so lovely meeting outside the Hotel de Vielle in Etaples. Sometimes we had to wait, Maybelle and I, so couldn't help noticing the finer points of the architecture. Very baroque but beautiful. That crowned King's face underneath the bell-tower, the balcony, pillars and porticoes, the huge doors with their pink and mauve painted panels, their mauve steel banisters either side and the top panes of the door, glass with a fancy iron grill. Yes --a beautiful pattern – or was everything simply beautiful because of the feeling: meeting this one? Something about him, the lad … definitely.

We would stand on the steps leading down on to the cobbles, after a time … in case they missed us, between the cream and red brick pillars either side. The pillars had scrollwork at the top, I noticed, either side the balcony and there were two more again going up from that. Flowers all over the place, the first time we met there. I shall always remember. Hanging baskets in the porch and then in the gardens, striped, dark-purple petunias, lovely big, orange, double-marigolds (huge really), red salvias, I think, silver leaves, small dahlias, big, purple sort of shooting flowers, pink daisies, white daisies with yellow centres, orange berries on shrubs, a big, well-shaped tree, two, little, dark-green umbrella trees to each side the path leading up to the four steps we stood on … patiently waiting. Expectant.

Tom made me smile. He couldn't make out exactly what the Etaples smell was, he said, "Sort of clean, smoky, food, flowers, sweet smell," he said –

"Yes and horse-manure. Nice though."

We walked up the street after drinking coffee in the patisserie just off the square. The cobbles leading up have an intricately, patterned design. Very satisfying to the eye. Some arranged in circular motives. Hint of pink. Yes, Tom says there's pink everywhere round here.

And then, we walked home eventually. All the way to Camiers. It's quite a way but we are young and you can get to know someone, walking in the evening. We passed our hospital but Mabelle and I refused to linger. We knew what was behind the trees for there is a bank of them all round the grounds. All kinds. The place is on a flat plain that slopes up to the road then goes into all sorts of dips and sweeps with a few pink and purple flowers blowing here and there. The trees hide everything. In little knolls. Massing down there against the estuary.

"Strong smell of horse-shit here," Tom laughs "And I know what the Etaples overriding colour was … guess!" "Can't." "Well CANDYFLOSS of course. Smoky."

Ah yes – we get it.

We are children playing in a summer setting. Transported over sea and land. Pixie-led, as they say in Ireland. The sun going down behind the trees as we march further and further along the road between huge mansions, parks and former playgrounds, the sea and the smell of the sea always on our left, the millionaires' paradise shut for the season or should I say commandeered as a rest-camp, back now up the pine-slippery, needled paths under the rusty-red trunks, the silent tufts and tails of green – is a great vermilion blotch, spreading, spreading..... dying. I see our backs. Our backs with our arms around each other dwindling into dolls in the distance. I hear our clear voices receding, receding. A wave crashes on a distant shore. Drags back.

EIGHTEEN

The station is really grand for such a small place: grey stone but with red brick up the sides in a sort of triangle pattern right to the pointed top of the building with such tall chimneys.

We are marched down the street, right turn at the bottom and halted outside the three sets of white-framed French-doors under a kind of platform above them then three more windows above plus a very small window under the apex.

We have to wait for them to open-up. 'STAND EASY! AT EASE.' No one appears yet through the narrow faded blue/grey wooden door on the right. Three long, wide, grey steps with a brown trim on the bottom two lead up to the entrance. Wonder how many boys have passed through here? Marched up these steps and through to the platforms the other side of the barn-like room I can see through the panes. Another three sets of identical French-doors looking out on to the platform. That is – when some bugger comes to open up.

The men are massed on the forecourt. Down the bottom of the road I can see the wide, horse-shoe-shaped door at the end of the Hotel de Voyageurs that faces up here towards the station. Dark brown. Almost like a barn door.

Here, on the right of the French-doors there is a stone banister and a more ornamental one on the left, then looking over there, a stone wall where the virginia-creeper growing over it has gone bright, crimson, <u>blood</u> red and even covers a small tree sticking up beside the wall, soaked in red, though that tree itself is now bare of leaves. The hedge leading down towards the main road is still green though. There is a small, wooden, lichened gate left open between the wall and the little tree. Open – as if pushed, it's bottom struts in foliage. Stuck – and left open, years back. Who has entered there all that time ago? Children playing – now gone? Like us.

Top end of the station-drive, on the right and opposite us as we wait, it says Ouvert de la Gare on a cream-coloured house with a glass-panelled top-half to its door. Window at the side. It has a red-tiled roof and a tree growing beside it almost obscuring this window. Not quite. I nudge Jim Fairhurst in the ribs and indicate with a knowing roll of the eyebrow that he should look and see the face peering steadfastly out.

"Probably won't move until the very minute strikes," Jim laughs and sure enough – when that happens, here he comes, full of importance to officiate behind the doors.

We are brought to attention, in sight of the lone country, this end of the village, leading across to common land and a hill beyond, shrubs, bushes spiking the air.

The train is approaching. We are brought through the station in perfect order. This has to have been worked out to a fine art. Forty men and eight horses to each truck but the mad scramble to get on board has to be taken into account. We are all loaded down with almost three-quarters of a hundredweight of kit per man and don't forget those forty rifles poking every which way. Captain– is a godsend and oh, the station smell in here: Camiers. Smoke and age, smoke and age. We are going down towards Boulogne before branching off up to St. Omer and then somehow to the Ypres sector.

My impressions are telescoping rapidly. One, two, three joined wooden slats leading down across the line, I suppose for foot-passengers crossing, then over the station-fence, out the back here, glimpses of hills indented with cream chalk behind red roofs. The railway is two-tracked, sleepers on shingle and the platform forecourt pebble-dashed. All extremely neat and tidy. Hedge on left, still green, the station-bridge, an ominous-looking structure with concrete slabs, steps leading down. 'Dannes Camiers' it states somewhere. Outside the French-doors there are weird decorative structures. An iron support with three rings, one above another. It's the same at the side of the building. I had to go for a pee just now. Some strange steel decoration: the metal support, three brackets encircling. And round there was the smell of Chrysanthemums. The smell of Chrysanthemums. Must be well into Autumn then. That's a Christmas smell at home.

I have heaved myself on, one of the last. Want to sit with my feet dangling over the side if I can. Don't like to be too crowded.

The station buildings look more forbidding this side. Six pillars holding up the canopy, gothic pointed roofing in between, two extremely narrow faded blue/grey doors on the left beside the three, large French-windows same as those out the front. I must say the old boy keeps it all very tidily anyway. But I wish he would put a smile on. Hardened to it, I expect, seeing so many off all the time. You would think he could acknowledge somehow though, wouldn't you? Makes you feel – what? De-personalised ... as if you are nothing in his eyes. Expendable. Blimey. Good old Fuck-Me. "Don't any of you lot shit on my Roses!" he says. We all know what he's getting at. We leave to the awful strains of 'One-Eyed-Riley.' Let's hope Monsieur can't understand the words. They're beyond all pales.

J.W. is stuck somewhere at the back of the truck. We shout for him to join us. Fuck-Me, Jim and I have secured our positions when the others thought it might be a disadvantage to sit right on the edge. Damned thing goes so slowly it doesn't even need brakes. If you want to shit, they say, once we get into open country, you can jump off, have one and run and catch up again, no bother at all.

J.W. manages it at last. He is red in the face from trying to get past far bigger fellows than himself. "Old bully-beef tins, fag-packets …goodness knows what, back there" he grumbles.

"Oh shut your face and give your arse a chance." Fuck-Me grins.

"One thing I'm glad of … won't have to do any more crawling through that bleeding gas-tent … eh Tom, boy? Eh?"

I try not to frighten him even further by saying he might now have to put up with the real thing. We all hated the gas-practices. Crawling on your belly, strapped into that hateful mask with all the real McCoy whirling and coiling round you! I'll say – it was horrible. If poor old J.W. had but known it …. I was as dead-scared as him. Hated it! All that green fog and having to crawl from flap to flap, full-kit, mask on. Felt as if I couldn't BREATHE. Wanted to rip it off. No joke. But poor old J.W. Blue-funk. Can't! No. No.

"Just keep to my heels J.W." I said. "Got to do it boy. Keep right on my heels. Don't lose sight."

He did it too. (Huh. So did I).

We must be crossing one of those ravines I saw when we were going up to Camiers from Boulogne. We are on that bridge ourselves then. How strange. When we nearly pulled to a stop just now, all the trucks knocked into each other: clang, clang, clang, clang. Some of the boys are playing cards on an old packing case left by the last lot. Fuck-Me and the rest of us are sharing one of the last Players Eloise managed to get through to me with her last letter. She didn't mention Rosalind or that she had seen her. I wrote to Mother and Father and then at last to Rosalind herself telling her I've got that photograph of her up the Golf-Links in my pocket still and asking her all the things I should have before.

It is pretty flat country, wide-flung mainly with dark knolls of trees here and there or a spread of them suddenly marching down over the shoulder of a rise in the ground. It's damned hot in this khaki and the ground all about has been harvested of course. There is a glow on the stubble. We clank on and on.

We are past St. Omer and have been hearing a lot of gunfire for some time. The train jerks to a stop and all the trucks go banging into each other again. Clang, clang, clang, clang.

All out and form up into full marching-order. Eyes front. By the RIGHT ... Quick march. We are young, we are fit and fresh. We'll get 'em. Someone starts whistling It's A Long Way To Tipperary. We all join in. The guns bang. Background noise. To be expected at this distance, we think. We hear a loud boom.

"TAKE COVER!" Hum. Drill. Right. In the ditch. How's that?

"All clear!" up again and formed in line. But there are two crumpled heaps in the road where we were standing before. Almost like two khaki sacks. Small. Folded. My stars! Bodies. Two blokes have caught it. This is no joke. One of the card-players ....

"Eyes FRONT! Quick march!" we sway off through dust and an orange haze where the sun shines over the stubble either side the road.

"Whizz-bangs!" Serg. utters. "Thank your lucky stars it wasn't a Johnson, else we'd have had four of 'em over us. Keep moving!"

And now, forget the spit and polish, the high-jinks with the rifle until you get in the reserve lines. Here it is somewhere else. Don't ask us where. We can't tell you. We don't KNOW except when we are back for a time right here again and look over to the shot-off tower of Ypres Cloth Hall to get our bearings.

We might be in the wood, zigzagging through the trenches or up on the mounds amongst the skeletons of trees. There's a place some call Dicky-Bush that's got a meeting-place run by ever such a good padre bloke where you can get to sing maybe or swig down some soup, spend some of your pay if you're lucky enough to find it. There's somewhere called Hell-Fire Corner and that's no laugh but here: HERE, I tell you what I detest most, apart from the lice of course that get everywhere; even round your balls ... no – it's the mud and the way, in places, it's up in waves and thick banks like some awful nightmare sea and the sight of the dead mules stuck in it and tanks upended, good for nothing any more – and the awful smell of death.

We do everything to order. Whistle! Over the top and running hell for leather, dodging through the enemy fire as best you can over the duckboards, heading for your position and then it's the diamond-formation with the three teams, one out in front, usually us, with

Captain –. Walking about directing us, cool as a bloody cucumber, little cane under his arm as if he's merely taking a walk round his estate at home and the firing, firing, firing, keeping them off, feeling NOTHING ..... it's either them or me and yes I've bayoneted and twisted the steel and pulled it out and chucked Mills bombs and fired and fired and fired and told old J.W. to just follow and DO EVERYTHING THAT I DO, so that he'll think he's dodging all the bullets going and so far, SO FAR, thank God, we <u>have</u> and to Keep Buggering On, J.W. just keep on. We don't know whether we're in Passchendaele , at Hell-Fire bloody corner, Dickybush – or where the hell we are half the time as I said, except when we see the shot-off tower at Ypres from a distance but not always the same angle because we lose a bit then advance, then lose and flounder in this bloody mud but we just go on. Where we're told. And we do. Yes somehow.

The guns never cease and when we're down in the dugout you can feel shells thudding on the roof. Thank Heavens there have been no gas-attacks on our sector yet. Down there it's a different world. You're not safe yet safer than you have been outside. It's a relief to squat round the packing-case under a lantern. We race piebald-lice against the ordinary and take bets. We are filthy. Our puttees are stiff with mud and it's getting cold now but a greatcoat hampers you. The long skirt drags down the cut out steps. How we all get in here I'll never know.

I'm an expert at digging a dugout and trenches. We all are. We're not in them for long and when we are it's to clean the gun or sleep. The rations arrive. We eat as much as we can but sometimes it's not up to much. The mornings are best if you can get a piece of bacon. We sit on the fire-step, backs to the mud sometimes, chewing then smoking a Woodbine – after a scrape – in cold water. I pity the older men with a thick growth. We are going to be relieved quite soon. Shit-house rumours. Things get passed down the line.

The job I hate most is having to go out on 'Burial Party'. Jerry sends up Very Lights at night, lighting up the whole scene. We have to get out of our trench on to the duckboards and flat on our bellies make our way over No Mans Land feeling either side into the pools of mud and water for heads and all the time waiting for the shout from the other side, then Jerry getting the drop on us. What do we do with the heads? Why are we …? Well, if one is alive, you pull him out and get him back, don't you? If dead? Oh, if dead – you push him down. Push him further under. Don't have time to worry that you might have got it wrong. Well if you do … that's private. Between you and God.

We are definitely going into reserve. Probably next week. But today Captain – and the three crews are going up on to that bare rise the other side from our present position under the trees.

We follow him almost to the top of the slope and spread out in the usual diamond-formation that he prefers. We are the arrowhead. I throw down the tripod and we set up the gun so that we will have a good, unimpeded view down the other side. He comes strolling along, head up. I love him. Cool as usual. Taking it easy. He is above us now, passing. He smiles and is going to say something encouraging. Strewth! Why doesn't he duck? His head's above the parapet. He's in the line of fire. Silly BUGGER! "CRACK!" He looms above me. He is falling. His tin helmet hurtles down out of the falling sky and its edge catches me in the mouth, taking my four front teeth half-off. Severing that string thing holding my top lip to the gum.

Oh, he's dead. He's dead. We grab him. We ease him down. We call the stretcher-bearers and he is taken from us. Taken away. I cry. We cry. We wipe the tears from our eyes. We fire. We fire. We fire. We scream our pain over the ridge. Gone. My mouth bleeds and bleeds. What do we do now?

Fuck-Me and I are on the hospital train to Etaples. He is due some leave but I am for the medics. I am to go straight there so he says he will wait in that patisserie for me before we set off down to Camiers to be deloused and have our hair cut. "Make a date with the girls", he tells me. "Tell them we'll meet them in here as usual. Can't wait. Give them my love."

The orderlies accompany me to the flap of a makeshift canvas dressing-station. There is devastation to right and left of the tent. Wooden planks and bits of steel, chair-legs and so on, strewn about on the ground, swept into enormous piles here and there, ready for carting away. Blackened by fire.

Ruth is standing just before the entrance. Too busy to notice me yet. She is dividing the walking-wounded into priorities. The smell of our wounds is terrible and some of the blood-soaked bandages around the boys' heads in front of me are leaking. We all stink. Are covered in mud, dust, lice and gun-smoke.

Ruth has gone as thin as a rake – in eight weeks. Her eyes have sunk right back into her head. Her hair seems thin and wispy under that cap. It is half-off. This can't be Ruth!

"This can't be TOM!" she cries. "My dear – what have they done to you?"

My mouth is swollen like a baboon's arse. It is painful and I dread the examination.

"You're badly infected"; she says and pushes me forward. I hope Judith will be at the dressing table. No. No sign of her – nor Maybelle.

They probe with steel instruments and the Medical Officer takes my jaw in his hands and examines the damage. He is remarkably gentle. "Nothing to be done concerning that - " (he means the string thing attaching my top lip to the gum) – "but we'll wash this, get the swelling down with antiseptics, then you'll have to come back for us to plug your teeth. What are you …?"

"A gunner," I say.

"Do you want home leave?" he asks. "This can get you a Blighty if you'd prefer".

I think of the Captain, of J.W. and Fuck-Me waiting in the patisserie.

"No thankyou Sir". I reply. How can I go home? I couldn't bear the questions. The ordinariness of things there when this …

"This time, three days". He makes out a chit.

"Thank you Sir." I say.

A male nursing-orderly takes over. He swabs my mouth and teeth (or what remains of them) in some kind of disinfectant. It stings like hell. I dance, temporarily from one foot to the other but keep my head up. "Try and stand still" he says.

"Sorry sir", I reply.

He smiles. He does his best. The agony subsides into almost a comfortable burn. He finishes up. Tells me the plugging won't hurt.

It's to prevent me getting toothache. I thank him and make for the exit at the back of the tent.

Ruth is outside the flap. Hovering. "I haven't got long Tom, I'm afraid ... but have to –,"

"Where's Judith – and Maybelle?" I try and enunciate between my numbed, swollen lips. It comes out as "Pllrs Pllytith –an Merrplll?"

I don't like to interrupt but if she's only got a moment -. She shuts her eyes, squeezing back tears. Her hands come up in front of her ravaged frame.

"Oh Tom" – she wrings out, shaking her head from side to side. "Oh Tom .... They're both dead. Killed by a bomb. We took a direct hit. Didn't you notice the damage .... All those piles of rubble?"

I can only stare at her as she goes to pieces in front of my eyes.

"They said we were undetectable from the air. How did it happen?" Her voice rises but then she is convulsed in a sob that racks her whole frame. I lunge forward and grab her to myself. I hold her whether she likes it or not, tight as I can against my filthy body. I screw my eyes shut. SHUT.

"I must go," she says, quiet now. "Got to get on."

I pass her the clean wipe they gave me at the dressing-table for her to mop her eyes and nose.

"Thank you, my dear". She says and goes softly away. Back to her charges. I can't move from this spot. Not yet.

We are down in a vast hollow. The sun is high up on the left, shining over trees. There is a bank of trees all the way round the hospital grounds. You would have thought the camouflage would have been perfect. The army tents and huts must look like part of the background from up there. Not to be.

Perhaps they were making or aiming from that sandstone-bridge over the estuary, as you leave Etaples. Very sleek water there, reflecting blue and silver with waterweeds on it. The bridge rises to a centre turret with gratings then the estuary flows out right with boats and yachts sailing like toys to the sea beyond. The sea always seems high from the road over there, where we used to walk. Sometimes you might even think the waters were blue hills, in the distance, kind of. No – the sea all right, we would agree. But the sea really DOES go up there. No – it's a cloud over it, coming down. There is a very, very pronounced smell of cow-muck somewhere here. The leaves have dropped from the trees while we've been gone. The small oaks and beech-trees are bare. Only these gigantic pines and yew-trees form the barriers. I CAN'T BEAR IT. Something is scratching and sobbing inside me to get out. The sight of the four of us walking down that road to the base-camp, arms around each other's shoulders, our voices echoing, in my mind's eye – is too recent. Too real. No ... too unreal. I feel in turmoil.

I turn and run up the slope on to the road where the smell of muck is even more pronounced. Some pink and mauve flowers are still growing under the sweeping branches on one of the knolls! I turn my head left to Camiers. The road stretches away between the massing firs. Shall I run down there? But no, I have to face Fuck-Me in the café.

I run, keeping my mouth shut as best I can against the air, now gone cold, back into the town, clattering down the thin street at the back of some municipal building, over those pink-patterned tiles she loved so much, duck left off my right foot, mustn't stop or flinch from what I have to do now and jerk myself upright to cross this other street and up the steps into the patisserie.

Fuck-Me is sitting in the corner facing the window. The proprietor is a tall streak of white apron behind his massive counter on my left as I enter. The brass bell pings. The brass fittings glint in the fleeting sunlight.

"Bonjour!" I say. "Bonjour M'sieur", he replies.

"Deux cafes <u>noir</u>, s'il vous plait", I say in passing and head for that table in the corner.

"How'd you get on Cherub?" he jokes.

"Patched you up all right – have they?"

I pull out the chair my side, hooking it round my foot to give it a smooth tug back and sit down almost in one move. Urgent.

"Never mind me Fuck-Me. Listen."

"What's up? … Has Jerry - ?" He moves for his rifle. As if to stand up, rush out.

The proprietor bends expertly over the table, depositing the cups. He leaves. No surplus fuss.

"Fuck-Me. Judith and Maybelle are dead." I say, as directly as I can. "Killed by a bomb. The hospital took a direct hit."

His eyes have opened to an unnatural length, like rugby-balls standing on the tip. His hair is up on end. Swear to it. My stars – he's white.

"Who told you that?"

"Ruth".

He turns away, pinching his nose. We just sit there. Ages. We don't drink the coffee but I pay for both of us on the way out.

"Merci M'sieur."

"Merci M'sieur."

We have quite a bit of pay saved. Never made it to Dicky-Bush. No leave until now. Five francs a day. Not bad. Get a litre of wine for half a franc. 'Oeufs et pommes de terre frites, 50 centimes', here and there.

The last thing we want to do now is eat. We head for Camiers. Fuck-Me makes no comment. He doesn't speak. Can't.

Hadn't felt the cold up till now but it is perishing in Camiers. Different cold to ours in Llandrindod. There it is dry, brittle, almost invigorating.

Fuck-Me and I are billeted in an Elephant Hut. That is – a half-circular frame, corrugated-iron roof and three-tiers of beds structured inside.

"Three-star hotel", I try to take the edge off his despair but Fuck-Me doesn't joke any more.

We would have preferred a Nisson-Hut and you couldn't say things are luxurious but hell - almost anything would be after the dugouts, the mud-ruts we've slept in. These huge things are an idea from Canada.

We are given the run of the 'facilities' anyway. The baths! That's the biggest luxury once they've deloused us. To soak, full-length in hot water, to duck your itching head underneath, to ease the pains. The pains.

Crimes, the posh hairdresser from Middleton Street at home is cutting hair in the barber's shop. I can't believe it. He clips the re-growth right to the skull. Fuck-Me and I emerge as convicts yet again into daylight. Old Crimes was quite pleasant. "Pleased to see you Tom," he said. "And I you, Mr. Crimes." I replied. "Fuck-Me". (I'll say it for him).

"I'm going over soon," he goes on.

"Shall I remember you to Arthur and Mary-Ellen?"

"Please do." I say. "- but please don't mention this." I point to my mouth. "I'll tell them later."

"Of course. Of course." He must have some connection with the chapels after all. He looked quite deaconish then. I grin as best I can. S'trewth I'm a mess to look at. It will pass. Have to.

Fuck-Me and I have leave. Neither of us wants to go home. We are going to Paris. You can get down from just outside Ypres now on the train through Amiens. We will be there for Christmas.

The idea came to me idling in the bath. Strange feeling of impermanence. Not as if I can rely on coming home to a hot bath every night: any time I want now, is it? No. Now only <u>this</u> moment to enjoy. The here and now. All confidence in the future went forever the first time we took the mouthful of rum and launched out of the mud into deeper, deeper mud, blood, and severed limbs sticking up as signposts to more mud and mud and MUD. Might as well make the most of the moments.

They plug my teeth. I am to use the antiseptic, take the tablets. The swelling is going down slightly but I am not so uncomfortable. I sit outside the Hotel du Lac, gritting my teeth against thoughts of Judith, Maybelle, Fuck-Me and myself chattering or merely being together quietly in the bar. My uniform has been steamed clean. No lice. I wear my greatcoat. It's going to be bloody parky back in the lines. This cold is like a vice. Can't sit out here long. But I have to write to Captain -----'s mother. I must. I will tell her what a good officer he was. How we all liked him. How brave -. I post it across the road at that Post Office. The lake lies black beneath the trees. Soon be dark.

NINETEEN

Back from Paris. Hated it. Shop-keepers scared stiff of those long-range Jerry shells that fall now and then. They can hear gunfire from the Cambrai area and the news was not good. They kept on, in pigeon-English about Ludendorf's mania to knock out Paris at all costs.

We couldn't do much. The money didn't stretch much farther than a few zinc counters and Fuck-Me wanted to drink. So did I. But getting around the place was depressing. All those huge stone corners leading off the Fauberg St. Germain dwarfed you and although they had art-worked most of the shop-windows with sticky-tape against bomb-blasts and you had to admire the ingenuity of some of the designs, most places were dark early and shut, shut, shut. Christmas, of course.

We had imagined lights, music, high-stepping girls and yes, they probably were there somewhere but we only had a couple of days and it was grey and cold down by the Seine.

"Hello Tommee-e-e, you come avec moi?" Time and time again, the skinny little girls would sidle alongside or stand, legs apart, brazenly in our path. "Oh-h, mon pauvre, mon petit hero", they might exclaim in mock sympathy but 'No thanks' and when we got back to the digs – and were sitting, smoking on the bug-ridden, scratchy blankets, we had to agree that really they were all cash & cunt. Couldn't wait to get out. Sordid dump.

It started to snow the day we left. Thin, small pieces drifting down outside the café where we sat across from the station. They had electric bars rigged up under the striped awnings to attract customers. 'Good idea' I thought. 'Have to tell Haydn Black when (and if) I get back'. There was something 'not me' about Paris. Had I been a student maybe or a rich American pretending to be a student, full of fun and horse-piss and high-falluting ideas about life – well yeah! But to be two five-francs-a-day squaddies, depressed as hell, one, eyes elongated with shock, the other with a mouth bloated into a Baboon's arse … no thankyou.

We spend the rest of our leave in Camiers. Recuperating.

But now. But now -. Don't ask me how we survived the winter. I couldn't answer. Sometimes your fingers almost froze to the gun and some of our fellows got trench-foot from standing or sitting in mud and water for so long. No escaping the conditions. I didn't. I mean I didn't get trench-foot thank Heavens. Got piles though. Most of us have those. Damned nuisance. Difficult at the latrines. You know what those are, don't you? Long planks with holes cut in over a trench. That's where we pick up the news. Gets passed down the line. You find that you don't care a damn about bodily functions anymore. No false modesty. Everybody knows everything. All a joke in the main. We just sit there hoping to blazes Jerry won't send over the mustard-gas when we are on the bog though. Just too, too much old boy. Chin, chin.

We've been up at Beuvry on rest and there's a hell of a flap going on. They want every man in the line; even cooks and mess-waiters. I'm temporarily separated from Fuck-Me and the rest because I was detached by one of the R.S.M.'s to help dig out a trench in front of Adinfer Wood. The Guards Brigade were holding the front line in Ayette but they had no defence behind except a sketch line of the Royal Engineers and no other troops but the sappers to man it. We dug the line in record time and those of us who had been seconded got off in another fifteen minutes to try and find our own lot, each man taking one tin of bully-beef, three biscuits and 150 rounds of ammunition.

I've found the others. We are manning the new trench they have just dug.

If the Boche break through, and I wonder if they have because no Very lights are going up and no S.O.S. rockets, he could very well come within twenty yards without our seeing him. We've got one N.C.O. and three men out front as a standing patrol but Jerry could quite easily have finished them off before we knew anything about it.

Hell, it's cold. We've been standing-to now for five hours. Nearly finished us. It is past midnight and our guns have just pulled out past the line the boys dug and have gone away to the rear.

It is two a.m. before the relief gets here. There is word that the enemy have attacked again. The 92nd Brigade can't retire so General Gough says we are to march back.

We are dead-beat and no one of us could have moved another mile when we arrive at Monchy-au-Bois, at six o'clock. We have had practically no sleep for two days. We sleep in our clothes, two minutes after arrival until half-past four in the afternoon, feeling absolutely perished and hungry when we wake up. We've been picketed out in a field and they tell us Jerry has been shelling most of the day. We don't take any notice even though he's still at it. Blast him!

Today, they tell us, the Guards and the 92nd Brigade are holding the line I helped dig last night and have evacuated all in front of it so that the retreat is going full swing. We are all praying for rain as the only thing to hold Jerry up on our right. We could have held him but he is round on our right flank and a retreat is imperative for General Gough wants the line to hold in one piece.

The roads are crammed with ammunition columns and lorries going west. Everything is a confused, tangled MESS and no one knows where the Boche is on our flanks. Thank Heavens we are not required to work tonight so can scramble down to the village to find some decent(ish) sleeping-quarters.

We move into some huts put up by the French Relief Committee for refugees who had returned to the area after having been evacuated once before. Sorry for them but to us the billets are the height of luxury: walls of corrugated iron, lined with wooden planks but each with three, warm and dry rooms. We plunder the culinary delights left behind without compulsion. Rabbits, hens and a sack of potatoes provide us with the first decent meal we've had for months. Fuck-Me and Jim Fairfield do the cooking. I can just about boil an egg.

We stay here a few days and there are one or two light moments as when, troops in the vicinity who are even less particular about what they pick-up as acquisitions and a battalion of the Kings Own Yorkshire Light Infantry pass through when there is a lull in the battle. Here they come in a long procession, wheeling barrows of vegetables and domestic objets d'art for which they can have no conceivable use. Four men and a four-poster bed are making purposefully for the Mess. Another man, with flowery chamberpots in either hand marches by, a feather boa rakishly draped round his neck. It is bizarre but a welcome diversion despite the blatant thievery. Thank goodness for the English. They make me laugh. Surreal sense of humour. I like that.

There is to be no more retreating and the line is to be held at all costs from now on. It comes slightly Eastward as it runs North but West of Moyenville that Jerry took the night before. It is hard to tell exactly where we are. Hell of a muddle.

One of the reinforcements who came up just now told us Lloyd George was seen getting off the boat at Boulogne a day or two ago. Something's up. You can feel it coming. Some think Gough and even Haig might have to go. Coming out of Beuvry we've just been given extra ammunition and a bag of grenades. "Right!" some major came flapping up and said to us – "Move forward till you meet somebody – our troops <u>or</u> the Germans". – so off we went for maybe two miles when some British troops came along and they told us they'd had to come back three or four miles, that only Jerry was in front of them, none of ours as we would no-doubt find out. "You'll soon find out," they said over their shoulders. They were looking for their own.

We stuck it out right there for a day and a half but orders came through to retire otherwise we would be unable to hold the trenches we had behind this line so back and back we fought a rearguard-action as far as Moyenville again. Boys were singing 'Keep The Home Fires Burning' – but tongue in cheek – when we got there. Then Jerry swamped us and we had to shove off though we were in position, not far from the town on the 28th (March now) when orders were issued yet again to file up on a sunken road and stay there. There was to be no retreating. Hold to the last man. Jerry was making another big bid for Amiens, it was rumoured. Wanted the railway. Wanted to cut us off from the coast. Hold. Hold.

There is some awful shelling coming over. Four deep booms from well behind the German lines and you know you are in for it, before the throbbing, rushing sounds increase and increase in power and horrible intensity. You know then, the damned things might be heading for you but the final vicious swipe of the contraptions as they tear past can give you a bit of a windy feeling in the guts before four huge expositions erupt in some abandoned homes behind you. Howitzer shells are different. With practice you can pick those out in the air if the weather is clear and dart for cover either way even though it only gives you a split second to decide but the Johnsons, or Coal-Boxes, as we call them, owing to the black smoke they give off when bursting, are deadly especially as four come over simultaneously as a rule.

Jerry is obsessional in some ways. Our day usually begins about half-an-hour or so before dawn when the order 'Stand-To' is given and passed silently through the length of the battalion front. This is how we are alerted. Sleepers are woken-up and those of us in the front trenches get the guns manned ready for responding to Jerry's inevitable machine-gun burst, pre-set before dark the evening before to fire on our parapet. It lets rip a devil of a stream of bullets, which skims along our top sandbags. Dirt gets flung into our faces and we all curse the 'bastard' in the filthiest language we can muster. That's where our team come into our own briefly as we return fire with the Vickers at a much faster tempo, shooting a hundred rounds or so across No Man's Land.

The officer who came hurrying down our trench to make sure we were in a state of readiness (sentries up on raised fire-steps peering over at Jerry's lines, the rest of the lads awake, even if relaxed having a puff at a pipe or fag, for instance – though no matches are used in the dark, only a simple lighter that can spark off a thick corded wick into a mere smouldering glow allowed), has gone, leaving a few N.C.O.s who are all over the place keeping an eye on us.

There is no special cause for alarm in all this as a rule. Intermittent rifle fire develops maybe – just to let Jerry know we are wide awake and it's no bloody good his starting anything – to which he then responds. Sometimes this obsessionality of his can be quite useful. In one of the past campaigns evidently, he would only fire the big guns at certain, regimented intervals – so when our boys cottoned on to this, we were able to knock out quite a few batteries.

Good old Fritz. We are glad when it gets light and we can make breakfast. Each section makes its own small fire. We are supposed to use charcoal officially but can't get the supplies so we plunder wood as a regular chore. We've never failed to produce a fire yet anyway and life takes on a bit of meaning again when you can smell the bacon sizzling and there is a billycan of fresh-brewed tea in your hand. Wisps of smoke at various points, show us Jerry making his own breakfast too. It's all mad. All this.

After the interlude, the officer comes back with details of duties and fatigues to be performed. Weapon-cleaning (especially ours) is vital but then pick and shovel work has to be done for trench-maintenance is constant: never-ending. They always need repairing, deepening, widening out, strengthening, either from the weather or enemy-action. Also we have to carry rations and supplies from the rear, interminably.

But not today. Hell they're sending over Minnies. There's the dull thud behind their trenches from the mortar gun! Damn thing is made from a steel drum, packed with high explosive and scrap iron. There one goes – sailing up in the air with a lighted fuse trailing from it. Which way will it go? Two seconds to decide. Please God

– not here. There she goes! Smack! Moment to breathe and brace yourself. Now! Block your ears. Keep down. Keep down ….. you'll be torn apart.

And we are out here dug in to the embankment of this sunken lane that gives good cover except Jerry's got a machine-gun into a farmhouse on our left, shooting down the road at us. It's murder. Not many of us left here. We're losing more chaps all the time. There are some battalions on our left and some to the right but Jerry has come bursting through on our left now and got behind us – firing into our backs. There's only the Company Sergeant Major; Fuck-Me, Jim, J.W., and me left alive here. He says to run for it after the next burst. Can't stay here. Can't do any good. Rats in a trap.

After the next – he gets up and does run for it: if _he_ can get through, he meant, so can we; but he's down, he's down. They've got him. Poor old beggar. He was a good man. Kind. Brave. Folded bundle now – in the middle of the road.

It's no use us sticking here, we say. When it gets dark, we'll go – but then we hear these Germans coming up. We wait until they turn the bend and are in range then … pins out of the Mills Bombs with our teeth (and what's left of mine) and wait, wait – THROW and now there's only this one got through and going for me with his fixed bayonet. I let him have it with mine. He's a tough bugger. Big in the chest. Unbearably intrusive. IN. TWIST. WITHDRAW. He sags, big as he might be and lands at my boot. I ease him away. Either him or me.

We keep quiet after that until about four o'clock the next morning when there is no sign of further activity, then creep out of the hedge and make our way back to the lines that are, after all this, only two hundred yards or so over there, though Jerry is only a spit away from us too. There is a very shallow trench running back so we crawl along it and that's how we manage to rejoin the remnant of our section.

We are in a terrible part of the line now, in front of Oppy Wood and Gavrelle. The Royal Naval Division had attacked from here last year and their bodies are still hanging on the wire where they were caught up.

The trench, now our support line, was called Naval Trench. This was their jumping off point. It is horrible to see the bodies, and worse, when we went up to dig pits for the Stokes-Mortar section, on fatigues, - we were actually digging through bodies everywhere. Fuck-Me is more depressed than me about it – if that is possible and as for J.W. well, I think he might go off his head if we are here too long. The bodies on the wire are a constant warning.

We had been relieved, luckily, the night before the attack on the 28th March. Just as well – for the bombardment started at dawn. The overriding impression was noise, noise, noise, incessant and going on for hours. Gough has been relieved, they say and Rowlinson taken command. Foch's doing. That's why Lloyd George was around, I'll bet. He's sent for fresh troops. Says unless we get reinforcements, Amiens is seriously under threat.

Thousands of guns are firing on the front over there. A terrific noise. Nobody can stand more than three hours of sustained shelling before starting to feel sleepy and numb they say. Bit like an anaesthetic. Usually our guns will start up, or have done on other fronts – to calm Jerry down – but no retaliation this time. He's got a 'free do' at us.

About nine o'clock the O.C. comes by in a hurry – getting all the cooks out into reserve again. They're even putting drivers on the big guns. Desperate for men. We have to hold.

He has split us up. Fuck-Me is to take Jim Fairhurst and two others back to the Naval Trench area – but J.W. is to come with me plus only a new recruit (one is all they can spare) and we're to take up position in the church-tower at Rouvrel, a small village in a sector farther east where Jerry is temporarily bogged down, hiding behind trusses of straw littering the farmland but trying to take the site. We have to hold.

It is literally all hands to the pumps for the allied boys. Don't know where we are getting the ammo. from but it is being brought up most of the day by just about anyone. Drivers, other gunners whose guns have gone west. We have no signals. No telephone-lines. Whiz-bangs sizzle and explode all around, Coal-Boxes, Minnies. The guns hammer, hammer, hammer.

In the tower, we pray separately that a mortar won't take us off. My fingers flick to and fro, forward back, the thumbs pressed down on the firing mechanism. J.W. feeds in the ammo. The new kid cools the gun. He fetches, he carries. 'You're doing well.' I say. He grins. 'Bastards', he tries out now he is in the thick and then louder. Bastards! As a bullet wings off the framed aperture that we fire out of. He's getting it.

It has been raining all day. The long, long spell of fine weather broke before dark and the intermittent showers that have been falling most of the day have become a steady downpour. It abates halfway through the evening when the fighting dies down and a watery moon comes from behind the scudding clouds. We have held on to our position but are relieved around eight o'clock p.m. and told to get back to the trenches, for a rest as there is little likelihood Fritz will attack for he is busy elsewhere. We lug the gun with us, to give it an overhaul before we sleep. The new crew have brought their own but the trenches are in an awful condition for the rain couldn't have been kept out. We have to place some wooden sleepers over the top of our bit to make a roof as best we can. We have to see to the gun. Imperative.

This trench is only three feet across and three deep. We are so tired, we just sit in the bottom, wet or not and get the barrel across our knees to clean it and make sure it is in the best working order for tomorrow – for who knows where we will be needed? We are in mud a foot deep. Backs to the wall. Gradually, our tin hats tilt forward as our heads sink to our chests. 'Only good effect of the rain', I think 'holds 'em up – the Germans'.

Jerry's attack either side the Scarpe, has failed. Fizzled out. A counter-attack North of Arras, by our lot has advanced the British line eight hundred yards and the Canadians, who have taken over from one of our divisions, have moved into a field of dead. Mostly dead Germans, thick on the ground as testimony to the ferocity of our defence. There are token bombardments and local skirmishes all along the front but it is becoming obvious that most of Ludendorff's effort will be directed on Amiens itself.

Serg. says Amiens has been like a haven of luxury behind the lines. Barbers where you can get a shave in hot, clean water and for those with a few Francs to spare, even the prospect of a long soak in a bath with every chance of a friendly Mademoiselle taking pity on your afterwards. "For a price, I'll bet", I interject ruefully remembering Paris. "Ah yes – but there are modest estaminets where all ranks, even those on meagre pay, can stretch to a feast of egg and chips and a few beers", he sniffs before going on eulogising about Chez Josephine, where Josephine herself dashes around at astonishing speed and efficiency as the proprietor. 'Chickens, chickens, chickens, her legendary pommes frites, seafood so delectable that by the end of the evening, the floor is a foot deep in oyster-shells and langoustines served up for the officers. It's a junior subaltern's paradise that.' (sniff).

"Sorry Serg.." Fuck-Me joins in. "That Frog despatch-rider was through here yesterday ... you know, him in the leather jacket, goggles etc. Anyway he says she's probably off. They all are .... All the civvies."

"Nah lad ... Not her, not Josephine. You heard wrong lad. She won't be going."

But she will Serg.

The bombardment of Amiens has begun. They've already holed the station roof. The town is empty. Paul Maze, that dispatch rider, Fuck-Me was talking about, told me a hush has fallen at Longueau, the important railway-junction just outside the city, that no more trains are running. The tracks are empty.

There are shells falling on the outskirts, shooting up high spurts of water and smashing to smithereens all those cloches they force melons and other vegetables under for the Paris spring markets – in that network of waterways made by the Somme.

The town itself is empty, some shops already ransacked. The front of the patisserie has been torn open by a shell and sweets are strewn all over the pavement and across the street.

The place is out of bounds to the troops (except on active service) with Military Police patrolling the town. They are protecting the cathedral hurriedly with a wall of sandbags. No one expected this before.

Paul found Josephine packing her cooking utensils on to a cart. As she left, she called "Tiens, grand" and threw him one of her last cooked chickens. He said he caught it like a rugby pass.

With the bombardment not yet inordinately heavy, the place by Good Friday evening, is still mainly undamaged for all that and although the town is already being evacuated it is still in reasonable shape. The enemy has brought up his big guns however to concentrate fire on all roads leading to Amiens.

All these attacks are Jerry's attempt to 'roll up' the front: to separate the British and French armies by bringing about a progressive displacement of The whole British line North towards the Channel ports. The worst days were the third, fourth and fifth of March but from the twenty-fourth to the twenty-sixth the danger has grown even worse.

On the twenty-first of March, seventy-six 1st class German divisions fell upon twenty-eight British divisions, Jerry advancing behind his surprise, artillery bombardment ... the 'creeping-barrage' our officers call it – across a front of fifty miles on that awful morning when there was mist thickened by gas: chlorine and phosgene with tear-gas shells exploding all over the place.

The gas is lethal of course and the tear-gas an irritant designed to make us take off our respirators. Oh – how horrible it is to be stuck in that mask and only able to see a few yards outside as the mist has now turned into a thick fog under a cascade of screaming shells, explosions and vivid flashes everywhere.

Useless. You're just useless then – but keep your head and just go on, on, on until you can set up the gun where you might be able to do what you must. Hold on. J.W...... at your heels. Can't hear him whimpering with the masks on.

The barrage, intermixed with blistering mustard-gas lasts five hours. Twenty to five a.m. until nine-forty when Hindenburg's operational order of the tenth of March takes effect and German troops emerge from their trenches, pass easily through the gaps in their own wire, cross No Man's Land and begin to penetrate our position.

We are dazed but enough of us defending plus our supporting artillery have survived to offer scattered resistance as Jerry comes forward. He is firing blind himself by the Pulkowski method that depends on meteorological observation, but his gunners have missed or overshot some key targets so as he comes into sight out of No Man's Land, our men on the big guns behind, with us on the Vickers, let them have it, while the surviving trench garrisons man the parapets.

Jerry keeps coming over a bank in large numbers about two or three hundred yards away and has already taken a front line in the 6th divisional sector. We resist, and resist and there still appear to be hundreds of the buggers coming on over that bank but they might just have well saved themselves the bother eventually. We've certainly halted that lot.

Although most of the British line has been overrun, the advance has been halted. Those Jerries who have not been mowed down are pressing again towards Rouvrel huh! – but Rouvrel is a stronghold for us now. The boys are in the houses and more machine-gun crews up in 'our' church tower, spewing such merciless fire that Jerry can make no headway there.

Fuck-Me and co. are down at Grivesnes and they haven't budged either. Jerry's advance at Morevil has not been nearly enough to achieve its object and north of Morevil, where the British and the French are joined at Hangard, the attack fell across the front where Villers-Bretonneux stands on the Roman road leading directly to Amiens. All the inhabitants have fled. The towers of Amiens can clearly been seen from the little town on its shoulder of flat land less than ten miles from the city.

The ground falls away on either side to the banks of the Somme North of the plateau and to the river Luce looking South; so the dead ground, rifts in the valleys: all clefts and gullies, are a great advantage for the enemy creeping forward to fight for the elevation above. A commanding position.

The battlefront runs across it, both valleys, and our troops are ranged in depth behind it. We are moved down to join them. We have to hold on to the high ground.

We are not an army, as the top brass back in Whitehall would understand it now. We have a brigade here, a brigade there plus divisions in name only, reinforced by battalions and even companies thrust any-old-how into the line: a mixture of units growing all the time as troops arrive from the North and men who had retreated South with the French army (who are worried about Paris) are brought back.

The fighting rages all day and the rain pours and continues to pour down but although we are pushed back in certain places, nowhere does the line give way and the C.O. is pleased with us. He says we have done as much as anyone to repel attacks and hold the enemy back. It has been literally – all hands on deck.

After dark, troops of both sides labour on through the mud, hauling up fresh supplies of ammunition for the guns, food for the men, carrying off the wounded, floundering back and forth with messages, orders, slog, slog, slog through the darkness and filthy mud to take up new positions or working to consolidate the positions now held.

At last we get back to our trench. Jim Fairfield is sitting on the near fire-step, head down. The two new members of his team are half-standing white-faced and silent beside him. They sink into the mud as J.W. my new No. 3 and I slide down the wall.

"Where's Fuck-Me?" I ask.

"He's on their wire ... stuck out in No Man's Land". Jim says. "He keeps calling. We couldn't get him. They wouldn't let us –."

"Calling? He's alive? What the hell do you mean?" I am glaring at him, I realise ... "What was he doing at the wire?"

"There was a lull. He thought we could get a drop on them as they came. He copped one – bad. Told us to take the gun and get back. It was impossible to make a move after. His cries are awful. "Tom", he lets out now and again ... or "Maybelle. Maybelle".

"Come on!" I say. "Show us the way."

"Tom, we'll be court-martialled. That's what the C.S.M. said. Not to think of it. Needed on the machine-gun. Too few of us."

"Whose with me?"

"I ... I'll come Tom, boy." J.W. bursts into tears. Jim stands, swaying with fatigue. "No J.W. you're No. 1 tomorrow don't forget if we are delayed for any reason." I say.

"And you three", I tell the others.

"Do everything he tells you. – He's a good man."

"Let me –."... My No. 3 pleads but "It only needs two of us", I tell him "and Jim knows the way".

Thank Heavens for all those burial-party sorties into No Man's Land. We know the drill. I confess I am praying to the Lord as we approach. I know Jim is. I can hear him murmuring "In the Name of Jesus, in the Sweet Name of Jesus" so I know we are one.

It is the most pitiful sound I am ever likely to hear, I hope. Every now and then. Very soft. Not whining ... just a deep groaning, labouring "To-o-om. Tom. Come and get me" and then after a silence, again "To-o-om. To-o-om!"

We know where he is. We plaster fresh mud on our hands and faces, the backs of our necks ... off the walls of the trench. The squaddies standing-to want to know what the hell we are doing. We indicate. They understand. They are on edge and upset themselves by the awful cries coming from the wire.

We ask where the N.C.O.s are and are helped to bypass any obstructions, are given whispered instructions as to how to avoid them forestalling what we have to do. We ask them to keep an eye open and if they see us coming back to get a couple of stretcher-bearers standing by. "No sweat", they comply.

No Very lights. Nothing. Jerry is busy cranking up his guns otherwise glad of the lull, I'll bet. Silently, we slither over the parapet and drag ourselves on our bellies over the mud. There are plenty of shell-holes to conceal us if the balloon goes up.

Out of the mud and up behind Fuck-Me in one movement. I have my arms around him trying to unhook him out of the tangled mess behind. He sobs. "I knew it," he gasps. "Boy – I know –."

"Sh ... Fuck-Me old fellah." I whisper. "Move your bloody arm can't yer. That's it. That's IT ... Come on. You poor old sod. Home to café and croissants it is. Sorry about this."

We've got him off the wire. He's bleeding from the chest, I think – and the neck. It's going to hurt him – but if we're lucky … it won't take long.

We turn him face down and grab him either side under the armpits and start running as best we can, bent double back the long, long stretch to our trenches.

We are nearly there, but suddenly caught in a bright beam. Had it. But no! A voice calls from the German side. "Hey Tommy!" but we slosh on.

"Drop me Tom. Drop me boy – run for it!" Fuck-Me gasps. Jim and I grip him tight. Tighter. We are nearly there. One up the arse I expect – as we take the last step. "Keep going Jim!" I say.

We have reached the line. "Good for you", calls the voice behind us! A Hun gentleman, I think. I thank the Lord.

We lower Fuck-Me into the trench where the C.S.M. is waiting with two stretcher-bearers. I don't care what happens now, except I have to give Fuck-Me a fag – before they cart him off down and out of the lines. I light up and press it against his mouth. His great, rugby-ball eyes shine, he smiles briefly, he coughs, he dies.

"Chest," says the R.S.M. after the inspection. "Fatal wound. Won't ask your names lads. Well done. Return to your section please."

"Thank you sir,"

"Thank you sir," we say and stumble away down the trench as they place a greatcoat over Fuck-Me's face and prepare to take him away. Away forever more. Do men cry? I don't know about the others but Jim and I are bawling like babies as we stumble back to the others. We will stop before we get there but now – now.

Rosalind

The 'United' service is at the Presbyterian Chapel today. All the various, non-Conformist denominations get together at times as things are so serious on the Front, whatever that really means, plus being Easter Sunday, we are all down here. The chapel is packed.

I love coming in. The vestibule is very welcoming, brass-handles to the doors either side and soft, clean hands of the gently smiling sidesmen holding them open for you after you've been given the hymnal and a copy of the Bible.

"Good morning Miss Hamer" they nod, "Morning Mr. Evans-Evans".

They all know us of course. There is room on the left at the back. We are shown into the long, yellow-coloured, wooden pew, sit and bow our heads in prayer. Mary-Ellen is in the third pew from the back, the other side the partition with Bernard and Colette Arrowsmith sitting beside her. Billy is at the end near the aisle. Arthur is seated in the Big Pew facing the congregation under the pulpit and slightly to the right. His hair is now silver. He has seen us enter. So has Mary-Ellen who half-bows her beautiful head, her own curls now almost completely silver, herself, smiling approval yet still managing to keep the profile turned to its best advantage.

The Reverend Stefan George will take this service, but during the Long Prayer, my thoughts wander. I sat with Tom once, over there beside Mary-Ellen. Billy was only a small child and Tom kept making him laugh.

When it is time for the 'collection' the sidesmen take round the plates then stand at the back, against the doors until the organ stops playing. They then walk down the aisles as swiftly as possible to deposit the 'offering' on the Communion Table to be blessed by the Minister above in the pulpit; but when Cyril, The Abbey, who was officiating on the side nearest the Edwards' pew, was heading for the front, Tom had caught him by the tail of his best suit jacket and held him back, one-handed while poor Cyril, knowing what had happened tried to pull free. Of course Eloise Edwards and Bill were in fits, though one look at Mary-Ellen's face had given me the shivers on Tom's behalf. Ida Owen was there too. Impassive. Head back, eyes sideways, hands clasped low in front. Oh Tom. I told Jenkin, once … but he twisted his thin mouth in disapproval. "Childish!" he had snorted.

I mustn't criticise him. We are getting engaged tomorrow. Jenkin doesn't want a long engagement. We are to be married in June.

Ah Stefan George is announcing a hymn. It is to be sung to the tune of 'For Those In Peril On The Sea' and the words have been written especially for this occasion when our troops are having to fight for their lives (and ours) so they say but I can't imagine it.

The papers are full of the 'gravity of the situation' and evidently Paris is in uproar after the Germans shelled that church on Good Friday.

We stand to sing.

> *Lord God of Hosts whose mighty hand*
> *Dominion holds on sea and land,*
> *In Peace and War Thy Will we see*
> *Shaping the larger liberty.*
> *Nations may rise and nations fall,*

Thy changeless purpose rules them all.
When death flies swift on wave or field,
Be Thou a sure defence and shield!
Console and succour those who fall,
And help and hearten each and all!
O, hear a people' prayers for those
Who fearless face their country's foes!
For those to whom the call shall come
We pray thy tender welcome home,
The toil, the bitterness, all past,
We trust them to thy home at last.
O hear a people's prayers for all
Who, nobly striving, nobly fall!
For those who minister and heal,
And spend themselves, their skill, their zeal —
Renew their hearts with Christ-like faith,
And guard them from disease and death.
And in Thine own good time, Lord, send
Thy peace on earth till Time shall end!

Stefan George stopped singing in the first verse and I did in the second. Suddenly realised I was not so much concerned with – 'those that fall' as with the wallowing in the idea of us all affected by tragedy and actually enjoying the sound of our own voices making music. Almost making ourselves sad – on purpose.

Arthur's beautiful voice blends with the facing 'audience'. He has a right to look and sound soulful. He has an underage son at the front. Mary-Ellen never sings but her head is proudly up. Billy is staring at Stefan George, unmoving and Jenkin is singing beautifully beside me. His long white fingers hold the hymnal at just the right angle to his bespectacled eyes, the loose-leaf entry for today's service held inside the hard, dark-blue covers. I read mine. It is a poem by one John Oxenham. New. I don't like it.

Things must be worse than Jenkin will allow must be. After all, they have never permitted newspapers to appear on Good Friday before and Winston Churchill, that new Minister of Munitions, has even been urging munitions-workers to carry on during the holidays, to speed up production to replace ABANDONED guns and the stock of ammunition. Steelworks, engineering shops and shipyards are also working through the holidays they said in the Wellington Journal and Radnor Times, to turn out tanks, aircraft and ships …. All more badly needed than ever – when we all thought it would be over long ago. Even textile factories carrying on non-stop because they want half-a-million uniforms for new recruits!

I wonder what we will do tomorrow? They are putting on extra matinees at the Kino and the Grand Pavilion over the holidays – and some famous comedian is going to appear down in the Rock Park Pump Rooms. Forget who. Barnes is it? No – can't remember - Yes I can …. Bobby Howes! – Perhaps I'll get Jenkin to take me there. There are all sorts of concessions being made this bank holiday. Race meetings … um.m. – but if we go, we'll have to use the trap for there are no charabangs or special trams allowed this year.

It's nearly two years since I last saw Tom. Sometimes I have day-dreams about meeting him then turning my nose up into the air and walking off just leaving him standing. Why didn't he keep in touch more often? Why didn't he come home?

We are meeting Eloise and Raymond Cox afterwards, up the Lake in the Chalet for coffee and ices. Since they've been married, she is different somehow. More subdued – yet still able to make you laugh – just raising one of those thin, black eyebrows. They are moving to Kent next week. Raymond has got a job teaching at a school in Dartford. Everything is changing.

I'm not going to tell her about Jenkin and I getting engaged. When we are married, I'll write and let her know. Don't want Tom informed yet. We are keeping it quiet anyway. Mam and Dada want it that way. They are afraid something might happen to put a stop to things before the bloody (sorry Lord) ring is on the finger. How Tom and I would laugh - .

Jenkin and I are walking through the Ridgebourne up to Pentrosfa, where we are having the house built. It is on a private drive up there. Exclusive. The Council have got the road up – or rather have dug into the verge beside Edwards' Bakery (no relation to TyCanol) here on the corner.

I stop and Jenkin stops with me. "Why are we here?" he asks mildly after a time.

"I'm just thinking what it must be like Jenkin."

"What, my dear?"

"Just arriving somewhere - say a field or something. Having to stop, dig a trench – then get in it and LIVE in it! Jenkin – how horrible."

"Oh, I'm sure it's not as bad as all that. They probably have plenty of Primus-stoves, you know- I'll wager they have it fitted out like no-body's business, Rosalind."

"But the fighting! - 'Going over the top' and all that, Jenkin … can you imagine it… what if -?"

"Oh … HA Ha … good Heavens Rosalind – don't let your imagination run away with you my dear. A lot of that is exaggerated no end. To sell the newspapers. I'll bet Edwards, for example, is having the time of his life out there. What …. Vin Blanc merely half-a-franc a litre – so someone told me. Probably flat out on the tiles most of the time. Do come on dear, lets see how they're getting on … then home to my place, eh? Mother's toasting tea cakes and boiling a nice fresh egg for us."

"Whoever thought it would turn so cold Jenkin. It was so lovely, all those weeks of early sunshine. Look – even the lilacs are out in full bloom and I actually saw yellow on the golden-chain tree at the top of the dingle –."

"Laburnum dear."

"What? Oh … laburnum, yes … but Jenkin it's gone so damp and cold. I'm quite chilled".

"Come along Rosalind. Let's get on, shall we?"

I don't feel like me. I am acting a part. Have sold out. Lost in unreality. It has no depth. It has depth – but I can't touch bottom to push myself out. How has this happened? I have betrayed myself and can't summon the desire to see a way forward. A blanket has been thrown over my head.

TWENTY

Tom

Easter Sunday morning we had been fighting for hours then ordered to join up with the Canadians right on our left flank, north of
Amiens.

Even by this day, although most of the residents had already gone,
there were isolated groups of refugees still trudging by as the 13th
Battalion, Rifle Brigade marched through to reinforce the line.

They had been marching for many miles and were shagged-out.
All at a low ebb. They were given a break in Amiens – so they just
lay on the cobbles in Main Street. We had got tangled up with them
so, done in ourselves, we crashed out as well.

The chaplain, Reverend Pargiter-Owen came along. He had seen
us shambling to a halt and when the boys got going again, I saw he
was carrying three men's rifles, they were so done in.

They were going in our direction so we tagged on but all these
French refugees were passing, poor little blighters, so the Rev. got in
front and asked us to sing: "Sing any old thing lads" … to try and let
the French see we were not downhearted.

Well we started. Marched through Amiens after all, singing and it brightened us up too, made us step out regardless. I don't suppose the Padre was very keen on the words to 'Mademoiselle From Armentieres' though and then my stars! - 'One-Eyed Riley' – but he didn't seem to mind. Kept us singing all the way through Amiens. Easter-Sunday morning Mary-Ellen. Flat out on the cobbles then 'One-Eyed Riley' with the Rev., - (a good bloke, always up front with the boys in the line, they say) - probably very far from the impression that we were hymn singing. His idea evidently was 'Where my lads are, I am'. Why can't they all be like that?

Another good one is Colonel Frizell, one of the Battalion-Commanders. He couldn't find his men when he got back to France after having his Blighty leave interrupted by the situation out here.

Eventually he caught up with them at Autreches, a long way South near the forest round Compiegne and intended to congratulate them on their excellent performance but as he stood facing them – he couldn't speak.

The men he stood before were hollow-eyed, bedraggled, exhausted and hardly enough left to make up a decent-sized company. Eventually, after a long, embarrassing silence, all he could manage to utter was

"Well done, men. Dismiss!"

Colonel Frizell had hoped they might snatch a good night's rest but it was not to be. Just after midnight they had to set off to slog three miles to Vic-Sur-Aisne to board buses to carry them north. They have picked us up en route.

During the rest of the weekend, fighting for possession of the woods and small towns in the Avre valley beneath it is fierce and different sites change hands many times.

By nightfall on the 31ˢᵗ, after the huge German effort along the line between Montdidier and Amiens – then beyond to Albert and the Ancre – only a piece of Morevil Wood remains in our hands. Jerry has captured Rifle Wood to our North, as well and that is almost on the roadside of the highway into Amiens. Cavalry have been ordered up to counter-attack and retrieve the situation tomorrow but I have to go north again, nearer the Canadians. Machine-guns are needed up near Arras, Lens.

Hellish tired. I am covered in dust, head to toe. We all are. This tripod weighs a ton. Jim's got the barrel and J.W. is staggering behind with the rest of it. Our new recruit is well broken in now, but he is limping. Got a sore heel. They can be the very devil – like my piles. The kid can hardly walk. Why do I call him that? He's two whole years older than me, he says. I feel ancient. I've got bloody thin – but so what? As long as my breeks don't fall off. Why do we have to bandage ourselves round with these perishing puttees? Mine haven't been unwound for days now. Like plaster casts. All the mud. We itch. The lice are everywhere.

Here's the Regimental Sergeant Major. What the hell does he want? He takes the gun-barrel off Jim and orders him away to another half-section who are without enough crew. J.W. and I are to go with him.

The limbers come up and we fall in beside the offside mule. Loaded with ammunition-boxes. There are trees banked on the right but common-land over on our left for a time. There are rooks around. One, two, three. The sky is very cold, pale silver, washed out after

all that rain with powder blue and grey-ridged clouds. A burst of pigeons goes up on our left. Flat country with a slight rise towards the
horizon, with one poplar left sticking up on the immediate skyline.
We trudge on. Don't like this area. Horrible feeling of hopelessness,
poverty. We pass peasants of some sort scrabbling about in the earth
on our right. Isolated gangs of them on a big flat field. Why are they
here? Senseless – emphasising a displacement that seems to have
come upon us all.

The ridge we are making for has come into sight ahead on our left.
Thought from back there it might be a slight rise but it is sharp and
high – all round. Black on green. Like coal. There are coal-tips all
around the horizon. Jerry is behind that ridge. We have to hold this
territory to stop him getting down to Arras and thence to Amiens.
We are really pushing it here, ahead of the line. Not far from Douai.
Dourges. A church in the distance with a hat on. One of those. This
is a non-place. Those pickers, grubbing in the black soil, didn't even
look up as we passed. No acknowledgement: nothing. Not even a
wave. We are the walking dead. That's how I feel anyway. Depressed
to hell in this ash-heap of a landscape. There has been massacre after
massacre here. You can feel it.

We manoeuvre over a canal, taking it easy with the mules for
the bridge is broken. They struggle and the muleteer is off and tugging at the bridle up front. I reach up and plant a hefty flat-hander
on the rump of the struggling beast. Stubborn buggers in the main
– but he plunges forward and up the bank. There is an avenue of very
big poplars leading down a track at the base of the ridge, a deserted
farmhouse halfway along.

We enter the yard. "Phew-w!" says the Sergeant Major. "Shovels
lads … get digging." There are dead Germans lying about, gone black
and stinking. We get them under while the R.S.M. surveys the ridge

and points out a hollow, some way up on a smaller rise before the big one behind.

"Up there," he indicates. "Make it snappy lads, before they realise we're set up".

He, J.W. No. 3 and I, energy quickened unbelievably, tear across another deep ditch with a stream at the bottom, out the other side and up, on to the exposed hill-side, up, up, up – and fling ourselves into the hollow. We set up the gun and position the angle to the rim of the height facing us. The limbers are down in the yard, sheltered behind one of the sheds.

It looms above us, black – no, mostly black but with green patch-es, and us halfway up this smaller heap in front of it. Is it an old coal-heap? No – can't be. It stretches too far – although the plain running off is as flat as a pancake either side. The main mountain comes down in levels, you can see that now and there are a few skeletons of trees on the tops. I can see a cathedral pile – way, way over to our left. Where? Not Douai. No … Arras. That will be Arras. Douai is over the other way. Just a spit up the road.

"Watch out … they've seen us," the Sergeant Major speaks softly out of the side of his mouth. He is my No. 2 on the gun! He looks at his watch. "14.00 hours", he mutters. He is probably thinking of his reports.

Jerry has appeared all along the skyline. The silhouettes are like black crows looking down. I depress the firing-mechanism, thumbs and fingers crossing and re-crossing, sweeping the barrel round from horizon to horizon. J.W. lies on my right with the water and the cool-ing apparatus. We kick aside obstacles left by our former defenders, now gone for good, cramming the debris into the bank with our boots. It is all expediency. No time for -. No time.

Rosalind

We have arranged to meet at two o'clock. Most people will be in then, resting after lunch. It will be quiet in the Dingle and around the Grand Pavilion before the matinee is due to start. We are going to see the film afterwards for the weather is still damp and cold, though not as wet as Good Friday and yesterday. Mary Pickford!

I am wearing a grey woollen coat with a fur-trim that falls all the way down over the breast-area and is free then to swish around over my boots, for fashions are designed in simpler and straighter lines now; for instance this dress I've got on underneath has a square neck-line, a blouse effect, cinched in with decorated panels but then these nice, soft pleats descending. Beautiful material. Dove-grey with the panels in the most delicate lilac and blue you've ever seen ... encrusted with pearls. Tiny, tiny pearls. I love it. I bought a hat at the Limes too ... off Nesta Davies – (don't care about all that now)... for the occasion. Jenkin and I are going to sit side by side on one of the benches up on the top, outside balcony of the Pavilion and then at half-past two precisely, he says, he is going to slip the ring on my finger. An emerald surrounded with diamonds. Twenty-two carat gold.

The hat is like a pouched cap with a high crown. Jenkin is thrilled with it. Says I look like a little coal-heavier. The boots are grey suede with such neat buttons you have to hook all the way up the sides. Both the hat (fur-felt) and the boots are pale lilac trimmed emerald. Oh dear – it's two o'clock. The black cast-iron stairway clangs under my heels as I trip up the steps. Mustn't be late. Can't help laughing – but he's a stickler for time. Mum and Dada say that's why he will be so successful in business. Tom hated business.

...Outrageous. He could be such a laugh though.

Tom

We are running out of ammunition. "You go ..." the R.S.M. orders me. "I'll take the gun."

I sidle out of my position and over the shallow side of the hollow. Blimey. I am running like hell down the hillside, crash-down under the bank of the small stream, up the other side as a bullet crashes into the mud alongside my scrabbling arm but I'm out and over, into the farm-yard and yanking a couple of ammo-boxes off the limbers. Have you ever seen them? Ammo-boxes! Well they're green and bloody heavy.

I get back over the ditch, shoving, cursing and heaving with the things held to my chest – had to ... if they hit the ground how the hell would I pick them up again? Then start back up the hill, ducking my tin hat down over my balls for Jerry has got my measure. Got the drop on me. The bullets are pinging like hailstones all round, jumping and whining. The first time: the <u>only</u> time, I've been frightened. I don't waste my energy cursing. I pray somehow. I am THERE. Throw myself over the side, boxes and all. J.W. makes a grab for the ammunition under my struggling carcass. The R.S.M. shoves over, J.W. hands him a belt, he feeds it in ready for use. No. 3 has J.W.'s water bag and lies now to my right. J.W. lets out a small whimper. The R.S.M. consults his watch. "14.30 hours" he states. Jerry is ranged all round the rim of this crater. I depress my thumbs and take the lot. Rat, tat, tat, tat, tat, tat, tat. Ratta-tat, tat, tat, tat, tat, tat.

If I get home in one piece, I'll settle down, live a quiet life now – after…. After …. Rat-a-tat tat, tat, tat … yes … I'll RATA, RATA, RATA, TAT, TAT, TAT …. I'll marry Rosalind Hamer. We'll be buddies for life. We are buddies.

"Cease-fire" mutters the R.S.M. It is silent. No one moves or shows on the horizon. We've held. We've held. <u>Done</u> it.

"Easy does it" he says.

" We won't be going yet."

Rosalind

"Two-thirty Jenkin."

He smiles and takes the emerald out of its little black bag. I extend my third finger, left hand. He slips it on. It doesn't quite fit: is too big. "Never mind," he says … it can easily be fixed Rosalind. Not to worry. Very few things go right, first time. Keep it on, won't you? We'll have a guard put on it tomorrow". A sudden chill goes up my spine. Nice to have second chances. Mustn't think though, Must not!

"Don't start that!" as Mam would say. "Just be glad you've got a nice, steady, young man to look after you."

"Don't sigh Rosalind", says Jenkin. "It will be all right dear. Trust me."

He thinks I'm sighing for the bloody ring. I suddenly feel real for a moment in a fog of unreality. Caught. Trapped. Betrayed – not by Tom, oh no … but a convention I was outside but now am hooked into. I have betrayed myself to appease the wrong people. Why have they demanded an appeasement for the real me? Mustn't think. Must not think.

Tom

We've been relieved and are on the road to Arras. Our billet is in this farmhouse at the side of the road. The yard is full of St. Bernard dogs. Never seen anything like them before. Big as ponies. I love them. Now <u>this</u> would be an idea – for back home. Breed these – along with the horses.

All sweeping spaces round here. Quiet at the moment but seas and seas of mud and mist hanging over clumps of trees and lines of very dark poplars where they are still standing. There is an avenue of silver birch on our left and about fifty yards this side the farmhouse but on our right, a figure of Christ on the cross. Here the cross itself has been carved out of wood and the figure, a lovely brown, semi-browny-grey, I think cut out of stone. There's a church beyond, up the hill and someone has arranged a bunch of flowers on the pedestal at the foot of the crucifix: red, orange and white. The grass at the verge seems to go up to it in a point.

There is very little cover. Open plains with some kind of rock-structure sticking up over there. Big farms and some Friesian cows in the yards. No Herefords (ha.ha). Brown and white cattle scattered about. Tomorrow we go back down into Arras for a couple of day's rest.

Yes we descend into this city through a canyon of medieval cliffs. Now on the outskirts. The air is very fresh and bracing and it is very quiet everywhere. White houses. Archways.

Down in the centre there are nine, great plane trees in a small municipal park (five at the front facing the main street, four at the back) arranged around the statue of a monk. There is a green lawn with seats but we throw ourselves down on the grass and sleep.

Eventually we find a billet in an abandoned house towards the outskirts, that has a pond in the garden with water-plants growing out of it in the shadow of an old church with a grey/blue slate roof and behind that again, the reddest, red creeper I have ever seen; almost plum-red with touches of orange in it. Really beautiful. The church has a tower and I wonder if it's the same one I saw from the hollow, halfway up that terrible mountain.

We find a means of washing and sprucing ourselves up with the aid of cold water and cracked mirrors. Told to make the most of things. Sergeant Major says orders have arrived. A big push is expected again for Amiens. We are going back south in the morning.

There is an auberge down the road: Le Regent. Small, almost a country atmosphere, dark inside until you approach the big window facing out on to that red creeper.

The most beautiful girl I have ever seen is sitting half-on to the window but gazing into the wall opposite where her friend sits facing her. It is a special snug sort of a place, old fashioned settles backing on to painted brick walls, leaving enough space for conversation over an ancient oak table.

I can't take my eyes off the girl, who does not turn or in any way indicate that she has noticed us enter. Good. Not at anyone's beck and call then. Her hair is waved back over her ears, cut short and in tendrils that curl forward again on to her jaw-line. The hair is dark-blonde but lit by the sun so that it shines very fair in wisps that half obscure the far side of her forehead. Her brow is round and golden over a straight short nose and her lips protrude, full and sensuous looking over the resolute little chin held proudly over a white, un-lined, clear-cut throat. She is slim. She is dressed in a loose, unre-stricting garment. Eau-de-nil silk-crêpe Rosalind would tell me I'm sure if she was here. I smile.

The girl opposite watches me closely as I slowly sink down on to the polished wooden settle, hands on my knees, sliding closer to the beauty, not taking my eyes off her profile for one second.

J.W. and No. 3 stand, watchful in the back of my eye merging with the brown shadows under the hops hanging from the ceiling on wide steps leading down out of the bar.

I reach the girl and put up my left hand to turn her towards me. To my everlasting credit, I do not flinch as the great sorrow in her lovely brown eye meets the heartbreak in the green of my own. The right-hand side of her face has been shot away.

I hug her to my chest as hard as it is possible without crushing her. She cries and cries into my uniform. Her friend sinks to the planks, head on her arms, rocking from side to side. J.W. cries. No. 3 and I don't cry but we shut our eyes before he sits over the table, patting the other. The bar is silent. When I look up, a labourer smokes hunch-shouldered and resigned over his cigarette as only the French are able, his companions gazing up, mouths screwed while the inn-keeper stands, legs apart, flapping a cloth staring straight at us, nodding, nod-ding. Approving. When we march out he says "Au revoir", not goodbye.

TWENTY ONE

There has been a temporary halt in the fighting and the situation has become reasonably secure. General Rawlinson has been sending congratulatory messages to all troops but I must say we would be more encouraged if we knew for sure that Ludendorff had laid off for a spell.

He had hoped to take Amiens on the 31st of March after the Mars offensive failed the day before they say. Hadn't expected that had he? Our furious defence must have surprised him: all those places he tried to break through along our line; but we stopped him. Finding out the full extent of their losses, he has now had to decide to restore his supply lines also to rest and reinforce his battle-weary troops. It is rumoured some of his own staff wanted to call a halt entirely but the old 'Ironsides' has made it clear he has no intention of giving up. He is adamant that his next bid to take Amiens must succeed and is preparing to that end. One of the Captains went out on a raid to capture prisoners to be interrogated so has even got the date: 4th of April.

Before dawn. We've been up, shit and shaved hours back now, guns prepared, just time to snatch a couple of biscuits and some water before the rum-ration comes round but <u>cloud-burst</u> and it starts bucketing down. We continue to stand-to, but without rain-capes for they would only hinder us if we have to fight hand to hand.

Half-past four and the enemy bombardment begins. Our hands are chilled-raw from setting up the guns and holding the position, feet like ice sinking deeper and deeper into the wet ground already drenched from the weekend and rapidly becoming a quagmire. Soaked and in need of sleep we crouch doing our best to cover our weapons and wait for signs of the attack.

SOS signals soar above our lines now the guns have started, flaring against the rain streaming down without end.

Dawn is slow to break and when it does come creeping over No Man's Land, there is a thick mist. We are stuck, peering into the distance as far as possible, eyes watering with cold and strain until ten past eight when we begin to see movement from the other side.

The barrage has been huge. Jerry has had his guns registered on our batteries, knocking out guns miles behind the line. He <u>started</u> on our front line then gradually lengthened his range until he got the artillery before gradually shortening it back to us again.

This goes on until eleven o'clock. Three times he has done it. Some heavies landed not far away from us but only managed to cover us with mud and shake us up a bit. Ah – here the buggers come now. Full marching order be damned. They mean to go for Amiens non-stop. Four divisions Serg. says – against only two of our brigades.

They are advancing in massed formation but we are cutting them down like the mowing-machine going through hay. Here's the second wave. "Steady J.W. Our lads are going over, stop! – Here hang on to the gun – I'm hopping up to meet them until our boys are out of the way". I grab my rifle, propped up ready. It is only the second time, apart from that Kraut in the lane, I have experienced proper hand-to-hand fighting with the bayonet. Hell's bloody bells – it's heavy. We are mad and fighting like wild things. Get back, you bastards, you baggy-drawed, piss-pot helmeted, dogs ... IN – TWIST – Out – OFF ... but he keeps getting reinforced and we are pushed back about 1,000 yards. Hope J.W. and No. 3 have saved the gun.

Don't like this. We have received a direct order to relinquish posts. We wouldn't dream of it without that directive because even though the fighting has been so intense and the shelling getting worse – it seems to me that Jerry is lacking spirit. It's hardly a mystery. They've been at it for two weeks same as us – but at least we have not been expecting tremendous gains – and they must be disappointed. They slog at you like robots. Open-mouthed. Heavy. Heavy. Sleepwalkers.

Those of ours down along the curve of the railway are in a bad position now and their Corps Commander himself has admitted he wouldn't be able to hold if strongly attacked. Standing fast against heavy bombs is a different matter to hand-to-hand fighting and Jerry is firing trench-mortars over the village they are holding at close range. He's aiming at the railway embankment of course to stop our supply-lines and that curve of the line has made it easier for him to break in on our boys' right flank and fire into their backs.

It's a good thing our commanders could see that coming and have set up a new line of posts and trenches behind on the hill.

We have been ordered to retire there but we hardly have time to draw breath for the C.O. doesn't intend for us to stay long. One good thing: I've found J.W. , No. 3 and the gun. The gun. I take the tripod.

There's a battalion in extended order behind a hill over there and we are told to go up ready to support but almost as soon as we set up the gun, Jerry gets our measure and is shelling us heavily with instantaneous-fuse shells. The buggers burst as soon as they hit the ground – then the pieces fly level with it. Deadly.

We are supposed to do what we can here then move a bit to the right to reinforce some blokes in a cutting alongside the railway.

This lot, we're covering now, went over as calm as if on parade – but shit! – look at that … it's all MAD … soon as they hit the skyline, Jerry's machine-guns opened up … they're going down, one after the other. Of all the pointless, fucking, blasted, bloody, senseless plans …. Who are the clowns leading us? Who the hell? WHAT the hell?

Now it's our turn to move. We start, bent double over the gun, (I've got the tripod as usual), tin hats tucked over the vitals, we get up near a bank and follow it along for a way but Jerry's watching us and following us up with shrapnel until, damn – now we are in full view on this bit of hillside sloping down to the railway where we are needed. Hell, machine-guns have opened up from Edgehill Clearing Station on our flank and Fritz is also firing point-blank at us with his artillery. Bullets are whistling past in every direction, clipping up the turf almost at our feet, shells bursting all the way.

"Keep dodging – like me, J.W." I shout as we dance from one foot to the other, running like hell for our position.

There are others running with us. Seems to be a few men at a time, taking advantage (like us) of whatever cover there is left – and they are still with us when we make it, unscathed, thank the Lord (and I mean that) to the troops in the cutting.

There are men lying dead all over the place and Jerry seems to be all around us. If you try it up on the railway-line they fire from Edgehill Clearing Station, then if we get up facing that way they get us from behind: from the other side of the railway.

We wait a bit and assess which side the heaviest fire is coming from then settle down facing the Clearing Station and blaze away at all the windows that we can see in the huts, but blow me, we've only been here a short time when word comes through that the 49th can't connect with those we are supporting down here, because of their own casualties. No bloody wonder. I think of the silhouettes on the hillside; but now we are told we have to go down after dark and clear Jerry out of the Clearing Station, then dig in, in front of it to establish a connection between the 49th and 52nd Batteries.

We do this in company with those left from the 52nd, using nothing more than a bit of rifle fire.

What a day. All along the front the fighting is going on well into the evening and after we finish cleaning out the huts down there – the English artillery get going – shelling Albert.

The medics have been amazing all through. They have been on the go for days now, across miles and miles of the retirement, making superhuman attempts to rescue the wounded. Stretcher-bearers are risking death or capture rather than leave the wounded behind and at the Casualty Clearing Stations they say it is terrible: every bed occupied in the tents, stretchers laid down in every available space and all they can do with the overflow is settle the wounded on tarpaulins in the open, covered with blankets to wait their turn in the operation-tent, a bed in a marquee ward or … the worst: a place in a convoy of lorries if the Clearing Station itself is forced to evacuate. The <u>lucky</u>

man is carried on board an ambulance train. Twelve trains a day are shuttled down the line, (the journey ever shorter as Jerry advances), to hospitals at the base. Etaples? Etaples.

But, it is the evening of the 5th April now. It has come down the line that Jerry's gains are so meagre, the map-adjustments need barely be made and Ludendorff's gamble has not come off, there has been no big and final breakthrough so forced to admit this failure he has said evidently that 'the enemy's resistance was <u>beyond our powers</u>' and has called off the offensive. The Allied line is HOLDING and Amiens is out of his reach. We all thought we were retreating, retreating but it seems we have been fighting back. And how! (as Jim would have said – when he got back from Canada that time). Long ago.

We are weary, weary, weary. There are very few officers and men now at the front who have been here since the beginning for the old Regulars were all but wiped out in the first three months of war. I can quite see how it happened too, after all this but at least the deadlock has been broken at last and it is the end of a very long beginning, even though, we in the field, have been the last to realise it.

It is rumoured Ludendorff is moving troops and guns North again though, there is to be another set-to even though no-one yet knows where or when. We have been told to brace ourselves.

Yes. Here it comes. It's to be back to Flanders. He's going for the channel coast beyond Ypres again. It should have been easier for him to attack there in the first place, any nincompoop would have thought, for the sea would have been only sixty miles away from the point of assault … but now, our front before Ypres where the BEF have been building up the defences since 1914 – is probably stronger than any part of the Western Front. We are familiar with every twist and turn of the trenches. Back we go.

It is to be Operation George. Ludendorff refuses to admit a setback and decides to strike on the 9th April.

Again he is helped by mist that cloaks his preliminary moves. He is also superior to us in heavy artillery and has brought the Bruchmueller battering train North from the Somme for the first bombardment.

The firepower is terrible and has won the swine an opening advantage. It must have had an effect on the generals. There is another 'Backs To The Wall' edict. We are to fight on to the end; every position to be held to the last man. No retirement.

There is a bit here and there however because Foch is feeling his feet now he is in overall command and thinks we British can survive without French help and must fight with our own reserves. He is right. We can … but it can be tough going, but the brave little Belgian army have come in to help and taken over part of our line where it has weakened and we've got the Royal Flying Corps in close support, buzzing and twisting about up there even in such bad flying conditions. We in the Machine-Gun Corps are in constant demand as the German infantry try to press home their attacks after the initial bombardment. 1914 style. Sod 'em. Sod 'em.

The battle goes on and on. To describe our days would be impossible. Sleep where you can. Eat where you can. Piss on the gun if we run out of water to cool her down, keep going, keep going. Stay on my heels, J.W. Do what I do. Duck when I duck.

On the 24th Jerry brings over one of his rare tank attacks but huh! – they're soon taken care of and checked by the appearance of ours that are superior in number and quality. Let 'em have it boys! Ya-ho-oo-o!

On the 25th the Regimental Sergeant Major we were with outside Douai returns to us. Jerry has succeeded in capturing one of the Flemish high points: Mount Kemmeland and now the Scherpenberg on the 29th - but this has marked the limit of their advance. Ludendorff has shot his bolt and must stop! German official history will record: 'The attack had not penetrated to the decisive heights of Cassel and the Mont des Cats, the possession of which would have compelled the British evacuation of the Ypres salient and the Yser position. No great strategic movement had become possible and the Channel ports had not been reached. The second great offensive had not brought about the hoped-for decision.'

The offensive against us in Flanders this time is said to have cost Jerry 120,000 men out of a total strength of 800,000 in his Fourth and Sixth armies and an intercepted report has it that his Sixth Army warned in mid-April that 'The troops will not attack, despite orders. The offensive has come to a halt.'

We are down on the Menin Road, leaning back against the bank. Ludendorff has buggered off South again. He really wants Paris – but we are going back to base for a rest and to be deloused.

The sun is up over Ypres, high and shining yellow on all the mud and dust along the way. The patches of grass left here and there along the banks are mangled, stringy and the dust has dimmed their colour to a sort of dishrag green.

We've just seen the notices stuck up there further along the road. The Regimental Sergeant Major has got the M.M. for holding our position in that hollow under the ridge! "But Tom –." J.W.'s mouth has dropped open reading that, but the R.S.M.'s head is grinning, pressing above him. We are puny against the size of him. "Tom – it was you -." I nudge him to be quiet before he can say any more. He looks at me – uncomprehending - "But Tom!" I roll my eyes up farcically and my tongue in my cheek so that it makes a bulge, signifying 'No use saying anything/that's the way it is/it's all a bagatelle.'

We are waiting for the Prince of Wales. He is coming down the road in his car. Ah – here he is. Stand up boys. Do your best.

They've got him done up as a General, red tabs all over him, greatcoat on, in an open-touring car. Poor little bugger. Must be awful for him. All of us, shagged-out, filthy, hardly enough strength left to stand – and then him having to appear like this. I like the Prince – think the world of him. He's a good 'un: look how he goes down the pits back home: further south, how he cares for the unemployed.

He spots the R.S.M.'s ribbons. Good. It at least gives him something to talk about.

"See you've been in the South African campaign, Regimental Sergeant-Major", he smiles. He is charming. Nice smile. Sincere, innocent blue eyes. His hair shines gold under that bloody cap.

"Yes Sir!" The R.S.M. is at full attention, towering above us all, chest out. We stand as straight as we can, staring straight at the bank opposite. Hell, I'm embarrassed. Can hardly swallow. If he speaks to me I don't know whether I will be able to form a reply. Mouth gone dry.

"And I've been as close as this to you before Sir!"

"Oh ... when was that Sergeant-Major? I've never been to South Africa."

"No Sir ... but your Mother inspected us before we went Sir – and she was pregnant at the time!"

The Prince laughs. "Oh good, good Sergeant-Major", he approves. The staff with him acknowledge that the lower-ranks have a certain acceptable entertainment value at times and smile a condescending approval. They move slowly on down towards the city. We sag back into the slope of the bank. Tomorrow we go to Camiers. Thank Heavens.

TWENTY TWO

It is near the end of May. The 29th. This is Ludendorff's Third Offensive and he has brought his largest concentration of artillery yet assembled, up to the front. He is hoping to crack the French defences with a new style of attack different to the old style (wave on wave of infantry following an opening bombardment) that had led to Nivelle's offensive, broken a year ago on the Chemin de Domes.

He is hoping a success now will create an opportunity to renew an offensive in the North, if he can draw enough of our Allied reserves to the front outside Paris. Using his long-range gun we call 'Big Bertha' he has brought Paris directly under attack from a distance of 75 miles. It is having considerable effect, objectively and psychologically. He has got 6,000 guns and an ammunition stock of 2 million shells. He fired them all off in a little over four hours on the 27th, in the morning, against the allied divisions. Our three British were practically exhausted in March and April and brought down here to maybe take it easier after a brief rest at base, but we are sixteen in all with the others.

Immediately after the initial bombardment ceased, fifteen German divisions of his Sixth Army with five more following crossed

240

water lines to reach the summit of the ridge where they rolled over it and continued down the opposite slope to the level ground beyond.

The plan was for Jerry to halt when they reached open country as a preliminary to reviewing the attack in the North – but this is where the bugger came unstuck. He felt the opportunity to maybe take Paris after his initial two-day success, was too good to miss and for five days has been pressing his divisions forward to Soissons and Chateau Thierry. His outposts are only fifty-six miles off the French capital.

The Allies have been committing our reserves as slowly as possible to deny Jerry satisfaction or to have to battle to the death (yet) but even so, we have been forced to engage three divisions yesterday and five today.

The American divisions are at last joining us. A brigade of the U.S. Marine Corps should be up in a couple of days, all being well.

It is now the 9th June. Good. Those Yank-Marines, turned out to be the most proficient of the Doughboy army and on the 4th June and days following have steadfastly denied Jerry access to the road leading to Rheims. If he had got through there he would have had the railway line, doubling his capacity to supply and feed his troops.

Now on the 9th – this is one of the worst days of my life. We have been at it hammer and tongs and this morning was no exception except by the time we were preparing to go over ... one of the N.C.O's came down the trench and told us the rum-ration hadn't shown up.

"I'll take the gun," he said to me. "Go back down the lines and find out what's happened. Bring it up."

I leave and start weaving through all the paraphernalia, dust and smoke until I get into more open country. I run down a lane and must admit … start thinking about Rosalind. Why, I don't know. There is no time for daydreaming as a rule.

'Get her mother to make the wedding-dress' I grin to myself. Yes. Serious. I belt like hell now to a corner. If he's not coming in sight round there, I think – I'm going back to the boys, rum or no.

Half-past eleven – and the only time I've been sick since the whole thing started. Frightened once – outside Douai – sick once: NOW.

The mules have taken a direct-hit. They are sprawled, dead here on tattered bits of groundsel: here on this flat piece of earth, blood and guts all over the place. The smell is awful. The supply-orderly is not dead. He is lying on his back, everything bleeding and exposed, even his balls, eyes rolling in extremis. He has been practically ob-literated. "Hrr, hrr, hrr, hrr, hrr, hrr," he goes. It's enough to make you want to put him out of his agony: to kick his head in. Poor soul. Poor soul.

"Did you?" I will be asked years later. "Did you?" and I will only say "I might have" and when I am asked again, I will say, "I might have".

And then I am violently sick in the bit of brittle hedge left stand-ing at the side where there was no shelter for the poor dear and re-membering my orders, yank the rum-ration off one of the sprawling mules and weave my way back to the section. Only about ten minutes have elapsed. How can that be? I wipe the vomit off my filthy face as I run. Nothing will ever be the same, surely, after this lot is over. Nothing, but nothing can ever seem important to me again.

Exposed like that: blown to bits and no medics handy, no hope of a stretcher. How could I have left him to go looking – in vain, most probably? Leave him going "Hrr, hrr, hrr, hrr," under the raging sky … the yellow air? Alone.

Rosalind

"The day every girl longs for," she says. "Such a beautiful bride girl. I always knew you'd look a picture. June is the month for weddings." June 9th.

This looking glass is too short to get the full effect but yes …. It is a nice dress. I look all right I suppose. She's got an eye I must say. Like the little buttons up the back of the material. White with a sheen on it. "A lily," she says. "Yes", I say but …. but.

Eloise told me he <u>had</u> written, before she and Raymond left for Kent. "Twice in the last few months –," … but I thought she was saying that out of kindness – to boost my confidence because she knew how awful it was for me – before.

Remember though – remember! That morning when I was up early and the postman was going away up the lane and Mam was coming back from the gate. What <u>was</u> it she had hidden under her apron?

"Who's it from?" I asked – "Mam?" and why did she slide away from my eyes?

"Oh it's nothing you want to bother your head about now," she muttered.

"Is it from Careless, the Solicitor, then?" I asked. They've been having some trouble with the lease and they don't like me worrying over their affairs I know, but something had upset her and I wanted to know what.

She didn't answer, just smiled and shook her head dismissing it: no further conversation on the matter. Echoes of 'Children should be seen and not heard' from our infancy – and anyway ... how DOES one think the unthinkable? Not of your own mother? It is nearly time.

They will be here soon. Pritchard's new, long car with the ribbons buzzing and fluttering, some of the early arrivals. There's Mam out the front now in powder blue, old-rose trimmings; bridesmaids on the lawn like a cloud of sweet-peas, the skirts of their dresses blowing east. There must be a breeze.

It will take about quarter of an hour to get there. I had better go down. One more look in the mirror though this glass is so old, blotchy and stained, I can hardly see myself properly but – there seems to be another face in there, way back no ... how is this? <u>Behind</u> me, over my shoulder. It can't be – Tom! It is! His face so white and <u>wretched</u>. Wild. In agony .... Panting as if he has been running, running.

I bring my head around. No one. But the door clicks to. It was latched before. An unearthly shiver goes through me, chilled. My hands cup my face beneath the veil. Too late. It has always been too late. They are pimping the horn joyfully. I have no guts to break this off, to deny my parents their delight in having chosen him well: this man I am to marry: to shame them in front of the wedding guests now thronging the space outside the gate. Yet am I not complicit in this myself: merely wanting the status: married woman so not on the shelf?

All is vanity. All. I was speaking to Stefan George, Wednesday, outside Ye Wells Hotel and he agreed on that. What brought it up? I know I wanted to ask him if Mrs. Edwards had heard from Tom but

I couldn't. What would he have thought? Though – no, Stefan would have understood. He would understand now, if I ran to him. If I ran this very moment. I should have spoken. I should <u>now</u>.

Eleven Thirty. It is cold in our chapel. I extend my left hand and Jenkin slips the chiselled gold band over the shaking, third finger. The die is cast, future settled. All over.

"I will," I said.

Tom

Thank Heavens Ludendorff has decided not to go for our rear – but is sloping off South hoping yet again to draw the French reserves after him and widen the salient bulging between Paris and Flanders. He's attacking on a tributary of the Oise now. The Matz.

It only lasts about five days and he breaks off pretty smartish on 14th June when the French counter-attack with some Americans and Jerry comes to a halt. He can't sustain the pressure and our side didn't know it at the time, but he had already decided to halt the third offensive we've just been dealing with on the <u>third</u> of June, not only because of the mounting resistance from us (the British), the French and also now the Americans, but also because, once again, his leading troops had overrun their supply columns that were lagging far behind the infantry and their supporting artillery. They had also lost another hundred thousand men or more and although the Allies have losses to equal theirs, we retain the ability to replace our casualties while they are even having to re-recruit from the hospitals.

Some awful kind of flu has broken out over there too. They say nearly half-a-million of them are down with it. Their resistance is lowered by their inadequate food, our M.O. says. Comparatively – we are supposed to be quite well nourished. ('nuff said).

We have a breathing space now while Ludendorff is evidently making up his mind which way to attack. Some of us even manage a swim; but there is more discussion about probabilities these days. Are things as bad in Krautland as we are led to believe? We know some kind of review has taken place in Spa ... but only that the Kaiser and Co. all agreed on 3rd July that to 'compliment the acquisition of territories in the East, the annexation of Luxembourg and the French iron and coal fields in Lorraine were the necessary and minimum terms for concluding the war in the West.'. (Fat chance). Their Foreign Secretary has had the chop for warning that the war cannot now be ended by 'military decision alone'.

But Ludendorff remains pig-headed about that and now on 15th July is committing practically all he has got left (fifty-two divisions) to an attack against the French, for the temptation of taking Paris seems to have proved to be irresistible. At first he made excellent progress but the French had had a warning from their intelligence and observation experts so on the 18th July they counter-attacked heavily with eighteen divisions under Maugin or Mangin one of their fiery little devils in the 1st line at Villers-Cotterets.

Evidently it was the day old Ludendorff travelled to Mons to discuss transferring his troops back to Flanders for the much-postponed new offensive against us again. This French attack brought him back – but no good. The French had five of these enormous American divisions (28,000 strong) with them, fresh troops who fought 'with a disregard for casualties scarcely seen on the Western Front since the beginning of the war' it has been reported.

They are now taking an increasingly important part in operations. Previously a few individual units might have been lent out piecemeal to the Allies despite General John Pershing's determination to concentrate the American army under his command as a single and potentially war-winning entity but now he has achieved his purpose of bringing the First American Army into being (better late than never).

On the night of July 18/19, the German vanguards that had crossed the Marne three days ago, have fallen back across the river and are in retreat, so the Fifth German offensive and what the French are calling 'the Second Marne' is over and cannot be revived, and neither can they undertake another Flanders offensive against us. For they require thousands of replacements a month if they want to do that and those figures are unobtainable. Their hospitals have already been returning seventy thousand convalescents to the ranks each month and the men are hardly fit to fight. Poor buggers.

There is some talk now that Jerry might be withdrawing to the Siegfried line as a result of the 2nd Marne failure and that some of them want to start negotiating but because we've been stuck in the lines and not exploiting the success (for some reason – don't ask me why) Ludendorff seems to think now that there is no justification for them to withdraw. It is reported that he has said there is no sign that we can break his line.

He would probably have been right in the war years leading up to this one but the old chump has got another think coming to him if he thinks he's right on that one, for we all know that he is unable to make up his losses and scared stiff of the sheer number of fresh American soldiers arriving daily at the front. For even if they are 'enthusiastic rather than efficient' (opinion of French and British officers) the effect of their arrival is a spreading malaise in his army over there. Evidently he recognises a sense of 'looming defeat' on the quiet. There are four million American troops now either in action or training.

One of our biggest advantages also – is the new technical arm: tank forces. They are vastly improved and far superior to Jerry's pitiful efforts in that field. His are a joke and we think he is barmy not to have developed better models. One of his worst mistakes that; for their A7V's have to be manned by a twelve man crew: pioneers running engine, infantry men firing the machine-guns and artillery men operating a heavy gun. Like something out of one of Billy's comics. They've only managed to turn out a few dozen anyway and are relying in the main on about a hundred or two of ours that they captured before.

(No, a hundred and seventy someone's just told me to be precise while we have nearly several hundred each – that is French and British).

All through July now, Ludendorff keeps making out he has the option of striking alternately against us then the French. He must be mad. You should see his troops plodding, plodding over the mud and ruination of the battlefield round the Marne and you would know that if we could only have a go right now, it would probably be over sooner than expected. It is hot and the air sings. The sky is too high somehow: indifferent.

Yes! Haig and Foch are concentrating a huge tank-force in front of Amiens: evidently we are going to try breaking back into the old Somme battlefield through the defences Jerry slung up after his advance in march … and we're going to get right into his rear area. One up the arse for you Fritz!

Suddenly the horizons come closer. More concentrated. No more time for bathing beneath pot-holed banks – where the river chatters over pebbles in the shallows and where there are trees left overhanging the water insects buzzing under the stretched leaves, a dragonfly darting petrol blue/green over the stream. Snatched hiatuses. Unreal. We have been glad of the chance to wash even though having to keep the everlasting look-out for the sniper in the bushes or behind the rushes on the other bank.

I have been sent to support the Canadians. I get on well with them. We seem to speak the same language. Most of them were at Vimy when they took the Ridge. I tell them we were diverted through there once when we were near Douai and I went up to see where it had all happened. Yes, up the little twisting streets through Vimi. There was a lot of pink about and then this sweet, little lady came along in a raspberry-coloured cardigan. We asked the way and she was so pleasant that she was almost dancing as she twisted herself to emphasise what she was saying and then we went up on to the ridge and over all the humps and bumps – covering the old trenches with huge hollowed spaces where shells had landed or mines exploded right to the grass edge overlooking the plain where thousands on thousands of boys had been killed: obliterated. Wave after wave.

There was a sharp wind blowing and looking back towards the woods we had come through we saw a vast cloud of white birds come down on to the grass there in the distance as I was thinking that whoever was in command on top here would have had the drop on anyone trying to cross that plane below – for miles: 'Canadian Corps, 9th April 1917 with four divisions in line on a front of four miles, attacked and captured this ridge.'

It was high up there. All around were the trees we had just emerged from. The sky was distant blue with pale Payne's Grey clouds. The trees massed dark round the edge of the plain below then over in the distance there were pointed coal-tips edging the flat country and more on the left near a small town. I wondered if it could be Douai. One of our small aircraft came grinding overhead. We waved. He waved.

Then we went back through the trees. There were many paths leading off the one we took back down and looking into that deep foliage it was like looking into a ghost-cemetery. I could almost see pale corpses of soldiers standing in there amongst the watery green boles of new trees growing: saplings. They could all still be in there with their pale, pale faces. So many trees. Paths through trees. Every inch fought over.

There was a terrible, sinister grey house at the end of the lane coming down from the Ridge. Grey, pointed bits all over it like a witch's hat (again): another Myrtle Villa? And an avenue of trees still standing leading down to where probably a great deal of fighting took place before the Canadians got up into the woods. The church was grey. There was a grey house with a cupola. Everything was grey even though the church tower, although grey, had a sandstone-coloured brick façade and in spite of the bricks being red on certain houses. Grey – and twenty-five past five by the clock on that grey church tower. Grey. Grey. Grey.

I listen to their tales: the Canadians. How it was. The things that happened. I don't bother telling them about the hollow outside Douai, or how on the way to Vimi, we scooted in and out of Lens under the continual surging and resurging: one minute we had it, the next – no… and almost a feeling of DESPERATION in that place. We were by-passing a park-space within a round ring of trees of different-coloured foliage, there was a dirty looking housewife scowling, elbows on the bottom half of one of those stable-like doors they have here and there, turning towards Vimi, a jumble of buildings and coal-tips, a very thin-spired church: needle-like, I thought. Trees,

trees, red roofs then on the right a huge coal slag-heap turning into a mountain. That's when the desperation-feeling hit me. Probably reminded me of my wanderings outside Douai – whether that ridge was an old coal-heap - and I can remember that right there on the way to Vimi, how I contrasted the feeling of desperation with how we had all felt at Camiers when we first arrived: our young mens' expectations, a feeling of comradeship, happiness maybe – at being together on some kind of romp! Everything had become focused that day.

These Canadians look on me as a rookie almost. They are a lot older than me in the main and seem to have adopted J.W., No. 3 and myself as some kind of mascots. I don't mind or care. They are tough, no-nonsense men and we get on fine. We laugh together. We play poker and they know we are up to the job. They have seen us performing, been with us when Jerry has tried a few (unlucky) sorties.

We are fired up waiting and the onslaught occurs on August 8th with the Canadians (plus us) and the Australian Corps supporting the tanks.

We are at them like hounds and the next four days are a haze of mad heaving over the tops of trenches where we have spent some hours sleeping; then running, dodging, flinging ourselves into position, firing, firing and Jerry falling back day after day. I am running somewhere under his barrage with the tripod and then we are setting up and some of his trenches are now behind us then right! Upsticks and on. On, on … keep to my heels J.W. and it is now the end of the month and the Allies have advanced as far as the outworks of the Hindenburg Line from where we had been pushed back in March; but although Ludendorff was advised that he could only retrieve the situation by retreating to a line on the Meuse, nearly fifty miles away, he wouldn't have it so during September they are to consolidate their position in and forward of the Hindenburg Line.

He doesn't know what he is in for. The Americans are taking an increasingly important part in operations and are now deployed South of Verdun opposite the St. Mihiel Salient, that waterlogged stretch that has been in German hands since 1914.

Jerry was preparing to abandon the Salient in obedience to general-orders to retire to the Hindenburg Line but on the 12th September the first all-American offensive is launched and surprises the Germans who suffer another severe defeat.

In one day's fighting, the American 1st and 11th Corps, attacking behind a barrage of two thousand, nine hundred guns, drive the enemy from their positions, capture 466 guns and take 13,251 prisoners. (The French though giving due to the 'superb morale' of the Americans ungraciously attribute their success to the fact that they have caught Jerry in the process of retiring). It is true that more than a few Germans are all too ready to surrender….. they will come at you, arms above their heads, crying 'KAMERAD! KAMERAD! – but Pershing's Army has won a decisive victory – no doubt about that.

For Ludendorff, past hopes of victories had been able to be foreseen by assessing force against force but the intervention of the United States Army has changed all the odds. Nowhere are the Germans able to conjure up sufficient forces to match the millions of men Uncle Sam is bringing over the Atlantic and the seeming pointlessness of their efforts is what has sapped the will of the ordinary German soldier in the firing-line. You don't have to be a psychologist to suss this out and the mood prevails during the whole of September and Jerry is back in most places along the Hindenburg Line marked out by the fighting of 1914. It has been strengthened a lot in the years following though, particularly in the central section – after they retired from the Somme last year.

On 26th September, Foch cries 'Everyone to battle' so the British, French, Belgian and American armies now attack in strength with 123 divisions with another 57 divisions in reserve against 197 German; but of those only 51 are fully battle-worthy according to our Intelligence.

I am going east with the Canadians, chasing the enemy back to his borders. We know things are nearly all up for Ludendorff but none of us can afford to relax, particularly now for no-one wants to 'buy one' at this late state in the game. I have even seen some of the hard-cases holding up an index-finger above the trench-wall hoping it will be in the line of fire from the other side: just to get a 'ticket' home rather than a 'wooden-overcoat', the point being that you are no good as a soldier if you can't fire your gun; but incredibly it is early October again and Ludendorff is said to be recovering his nerve: beginning to talk of sustaining resistance and rejecting President Wilson's peace-conditions that we had heard were pretty much on the cards.

These conditions are now restated, appearing to demand the abolition of the monarchy as one of those 'arbitrary powers' menacing the 'peace of the world' – to that the American President has declared himself an implacable enemy.

Blast it all, Jerry even seems to be recovering something of his spirit and they are resisting our advance savagely as we push them further towards their frontiers. They had a moral collapse in late September when troops returning from the trenches had taunted those going up with cries of 'strike breakers'. That must have been horrible. They are in the shit at home with all that Communist agitation feeding on the poverty: but even so – not to back their own troops! Disloyal. Can't bear that. Poor sods.

Old Foch was frothing at the mouth for a time there in Flanders, they say, because the French got held up for a time with the added resistance plus plenty of water-obstacles and now Ludendorff is defying his own Chancellor's authority and composing a proclamation to the army, rejecting Wilson's proposals for peace, characterising it as a demand for unconditional-surrender. 'It is thus unacceptable to us soldiers. It proves that our enemy's desire for our destruction, which let loose the war in 1914 (! – my exclamation mark), 'still exists undiminished. (It) can thus be nothing for us soldiers but a challenge to continue our resistance with all our strength.'

Someone manages to suppress this document before it is published but by mistake one copy reaches German Headquarters (East) from where it is conveyed by an Independent Socialist signal-clerk to the party in Berlin.

It has been published by noon and the Reichstag turns into frenzy, enraged by the insubordination that characteristically Ludendorff tries to retract but the Kaiser is then confronted by Prince Max with the demand that he should choose between himself continuing to serve him or Ludendorff.

On the 25th October both Hindenburg and Ludendorff arrive in Berlin, both having left Headquarters against the Chancellor's instructions ... where after Ludendorff has been ordered to report to the Kaiser, he is forced to resign. His resignation is then accepted briefly and without thanks. Hindenburg's offer to resign is declined however – and when the two soldiers leave the palace, Schloss Bellevue, Ludendorff refuses the offer of a lift in Hindenburg's car to make his way alone to the hotel where his wife is staying. Throwing himself into a chair, after a period of silence he predicts that 'In a fortnight we shall have no Empire and no Emperor left, you will see.'

Exact to the day, Wilhelm 11 abdicates on the 9th November. Germany is now standing alone for their supporters have all sought terms of their own for peace and under pressure from the British, French, Americans and Belgians stiffen their resistance yet again as the armies fall back across the battlefields of 1914 towards the Belgian and German borders.

We are outside Mons, being extra careful not to stop a stray or unlucky bullet. Both sides know now that we are nearly at the end of the war. We have had it pretty tough along the way, particularly at all those rivers and canals and we took a lot of casualties. Some famous Welsh poet caught it at the crossing of the River Sambre only a day or two ago. Hard luck – but when your number's up, it's up. The Canadians keep your spirits high. They have black jokes for everything – almost beyond belief. Good hearts though.

We are in wet open fields, this side of town. A house is silhouetted dark against the light so that you can see through the windows to the other side: like a false-fronted building in a cowboy film. Everything is stale almost unreal. But the post has caught up with us at last. I have quite a bundle. One from <u>Rosalind</u>. I'll keep that one till last. I sit on a mud-step, back against the mud-wall of the trench, cold, a woodbine in my mouth, grinning. This is good, good. Keeping hers till last is a bit like keeping the tastiest portion of an excellent meal until the very last exquisite bite is lifted off the plate. I shiver. Only hope we won't have to spend another winter out here.

Billy has sent me some comics, bless him. I read his letter before taking a cursory glance through the once so-treasured pages of The Magnet. I have to laugh out loud at one of the inserts, halfway down the middle column of one of them:

'Does Your Soldier Pal

Write to You?'

Notepaper is "some" price these
days, but none of us would grudge
Tommy all the paper he needs on
which to write those cheery letters
of his if paper were treble the price
it is today. Still, it's no use simply
"gassing" about it; it's up to each
one to do his bit to pay the piper.
It costs the U.M.C.A., who supply
Tommy with fine stationary, no less
than 60,000 pounds a year. Sixpence will
supply your own or somebody else's
pal with enough notepaper to write
one letter each week for a year.
Going to let him have it? Of course
you are!
So send sixpence along today to
YMCA (Stationery Fund), Tottenham
Court Road, London W.C.,
mentioning that it comes from a
reader of this paper.

Letter a week eh!

Then Gussy is in the one for Oct. 5th. Turning out his pockets.
"Fallen Fortunes" it says and underneath "STONY!" in large capitals.

I spit out the stump of the cigarette hoping it's not an omen but
grinning (sardonically I realise).

Eloise's letter is next. She has married Raymond Cox then and they
have moved to Dartford after spending some time in Birmingham.
She says she bumped into Rosalind before leaving home and to <u>be</u>

prepared: that I will be getting a line from <u>her</u> soon, <u>Dear Tom.</u> As if Eloise really cares about something I am not yet aware of; maybe Rosalind is sick, has TB ... or -.

I rip open Rosalind's letter. She feels she ought to tell me – what? WHAT? I read on. She has got married. Married that Jenkin Evan-Evans!

The big Canadian N.C.O. looms over me. "What's up Taff?" he grins. "They caught up with you at last?" (seeing the letter dangling between my knees).

"Had a 'Dear John', that's all", I spit sideways.

"Ah-h ... women! Treat 'em rough and tell 'em NOTHING! Only way ..." he clumps off bent double behind the parapet. I am numb. Can't believe it. Another letter will surely arrive any moment saying it's all a lie. But I am numb and have a weird sense of foreboding for the future. Ishmael.

In Germany itself, we read in copies of Army newspapers, that resistance is crumbling. There are mutinies and demands for the Kaiser to abdicate. By the 7th November a German delegation has already crossed enemy lines to meet the French representatives in the Forest of Compiegne outside Paris to settle the issues of Abdication and the Chancellorship succession; but while all this is going on some of our troops are advancing into the Western Rhineland provinces and have established bridgeheads across the river at Mainz, Coblenz and Cologne. They are surrendered under the armistice terms.

We are in Mons, or just outside it, on the 11th – when it ends. No one is putting his head up but there is a strange feeling before one or two things are thrown in the air out of the trenches up front and there are shouts. "It's over! It's OVER!"

The Canadians are tough men. They can be wild. They shoot some of their officers in the back: those who had been swine or given the wrong orders. I say nothing, merely chew my cigarette-end round and round and get on with my own business.

The city changes. They have brought out a roundabout, all blue and pink gilded gold and decoration: a work of art. We throng the streets. Two women walking a St. Bernard dog hug us, kiss us as they pass. We allow girls to lead us off, or stand mute in the square watching the Noah's Ark turn to its piercing musical accompaniment, dumb, exhausted, anaesthetised by experience beyond immediate absorption; and of course I can't comprehend this Rosalind thing: this betrayal.

The Carousel is a squeaking, squealing focus of light and movement on the cobbles between the tall, brown-framed, pointed houses (or what is left of them). I stand, hands in pockets, cap on the back of my head, half-tight on red wine watching the revellers, the crowd. In the shadows the other side I see a familiar face laughing for a moment. Head back on a huge frame, concealed and yet <u>there</u>. My numbness drops from me as I take my hands out of my pockets and clatter across the cobbles to where he is standing; but there is no-one standing anywhere near where I thought he was.

"Ou est l'homme -?" I ask some local townspeople who are quick to tell me that they speak English.

"No – no-one was standing by the pillar M'sieur."

"Yes – we are certain".

I trail away, back to the billet. How I would love to have seen Jim. How we could have fathomed things out.

TWENTY
THREE

J.W. and I are 'Slip-Men' that means we have a job to go to as farmers' sons when we get home. We will be officially demobbed, (Z-reservists) later, meanwhile guns have been handed in and we can go.

We are at the station in Mons waiting for the train West.

The apron in front of the glass doors of the main booking-hall is heaving with khaki uniforms, some men still uncertain when they will actually be allowed to leave. I look up the line and watch our train coming on. Some white birds go up in an explosion off a dark roof, their wings flashing silver then grey as they wheel as one and take off East. Goodbye. I never want to come here again.

J.W. and I climb aboard and find an empty compartment. We sit, facing the way we are going, kitbags stacked on the mesh racks above the wide mirror. We don't say much. I like that about J.W. There are never any awkward silences. He is sympathetic to a person's mood and never sulky.

Almost imperceptibly, we pull away from the platform, the train gathering a normal speed unlike those from Camiers to the front.

Why was there that slowness but now -? One, two, three, FOUR! One, two, three, FOUR! – we rattle through Mons and out into the French countryside: the fields and swamps of mud that we have so recently fought every inch to acquire. We say nothing to each other such as 'Oh look – that's where we did that' or 'do you remember ...?' Pointless. We dream our own dreams – (well, I presume J.W. does, I have none), think our own thoughts. Jim and No. 3 are having to do more time. They saw us off last night in that licensed café in the square. We shook hands, that's all and wished each other well.

The sky is iced-cobalt streaked with clouds like cotton-wool on our right but beyond Lille now on the left, prune-coloured towering clouds like bursts of paint dropped on to wet, absorbent water-colour paper. Massing high to Heaven. I wonder if there is a factory in the vicinity causing this phenomena – or is it a natural result of atmospheric conditions?

Someone opens our door and kindly throws in a newspaper. People do that sort of thing when they see us in khaki.

The Kaiser's lot have scuttled their fleet in a British harbour: a small island off Scotland somewhere. All those magnificent battleships. It is awful somehow to think that if he hadn't been so envious of our maritime strength and tried to build up his navy to match ours – all this could have been avoided: all the fighting, killing, mutilation – started most probably by the neurotic climate of 'suspicion and insecurity' from that the war was born in the first place, it says here.

'The unmarked graveyard of his squadrons inside the remotest islands of the British archipelago, guarding the exit from the narrow seas his fleet would have had to penetrate to achieve true oceanic status, remains as a memorial to selfish and ultimately pointless military ambition.'

So there you have it.

The leaves are orange, brown, yellow but there are twigs gone mauve, gone red with silver birch trees dotted over yellow in half-crown shapes but rusty in their tops. Yellow froth on bushes … some kind of broom? no – gorse. Grubby little sheep and cattle like moving cave-paintings, hump-necked, cloven-hoofed, pushing forward, foot after foot as we hurtle past and stubble blown sideways: blond whiskers pointing our way West. Yes long pieces – left lying – all one way. Green grass; and flags flying over churches in the distances.

The cold sky is reflected into a darker cobalt channel of water before the sea-line is there in the distance over on the right. How quickly we have made it back over horizons it took months and months to reach, going the other way. There are golfers out too: bags over their shoulders, diamond-patterns down the sleeves of grey jumpers. The war is old hat already. Where have we been?

The sea-line is dark-blue then lined pale almost lime-green approaching Boulogne. The sky has turned Payne's Grey as we get nearer, echoing in colour the sound of the silenced guns. A clock with brass hours glints from beneath a burnt-mouse coloured, grey tower. The station is all chiselled fringe over its platforms and decorative steel girders.

The remembered smell of fish and sewage is strong as we go on board the boat and follows it as we sail out into the Channel leaving the sinister dark silhouette of the iron-filings works still clawing its way towards the city with that extended feeler.

"Look – there's that rock you noticed – coming in!" J.W. alerts me but

"Yeah." I say. I can't be bothered and the piece of old sea wall slips quietly past on our left. I am hollowed out. It is too long ago: everything. Some part of me almost longs to be home, to see old faces: another part dreads it: can't bear the thought of smiles even, women standing behind tables making the wrong remarks, asking the wrong questions, raising the tea-pot: smiling, smiling.

There is a fresh breeze and silver water chopping under the boat though from where we plough forward towards Folkestone the sea is a hyacinth-coloured pond as if alive with white swans massed and rocking up and forward, up and forward towards the far coastline: necks erect and arched for the wind is whipping the tops, emphasising the troughs, changing the light; even the colours. The sky is ultramarine or steel grey, the light yellow or pale green, slanting.

At Folkestone we are given passes for rail-fares, some pay owing and enough for twenty-eight days' paid leave. We are asked whether we would like to be paid one pound or keep the greatcoat. I say I will keep the greatcoat – on principal. J.W. does the same.

We have arranged on the crossing that he will spend the night at TyCanol and I will run him over to his place in the trap, tomorrow so now I wire ahead to tell them to expect us.

We take the train to Victoria then make across London to Euston. "Crewe", we agree, "Shrewsbury then down the line to Llandrindod Wells". We are still not saying much. It is late afternoon and getting dark when we find our seats on the right train. All the time we are patted on the shoulder as people pass. "That's right mate!" they say or "Well done lad". We smile. We move on.

It is pouring with rain when we arrive.

Father is on the platform. Benign and silver-haired, moustached beneath the station lanterns. Bill Whitford the stationmaster is with him. Father steps forwards and shakes hands. I introduce J.W. and they both say "How do you do?" I am a good foot taller than Father now. "Nice to see you, Mr. Whitford", I say and he says "Welcome home Tom."

Arthur Addy sits in his taxi, face beaming red and shining under the lamps that side of the small booking office. Father gets in the front, J.W. and I take the rear seat. We pass up Station-Crescent, rain lashing down, the pavements wet and shiny beneath the twisted, barley-sugar pillars holding up J.O. Davies shop and those further up the street. Father turns and asks after J.W's father. J.W. replies that he is sorry but he doesn't know. Father and Arthur Addy discuss a meeting they have recently attended. My heart thumps. I feel vaguely guilty for some unknown reason.

The lamplight streams out on to the slate path leading to the front door. The women are standing behind the big, oak table laden with a special tea – for us. I can't bear this: the ordinariness. Mother, silver-haired herself now, wears good-quality black with a print pinafore covering most of it. Ida Owen, beside her, is short and wide in dark mustard-coloured wool, again swathed in the ubiquitous cotton patterned with small black, maroon and white flowers.

"You're back!" says Mary-Ellen and comes forward to take my arm briefly and peck me on the cheek. I bend to receive this kiss.

"You've grown." She laughs. I introduce J.W.

"Know yer Father." Ida announces abruptly.

We are told to wash our hands then to come and sit down to tea.

"We'll use the facilities first, Mother – if you wouldn't mind" I say. She reddens. We don't usually remark on bodily-functions but J.W. and I are used to a different code of behaviour. I take him 'across the way' then into the back-kitchen where we wash and brush over our cropped skulls.

"Just having a swill, Mother", I call through but this is not the language they use in this house. There is now a feeling of slight disruption: change in the offing.

"Note my new table-cloth Tom, dear", Mother advises as J.W. and I sit, side by side, our puttees stretched over the grey stone flags under the table.

"I embroidered the border dear. You must see it afterwards. Look now if you like. See – the word P E A C E at every corner. I only finished it last week!"

"Very good Mother". I mumble through the egg and cress. "Wonderful!" says J.W.

Bernard comes in. "What's thee done to the teeth, boy?" he asks in the 'Radnor'. Amusing as ever. Expansive, extraordinarily handsome, urbane.

He approaches and shakes hands. I introduce J.W. "How d'you do?" "How d'you do?"

"Know your father", Bernard says. "Saw him at the auction in Builth last week".

"Every bugger seems to know your father, J.W." I say before I can think. Mary-Ellen nearly drops the teapot. The red rises past the black-band right up to her forehead.

"Sorry Mother", I laugh.

"Forgot where I was for a second". J.W. laughs. Bernard asks if I was in a fight. Is that how I lost my teeth? But I have underestimated J.W.

"Tom's C.O. was shot almost on top of him. His tin hat fell off as he fell and knocked Tom's teeth out. <u>That's</u> how Tom lost his teeth, <u>and</u> that string thing that holds down your top lip. That's gone too."

Father has taken his seat at the top of the table opposite Mary Ellen. He gives me a searching look from under a puzzled brow. Doesn't know what to make of this. Mother leans over and pats my arm.

"Hopkins the Dentist, dear ... tomorrow. Oh and you will have grown out of all your clothes. We'll take a trip to Vaughany-Jones' also."

"Not tomorrow Mother. I'm taking J.W. home, remember."

"Thursday then dear. Yes. We'll have you fixed up. Don't you worry."

"I've a clothing-allowance. They gave it us at Folkestone with the pay owing."

"I'm sure it will go some way -. Yes Ida. More tea all round. That's right."

The door crashes open and Billy comes hurting into the room. He jumps on me, hugging me and patting me on the back, the shoulders, the face. I stand up dragging him with me. We stand under the lamp. "You're home!" he sobs. "Tom – is it really you!"

I introduce my friend but remain standing for a moment. Under the lamp I feel the haggard lines of my face displayed, emphasised to a degree no-one would have noticed out there in France, I feel the terrible thinness of my body and this hardness settled on me as the thrown cloak of some departing prophet: an unwillingness to participate in ordinary, polite, family matters. Little Billy is the only one here I can stand the sight of (apart from J.W. of course.)

And thank Heavens for him: that he is here for the night. Had he not been, I might have gone rushing out into the air, anywhere to get away from the ordinariness that I can no-longer stand. The river-bank seems preferable to sitting: actually sitting in a chair and looking into the fire or at the wall-paper while they speak: they utter words, they make little noises, rustling materials or papers with the fire spitting and then the kettle starting up as it gets hot and hotter over the coals or stands singing on the hob. And WHY?

No – down there, under the willows along the bank, a man could sit and gaze into the black water. Gaze into death-and-maybe and all this myth of life and the ridiculousness of how it has been. Oh yes, but it's not the thing to do here. Not back home. No trenches. No – it would be too unusual a thing to do to go down there and insist on sitting by the bloody river of all places rather than thankfully lowering yourself into a real armchair boy! By a real fire. Aren't you glad to be home? Aren't you grateful you're not one who ended up with all his guts spilled out on that square of groundsel and tired green just off the battlefield? Aren't you so glad you're not one of the drowned-in-mud of Flanders or the poet caught nearly crossing the River Sambre so near the end? Aren't you <u>lucky</u>?

It is so good to be out. The morning is crisp, frosty and fresh. The high-stepping cob bowls us along at a cracking pace.

J.W. and I had an excellent breakfast and we are clean even if haggard and hollow-eyed. We head up Llanyre Pitches, along Gravel Road and out towards the hills.

We pass the entrance to Rosalind Hamer's family-farm but J.W. makes no comment and neither do I. He knows. I told him in Mons.

His house is small and grey and lies in a hollow surrounded by spruce as a windbreak. Both chimneys are smoking. The fires are stoked. Billy rode over on Flash yesterday to tell them we were on the way. And now we are here.

Temporarily I knot the reins to a hitching post and J.W. and I approach the front door. He opens it and his mother, standing by the fire drops the clothes she is about to air on the wooden clothes-horse and lets out a huge cry of welcome. J.W. rushes towards her and bursts into tears. She takes him in her arms and rocks him to and fro. His father rises from an old battered settee and turns J.W. towards him, kissing him, hugging him.

I stand, back to the closed front door, eyes wide, mouth open with some kind of pain in astonishment. J.W.s father turns and fixes me with a look of pure compassion so that I feel an almost unrecognised feeling of vulnerability. What is this?

He quietly approaches and smaller than me though he is, reaches up and enfolds me in his countryman's arms. Crying. He brings my head to his shoulder and I <u>sob</u>. I start to cry. He tugs me to the settee and I am half-sprawled across him, my head on his breast, crying like a baby. He strokes my head and soothes me with noises I have no remembrance of hearing before.

"Tom saved my life," J.W. tells them as we stand facing one another before I leave. "But for him, Mam and Dad, I wouldn't be here."

I shake my head. I feel that I cannot speak. We shake hands. All of us. I manage to get out "Goodbye J.W." and he throws himself against my chest.

"Goodbye Tom," he cries and I leave, having forgotten that the cob was merely tied to their post. The day is duck-egg blue over the hedges. It will be a short one: dark just before four o'clock and I have to get through the long night ahead. How?

I had forgotten the therapeutic effect of the War Office but after tea I wash, pass a damp hand over my shaven head, tug my collar straight and head up the road to town. I can't stay in. Not with the lamps lit and the kettles sizzling on the hobs. Something seems to prick the rooms with an unknown scale of notes beyond silence: an advancing, a continual advancing-descent of invisible needles behind the scenes: deadening, defeating, robbing you if you sit down, of life and energy.

My tunic and puttees over the breeks will have to do. No one will see me going uptown in the dark and the boys won't care. No one here now would dare to ask me where I am going: what I am about.

Thank Heavens they are still there above Old Humphries' business. Chinny and Morley, Lance, Ivor, Lional and Stan. They whoop their welcome when I push my head round the old wooden-planked door but can I explain this? They ask no awkward questions: none of them comment on my appearance and thank the Lord, Stan is back. Good old Stan, just sitting there grinning quietly over the half-chewed cigarette bobbing up and down in his mouth. We look at each other now and then. He knows. I know. He was with the Borderers.

We adjourn to the Llanerch after a time.

Rosalind

Jenkin's sister and I have just come in to Vaughany-Jones' Gents. Outfitters to buy him a victory-cravat. Just for fun.

We are in the lower section of the shop but there is someone in the 'holy of holies', a tent-like structure where they do the fittings, half-concealed by that heavy, lined curtain they can pull across.

Vaughany is very proud of this arrangement. He had the curtain-rails put up and the brocade cut and lined by the Manager of the Greenlands branch recently opened in Llandrindod. Greenlands of Hereford, no less: Mr. Robinson officiating. He does all his own measurements and hangings while Mrs. Robinson runs up the curtains and loose-covers on her treadle sewing machine.

You hardly ever see her and they say that he even makes the poor soul pay for all her own Silko's and cottons – out of the housekeeping money! She has become a great friend of Sally Harris who lives at the bottom of her road – in one of old Edwards TyCanol's houses left him by his father. Stan Harris's mother.

Mrs. Robinson and Sally Harris are shocked, they say, by the amount of drink Stan puts away. Poor old Stan. He's had a tough time. They ought to make allowances.

A thin, young man in khaki is in the inner sanctum with his back towards us. His shoulder blades are two sharp plates beneath the serge. His head is cropped and as he turns briefly to speak to a seated figure beyond my gaze, I notice he has some teeth missing in front. It doesn't matter. I have never seen anyone as attractive in my life.

There is an independence-in-the-face-of, a feeling of absolute self-containment. A – what? You can feel it coming off him: the appeal. He is even more attractive than Tom Edwards. He IS Tom Edwards! Thank goodness I am more or less hidden behind this pillar.

Mary-Ellen leans forward and speaks to Vaughany. "The whipcord, I think. Yes … (hem, hem) … I'll remove myself shall I, while you measure up?" She laughs pleasantly and I see her little button-boots retract as she prepares to stand.

I grab Jenkin's sister's arm unceremoniously and propel her back out on to the pavement. Jenkin laughs. "What – out already girls?" he says but then he sees my face. I am frantic to get away.

"Who – who was that wonderful-looking young man, Rosalind?" Jenkin's sister gasps.

"Tom Edwards", I snap.

"He's lost his teeth!" she giggles.

"Wonder how?"

"TOM EDWARDS", Jenkin barks. "Is he back already?"

"Well Stan Harris has been back two weeks", I explode but he cuts me off.

"Teeth gone, you say. Huh. Probably lost them in some drunken brawl!"

"Jenkin, how can you! - and of course they're allowed home if they've a job to go to –."

"Stan's not working – except his elbow!"

"I don't know about that – but Tom will be – you can bet on that!" I cry and thrust my purse into his sister's arms.

"Here. You go and get it." I can hardly be bothered to speak. Don't care what they think. I run across Middleton Street and down the quiet path beside Plas Winton, the big, chateau-like hotel on the corner, leading to the Dingle.

The sky is crashing down on to the Church of England roof at the top of the street and Plas Winton's red bricks, decorative tiles and ridges topple into my eyes against the rushing, harsh blue. I must be alone.

I'll make for the Park and sit by the stream under the laurel bushes. All the demons of hell are raging in me. My skin will never contain the way I feel. I will rip apart: scatter back to the basic elements of my being and hope someone ... <u>anyone</u>, will crush them under their heel. There is rust, rust red all around, yellow then rushes, reeds, blue puddles in the middle of grass-patches, reflecting bland, bland blue: a senseless jigsaw. What am I to do? How can I gather enough of myself together – for it is leaping about me ... I can't even BREATHE – to think it out? I can't exist in this emptiness but how to outrun myself? Where shall I go? Who will understand? Who will help me? Help! Help! P-L-E-A-S-E.....

TWENTY FOUR

Tom

Hopkins made a good job of my teeth. He's a genius. You'd never tell. Maybe it is because I'm so young and my face hasn't fallen in but the teeth fit and I've got used to them now.

At first it was as if I was chewing the whole plate, teeth and all when I tried eating but persevere and you're there! They're good for taking the piss too, when the boys and I are in the back-bar of the Metropole Hotel if some client in there is putting on the dog – I just look straight at Lance or Stan, Chinny if he's there and drop them farcically. We are always laughing.

Hopkins was quite blunt about things when I had the first appointment.

"Have to take them all out Tom." He let me know at once. "Front are done for … and the plate will fit much better – if you give me a clear field."

I'm not sorry I agreed. I've had them for well over a fortnight now and no bother. My appearance is improving too. I'm filling out and the hair is growing and I've got into a good working routine: up at six o'clock, feed and water the cows who are in now for winter, ditto the horses and the bull then do the milking, in for breakfast while Billy Mills sees to the milk-cans, bottles etcetera, back out, harness the cob and hitch him into the float, up-town with the first delivery, Billy Mills and I going like hell, then home again to muck out the cowsheds, stables, bull-pen, suckle the calves, muck them out, sweep the yards, Billy Mills and Ida Owen scalding the milk-bottles, cans and churns, saw wood into logs and stack them in the woodshed, get down the water-meadows and cut back any thistles with the bill-hook, trim the hedges, cut fresh stakes to strengthen them and fill up any gaps, before coming up for lunch, out again to do the afternoon milking, harness up the cob, back to town with the second-round, home, scald the bottles, cans, churns, muck out the cowsheds, stables, calves-pen, bull-shed yet again and bed them down for the night so up into the loft, pitch down the straw, fill the bings with fresh bedding for tomorrow (that is the long passages in front of the cow-stalls) then in for tea. This is the slack season.

I might sit for half-an-hour at the most under the Aladdin Lamps, after the meal with the others talking around me but then I wash, change my clothes, adjust the knot in my tie by peering into the little square-framed looking-glass beside the back-door and as near to six o'clock as I can make it – I am gone. I cannot stay in. Never, until I am an old man, will I be able to stay in the house during the evening again. It's not worth asking me why. I don't know and I don't want to know. Don't bore me with explanations. I don't bloody well care.

It is the week before Christmas. At one time I would have been thrilled. Snow and ice in the steep streets, windows bright with lights and decorations, tinsel and silver stars behind counters in the cafés and huge firs garlanded and glowing darkly in the corners of the luxurious hotels – but now…

I don't want to remember last year or the year before. Christ's coming, yes. But the rest of it, the packaging, the parasitical posturing, the knowing what's behind it all … the greed, the abominable envy: DEATH and the stink of death … and coming down the road in the snow and I thought "Yeah … what would they do? What would they DO? If it was all just suddenly snatched away and they were given a shovel and told to dig out a hole in the ground now: now this minute – and LIVE IN IT … and keep ducking Mother, Father, in case you cop a bullet up your arse.… oh sorry for the crudity: sorry, sorry, sorry. I must stop it. Must stop it."

There have been echoes of a former excitement. I went into C.C. Hughes's to buy a present for Billy last week and ranging round the counters, the shelves, there was that smell: of the shiny covers of annuals, books, teddy-bears, dolls … and a sudden fascination of something made out of painted tin or gold-net. Yes as intangible as the feeling that comes once and once only as you look at the first piece of fresh, sparkling tinsel of the season, I got it for a second: something of before, long ago.

I bought him a farmyard set and a whole army of lead soldiers in different uniforms and just for fun some sugar-cigarettes, white with pink tips. I love C.C. Hughes's shop. It has a dark, quiet glow. There is a kindness in there. No one ever bothers you or implies that children should not handle the toys or that they should hurry up and out. I will get Ida to wrap everything in fancy paper. She's good at that.

Eloise and Raymond Cox are coming for the holiday. They are to have a bed put up in the parlour so thank Heavens that's one depressing hole we won't have to sit in. The family are to make do with the big kitchen and the 'lean-to' as Ida insists on calling the back-kitchen. Preparations are in full swing. The piano has been moved in so that we can enjoy musical evenings. I am wondering how the hell I can get out and up town without upsetting any arrangements but it will have to be resolved somehow.

It is the day before Christmas Eve. I am sitting enjoying a cigarette in the shit-house when the latch goes, the door opens, Billy's hand comes round and he throws me an envelope that must have come with this morning's post. He doesn't say anything and neither do I. The door bangs shut, the metal latch jumping up and back into place. Mary-Ellen hates me calling it the shit-house.

It is a note from Maggie Price asking me to call this evening if I am able. I wonder what she wants. I feel around inside the envelope in case she has enclosed a fiver and laugh. I always do this now. No –nothing doing. I only saw her the other day so something must have come up in the meantime. Surely it won't be a party – when I get there? No – she would have said. We are going to have a round of golf when the weather is fit later on. She, Nesta Davies, Haydn Black and I. I look forward to it. Maggie Price is a good pal.

I feel good. Still as thin as a rake: but good. It is satisfying to be clean and comfortable in your clothes. Mary-Ellen has fine taste and I like these whipcord trousers and the tweed jacket. I particularly like the pink tinge to this shirt and the cut of the collar, it goes with the different greens in the heather-mixture tweed of the jacket and the overcoat: so light after the greatcoat and yet so warm. I have a mole-coloured trilby hat also. Quite the masher! Leather shoes with punched holes in a pattern across the apron: dark as bog-water. Good, good, good.

Black ice going up Park Crescent but I make it to Maggie Price's door beside the old shop and press the bell. She comes down, switching on lights as she does so. T.P. Davies, the chemist just a few doors down has his windows all aglow for Christmas with those red and green giant bottles they usually display – but these are enormous -.

The door opens. "Tom <u>dear</u>, how nice of you to venture out in this. Do come in.."

She ushers me along the familiar hallway and upstairs. We pass along the landing to the front room over the shop and she takes my coat and invites me to sit down. I do, out of politeness but stand up again when she leaves the room. Where the hell is she?

Suddenly she is in the doorway. I have never seen Maggie Price looking anxious before but now she seems nervous or -.

"Tom", she says. "Tom … there's someone here who wants to see you." She turns and goes out again. What in hell is going on?

There are light footsteps hurrying and then Rosalind Hamer is in the room. A beautiful woman who I don't know in hay-coloured silk, hair short and brushed back. Deep-bosomed, slim in a loose-cut dress. I stand straight. I am at attention, chin up but in, eyes front. She throws herself at my chest, arms fastening around my neck trying to pull down my head.

"Oh Tom. <u>Tom!</u>" she cries.

How can she do this? What can she expect of me now? After all … after all the horror and the pain …. Then the betrayal. The <u>betrayal</u>.

I detach her hands, her arms, her body from mine and walk to the door where poor Maggie Price leans, hands behind her back. I am angry with her too but now all I want is to vanish from sight.

"I'll get your coat," she says apologetically. "I'm sorry Tom –."

I take the coat, tight-lipped and make back down the stairs without speaking. I can't. I am shaken to the core. Rosalind! Rosalind!

Maggie Price is leaning over the banisters but I don't look back. I leave, closing the door without banging it. The street soars into the frost and stars. Where now?

I can't face the War Office at the moment or the back-bar of the Met. I am walking fast, even as I think. I am heading up past the new shop: Greenlands of Hereford, towards the Common and the Lake.

This is the place to be with the black wind blowing the stars and the branches groaning and twisting over the slopping water, the great rhododendron bushes a border of moving, shiny foliage around the perimeter and massing on the island in the middle of the lake. The streetlamps are mellow and sparsely placed but the lights from the town make a glow to the left as I turn to walk right round. I might even go up to the heights above. A wild place. Half tamed but with reality underneath, not too far from the surface: mood match. I would like a gale to arise and blow everything flat. Me too: pinned to the ground; or a huge storm, thunder and lightning. I would run laughing right over the golf-links welcoming whatever might come. I would welcome death: complete annihilation from this world. There must be another: something beyond this shit-house. Yes SHIT-HOUSE, Mary-Ellen, SHIT-HOUSE!

Sleet in the wind now and beginning to slice down savagely. The heavy shadow of the gazebo halfway along the far-side path facing the Common is a more solid shape in the middle of the threshing branches. I stumble through the gap in the rough wooden pole surrounding the structure and duck in under the pointed roof. The slapping water is about a yard away as I sink on to the slatted seat.

I sense a movement to my left in the corner. The second I realise someone is there my hand reaches for the throat: a reflex-action. Life has depended on the quick-think/quick-response for the last year.

There is no armed resistance; only a gargling-gasp of horror and two little hands scrabbling at mine. It is a girl.

I release her. "Who the devil are you?" I ask as if I have a right to, before apologising, explaining my reaction as best I can. She is very understanding

...... she gasps, then recovering,

"You're Tom Edwards, aren't you?" she asks.

"Don't apologise, please. I can well imagine."

I can't see in here, especially as she stays huddled into the corner, that she has been crying but I can hear it in her voice.

"What's the matter with you, why are you out on your own on a night like this?" I am really interested. She has a gentle manner but there is a feeling of the chips being down: here is someone not about to spin me some tale of life's essential goodness: roses all the way.

She is to marry the young fishmonger. Yes, she is fond of him but she hasn't lived. She would like to have done more with her life, studied maybe – gone to the County School, passed exams then gone abroad or something.

"One-armed Davies?"

"Yes, him. <u>That</u> doesn't make any difference. It's not that. It's <u>me</u>."

"Recites at the Eisteddfods, doesn't he?"

"Yes, that's him."

"So -."

"I just had to come out. To <u>think</u>. Am I going to go through with it – or not?"

"Hm-m-m. When's it planned for the 'er <u>happy</u> day?" (Sniff).

"June."

"Serious business - considering the nuptials. I can see now, you're in a delicate situation hovering on the brink of … deadly wedlock."

She begins to laugh.

"Oh – you've got a funny way of putting things, Master Edwards."

"Less of the Master. Look – I know you, don't I? Where do you work? I've seen you somewhere. I'm sure."

She has taken shape in the dark now. He recognises the black eyes, the intense stare.

"The Chalet", she answers.

"I serve teas."

Ah yes. I bring to mind the neat figure, bun at the back of the black hair, hurrying away with orders.

She has a longish, pointed nose like a field mouse, no – a badger maybe? I have looked her over on more than one occasion having been in there with Maggie Price and Nesta and even had the cheek to think to myself that the piercing beauty of her black, honest eyes would not have been a sufficient attraction for me because the nose would put me off. How shallow we are, how conceited ... or is it nature's safeguard against the wrong mate I think now? But she is asking me why I myself am strolling round the lake in pouring sleet and rain.

To my intense surprise, I tell her. She has all the right attitudes. I think she must be the most kind and understanding female I have ever met. There is a quietness, a natural grace-without-prudity: a camaraderie I have not encountered before even though tonight she is merely a huddled form bundled into a dark corner with sleet pouring down outside such a flimsy shelter. She embraces me without touching. I am engulfed in the aura of another person's essential goodness; a reminder of J.W. sometime in those hideous mornings sunk in mud.

TWENTY FIVE

It is August and Carnival in town. Hot – and already I can hear brass splitting the air as the bandsmen march ahead of the procession. They change then: no longer Tom Davies the Sadler or Giles the Fish, Crane, Pritchard, whoever … now. Soon at 2.00 p.m. precisely when the order is given, the fat little legs encased in navy-blue with the red stripe running down the outside leg, will stride forth under the little beer-bellies, the cheeks will balloon ferociously and the massive arms thump the sticks on to the big drums in absolute time, musicians to a man: artists all …

Forget the counter-jumping and the fore-court trading, forget the bills spiked on the old ink-stained desk, up boys up and wet the mouth-piece, spit and raise the gorgeous, rounded shining shapes and march, march, march. We are off.

I dig my heels into the massive, black flanks beneath my heels and the great horse dances, arch-necked. We are showing-off, he and I. I am got up as a cowboy, curly slim bathroom-mats, one fronting each leg, as chaps, Stetson knotted with a bootlace beneath my chin, red neckerchief casual over a green-checked shirt, sleeves rolled up, to look the part.

Everyone joins in when it's Carnival and this year it is going to be the best ever so it is hoped. I wasn't all that keen to enter but it would have been churlish not to, Bernard seemed to think, so here we are. He is back there somewhere on his dark-bay mare dressed as a character I haven't caught up with yet off the cinema-screen.

It is a huge procession. There are dancing drum-majorettes just behind the band, in flimsy, orange georgette-squares and triangles made up into short-skirts over kid boots buttoned up the front. They step, they stamp, twirl and step again, there are lorries festooned in bunting and crêpe-paper, inching forward under a riot of balloons, men blowing whistles, laughter, shouts and singing. There are a whole crowd of people with their faces blacked under curly wigs and red-striped top-hats, stars and stripes on their satin suits and dresses singing 'Swanee River', and all kinds of single entries: elves, fairies, absent-minded professors, snails… even a huge moving tomato and all jostling, jostling back there, placards and streamers waving and streaming, flags, whistles, mechanical, feathered birds. The mounted section, that is – us … are together before them in a side-stepping, plunging, neck-throwing group.

"Tom! Tom!" I hear rising from the pavement just along from Norton's Automobile Palace after we have turned along out of Beaufort Road. The hoofs are all crashing along the tarmac but I look down left and there is little Petra Davies, Nesta's kid sister, standing, desperately trying to catch my attention. She must be twelve years old now.

I bring the horse's head down and move over to say hello. She is ecstatic. "Thith ith my new friend …. Vera Robinson!" she gasps. "Her father is Mithter Robinthon – from Greenlanths –."

I laugh and say hello but have to go. The great horse is bucking to and fro and no-way can I hold up the procession. 'Nice looking kid, Pet will be' I think to myself … 'and her little friend. Pretty little heart-shaped face that one: so white – and those huge blue eyes! Knows how to use them too! Even at that age. My stars!'

I move into the distance with the others, jostling, jumping, away, away.

Three weeks ago, she told me she was pregnant, had been since April. There's no doubt about it, it is my child.

We were sitting in our place round the lake: the gazebo and she asked me how I felt about it. I just sat forward, my head in my hands.

"You don't want to be a father Tom, do you?" She went on kindly so I told her the truth, I said "No." - I couldn't bear the thought of it: couldn't really stand kids or having them round me too often and didn't want to offend her but didn't want to get married either.

I was not to worry about it, she told me. She didn't cry or anything. Said she was glad I had told her the truth. Said she was going to discuss it with Davies and if he still wanted her, they would bring the marriage forward.

"You're a pal", I said.

"Best I've ever met."

Neither of us waste words. We left it at that. But it got out. Mary-Ellen asked Father to 'speak' so I was called into the parlour.

He was amazingly tolerant. Did I want to marry? No. Was I sure? Yes. How did the girl feel about it? Extremely understanding. Had she plans? Yes. What were they? I told him. Um-m-m. He said he would have a tactful word with young Davies's father and see if he couldn't contribute to the expenses of a hasty marriage. Thankyou. He was practised in this obviously. Bernard?

TWENTY SIX

There has been hatred emanating from the back-kitchen. Mother and Ida Owen. Particularly since the interview in the parlour. 'Men and piggery' heard in mutterings, doors slammed, plates put down with a thump. Icy silence from that end of the table where Mary-Ellen sits upright; but yesterday was the Carnival and today all the doors are open allowing a cooling draught to freshen the atmosphere and wash like Ithon water over the great, grey, stone slabs of the Big Kitchen floor, the red tiles of the 'Lean To'.

Today Mother told Ida off for her nastiness, that she was to treat me with more respect – or else! I am gratified and Mary-Ellen has been kinder towards me than I can remember: ever.

The big, fat cabbage-roses are blooming still, all up the porch outside and the garden is full of blue spires, dark red petals and bees buzzing in and out of bell-shapes and flowers with stiff petals like baby's rattles flung on the ground. The smell of flowers pervades all the rooms and the breeze from the hills moves green and smokey blue through the house.

Mother's Canadian cousins are here to supper. We are relaxed around the table. Mother is even asking me if I think I might like to join them on their half-section, high on the heights of Manitoba next year? It might even be a good idea: give me work-experience in a different country, different environment; help me to settle down and decide what I would like to do in life. Why ... I might even consider being a fruit-farmer eventually.

I am puzzled. I think of my plans for breeding Welsh Mountain ponies mixed with an Arab strain; but of course, she may be right, it would be an adventure. I remember Jim Corp: his trips into the wild ... but how long would I be expected to stay? Are they suggesting I go for a sort of holiday or what? Hm-mm. I remember Jim's not altogether welcome returns. Tonight, the 'uncle' makes it seem quite an attractive proposition but I wonder how I will feel tomorrow and now that I'm back home and busy every minute of the day – who is going to do my work? How will Father manage with all his meetings? Bernard won't do it and Billy's too young. There is only Billy Mills.

March came in like a lion. It has been decided. I am to go. The Old Man is giving me £50 and paying my passage on the White Star Line – I think. (Can't be sure of that yet). But Liverpool to Montreal via Halifax and Quebec. I imagine the great liner waiting at Liverpool alongside the dock.

Mother has been up to Vaughany-Jones' and bought me a whole trunk-full of clothes. I am standing in my bedroom now looking down. It is open on the counterpane and full to the brim with vests, long-johns, warm underclothes, flannel shirts, night-clothes, pull-overs and every conceivable item of clothing the 'relatives' could suggest for a <u>long</u> sojourn in the Canadian-climate, before they departed.

Yeah ... I can see it now looking down into all this lot: 'Go son – and please don't come back. Make it permanent.' Mary-Ellen can't stand the disgrace. There have been those one or two fights in public-places: swift reckoning with an extended fist rather than arbitration, conciliation; there is the bad-language, the lack of proper proprieties observed, the never-ending line of girls in waiting, the PREGNANCY ... No. - Never mind dear BernARD: <u>he</u> plays the game, <u>he</u> manages, is acquiescent, will be a <u>success</u>, while you: YOU – are Ishmael, only fit for the Llanerch Hotel, back-bars with good-for-nothing cronies: Stan Harris etcetera. <u>Never-mind</u> he fought in the War. We have to obey certain standards of behaviour. Goodness knows where all these wild ways of yours have come from. Go away!

'Yes', I think. 'Remittance-Man to Canada'.

I am sitting at the foot of the ladder leading up into the loft above the Little Barn facing the open back door. The door is in two-halves actually, top and bottom like the bloody place I glimpsed that time on the outskirts of Lens. They are both wide to the fresh air.

I have shut the great black double-doors at the front facing the yard for I don't want the Old Man wandering over the stones just to silently reprimand me for sitting here on this plywood crate, smoking. He won't say anything now but even so he ought to know I'm not likely to set the place on fire am I? I'm the first to tell any tramps we allow to spend the night in the hay, not to smoke; even take their matches off them so he might credit me with some sense.

I remember that day after the carnival when I made up my mind. 'Yes I will go.'

The Summer was at full-stretch, all the oaks standing over their shadows down the slope and there was that silence when a solitary crow, black against the sky yet singead-bronze at the tips of its feathers nearer to, might flop over from the three hills before the double 'bong-bong' sounds from the gas-works down near the Crossing hit the air. Soporific at that hour. 12.00 noon, sun just going over. Hot.

The stone-flags are cool today though and it is pleasant with the dust-motes dancing where the light comes through the cracks. I remember the games we had in here, the fun with Eloise and Ivor, though how we didn't break our necks jumping from the bays on to piles of hay pitched on to these stone flags, I'll never know. Those rope-games too. Slinging a jo-ho line between two uprights holding up the beams, then sitting on it and someone else pushing you until you were swinging right up there near the roof with only your hands clutching the thin rope either side. You didn't dare cop out either or the others would soon have labelled you 'Cowardy, cowardy, CUSTARD'. I suppose I would have done the same. Kids.

I seem to remember sitting here, facing the other way, Eloise and Ivor coming down that ladder -. Crash! …. What was that?

I am going tomorrow. First thing. The Old Man is coming to Liverpool with me. We will stay with Auntie Luce and Dora for a few days, take in some concerts: they support the Liverpool Philharmonic Orchestra and they know how we love going along there with them. It seems ages since I saw them last. I used to love going up there on holiday before the war. Dora is my very favourite aunt-figure, I think. Kind, loyal; but I hope they won't all want to come traipsing down to the boat to see me off.

Last night was a 'special' at the War-Office before we adjourned to the Llanerch. The boys want me to do one last magnificent 'jape' for them before going. I told them Father is treating me to the Grand National at Aintree on the 26th so Chinny thought it up. It's brilliant! First-class … if I can bring it off.

"Look!" – he said, "That miserable old bugger Humphries, downstairs – miser that he is, ALWAYS has a flutter on the National. He's been trying it for years – so here's what you do, young Edwards … we'll let you know which one he's backing – got it? No – phone us the night before …. Then when you get to Aintree … HA.HA listen to this – get yourself to the telegraph office ON THE COURSE …. Their STAMP see? HA.HA … and send the miserable sod a telegram saying his choice has romped home first past the post plus the odds. It may be eleven to four on Troy Town, the favourite – but he's not backing that. He's got his eye on some rank outsider – he's convinced he's going to win. I'll get the name out of him somehow and let you have it before you go. Do it! Will you? One last blow for sod 'em all!"

I have to laugh. Can just see Humphries getting the wire, tugging that filthy, old, black, alpaca jacket off his chair-back, and on over the moth-eaten cardigan before flinging himself open-mouthed and roaring up the stairs, crashing into the War Office with the boys lounging, half-soaked trying not to squeal out laughing; but he won't notice the laughing.

"I've won! I've WON the bloody National!" he will gasp …

"Come on boys … down the Met. With you. I'm PAYING! My treat!"

First time in his life to call a round! I can just see Chinny wiping his hand across his face, Stan quietly grinning, Morley bent double laughing, laughing. They will stagger behind old Humphries down Temple Street, him waving the telegram, the others clutching their stomachs. Oh yes. Yes. I'll do it. I won't let them down. He's not backing Troy Town but I <u>know</u> that's the winner all right so the whole thing is bound to be a gas.

T W E N T Y
S E V E N

And then I see my back-view on the dock gazing out to where the sea widens to the horizon. The great hulk of the steamer looming to my left, its hull and superstructure gleaming white in the clear April light. I am alone, hands in my pockets, the smoke curling blue from the cigarette in my mouth rising into the still air. Time to go on board. I was 20 last October. Not a bad age to be – but now? Now?

About The Author

Writing under names Ivonne Piper or Mary Parker:-

Had short stories broadcast and published (BBC Wales: Morning Story, Stand Magazine, Planet and Swansea Review.)

Winner of Welsh Arts Council prose-prize 1973. (Piece published in Planet 16.)

Television play accepted by Harlech Television Co. in mid-70's.

3 articles published in Irish Times – early 80's.

(So far) 43 poems published in various magazines, a newspaper (London Welsh) and 3 anthologies (People Within, Cheltenham Poets and In The Company Of Poets.)

Poems published in Envoi 46, later placed in UCLA archives.

Poem broadcast, late 90's – Radio 4.

At present working on an esoteric literary work entitled Reality/Unreality also towards a collection of published and unpublished poems and short stories.

Printed in the United Kingdom
by Lightning Source UK Ltd.
118495UK00001B/241-246